"Reminiscent of Georg Grosz ... *Death in Breslau* isn't just an exciting mystery, it's the story of lost Fatherland ... wonderful."
—*THE GUARDIAN*

"The city of Breslau is as much a character in this thriller as the parade of gothic loons that inhabit it ... This addictive soup has an air of the burlesque about it."
—*THE DAILY TELEGRAPH*

"Krajewski relishes the period detail as takes us from bloody interrogation cells to Madame LeGoef's sweaty bordello ... above all you get the sense that Krajewski is enjoying teasing and tormenting us with numerous examples of the violent coming together of eroticism and the body-politic. In this respect, *Death in Breslau* is strongly reminiscent of Alain Robbe-Grillet's *Repetition* ... What's haunting about Krajewski's book, however, is that the worst was yet to come."
—*INDEPENDENT ON SUNDAY*

DEATH IN BRESLAU

MAREK KRAJEWSKI

Translated by Danusia Stok

MELVILLE HOUSE
BROOKLYN · LONDON

MELVILLE
INTERNATIONAL
CRIME

DEATH IN BRESLAU

Originally published in Poland as *Śmierć w Breslau* by Wydawnictwo Dolnośląskie Co, Ltd. © 2006

Published by permission of Wydawnictwo W.A.B. Co, Ltd.

Translation © Danusia Stok

This publication has been funded by the Book Institute — the ©POLAND Translation Program

This edition published by arrangement with MacLehose Press, London, an imprint of Quercus

First Melville House printing: August 2012

Melville House Publishing
145 Plymouth Street
Brooklyn, NY 11201

www.mhpbooks.com

ISBN: 978-1-61219-164-5

Manufactured in the United States of America
1 2 3 4 5 6 7 8 9 10

Library of Congress Control Number: 2012943812

INSTYTUT KSIĄŻKI

©POLAND

All-seeing Time hath caught
Guilt, and to justice brought
The son and sire commingled in one bed
 Oedipus the King, Sophocles
 (translated F. Storr)

DEATH IN BRESLAU

I

DRESDEN, MONDAY, JULY 17TH, 1950
FIVE O'CLOCK IN THE AFTERNOON

The July heat was unbearable. Director Ernst Bennert of the Psychiatric
Hospital slid his hand over his enormous bald skull. He examined his wet
palm with care — like a palmist. The mound of Venus was sticky with
sweat, tiny drops glistening in the life line. Two flies dug convulsively into
a stain left by a glass of sweet tea on the oilcloth. The light of a merciless,
setting sun flooded the window of his consulting room.

The heat did not seem to trouble the man with a shining black mane
who was also sitting there. He turned his chubby face — adorned with a
moustache and sprouting stubble — to the sun with evident pleasure. He
rubbed his cheek with a hand on which flexed the tattoo of a scorpion.
The man looked at Bennert. His eyes, dimmed by the sun's glare, became
suddenly attentive.

"We both know, doctor," he said with a distinct foreign accent, "that
you cannot refuse the institution I represent."

Bennert did know. He glanced out of the window and, instead of the
once splendid but now ruined tenement house on the corner, saw the ice-
bound panorama of Siberia, frozen rivers, heaps of snow and human
limbs protruding from beneath them. He saw a shed in which skeletons

1

in torn uniforms fought to get to the iron stove with its smouldering fire. One of them reminded Bennert of the clinic's previous head, Doctor Steinbrunn, who, six months earlier, had not agreed to the Stasi interrogating a certain patient.

He rubbed his eyes, rose and leaned over the window sill: the sight was familiar – a young mother scolding a disobedient child, a whining lorry, loaded with bricks.

"Very well, Major Mahmadov. I will let you into the ward myself, and you can question the patient. Nobody will see you."

"Just what I mean. See you at midnight then," Mahmadov brushed the fragments of tobacco from his moustache. He got up and smoothed his trousers. As he was pressing down the doorknob, he heard a loud thump and turned abruptly. Bennert smiled foolishly, holding a rolled copy of *Neues Deutschland*. Two dead flies lay flattened on the oilcloth.

DRESDEN, THAT SAME JULY 17TH, 1950
MIDNIGHT

The patient Herbert Anwaldt had survived "the house of torture", as he called the psychiatric clinic on Marien-Allee in Dresden, for already five years, thanks to his imagination. Imagination was a filter for wondrous transformations; the nurses' jabs and punches became gentle caresses, the stench of faeces became the scent of a spring garden, the cries of the sick became baroque cantatas and the shabby panelling frescoes by Giotto. Imagination obeyed him. After years of practice, he had managed to tame it to such an extent that he had entirely extinguished in himself something, for example, which would otherwise not have allowed him to survive incarceration: desire for a woman's body. He did not have to "extinguish the fire in his loins" like a sage from the Old Testament – that flame had long ago gone out.

Imagination did, however, betray him when he saw small, busy insects scuttling across the room. Their yellowish-brown abdomens flitting in and out of the gaps between the floorboards, their flickering antennae sticking out from behind the washbasin, the individual specimen crawling on to his eiderdown: a pregnant female dragging a pale cocoon, or a handsome male holding its body high on quick limbs, or the helpless young tracing circles with thin feelers – all this would lead to Anwaldt's brain being shaken by an electrical charge of neurons. The whole of him would curl up painfully, flickering feelers would burrow into his skin and he would be tickled, in his imagination, by thousands of limbs. He would then fall into a fury and was a potential danger to other patients, especially since the occasion on which he had discovered that some of them were catching insects, putting them into matchboxes and hiding them in his bed. Only the smell of insecticide would calm his jittering nerves. The matter could have been dealt with by transferring the sick man to another hospital – one less infested by cockroaches – in another town, but here unanticipated, bureaucratic obstacles would present themselves and successive heads of clinic would forsake the idea. Doctor Bennert had restricted himself to transferring Anwaldt to a private room disinfected somewhat more frequently. In periods preceding the swarming cockroaches, the patient Anwaldt would be calm and occupied himself for the most part by studying Semitic languages.

This is what he was doing when the nurse Jürgen Kopp was on his rounds. Even though Director Bennert had unexpectedly relieved him of the day's duty, Kopp had no intention of leaving the hospital. He closed the door of Anwaldt's room and went to a department in the next-door block. There he sat down at a table with two colleagues, Frank and Vogel, and started to deal cards. Skat was a passion shared by all the lower ranks of the hospital staff. Kopp bid a spades and turned out a jack of clubs to draw trumps. Before he could take the trick, however, they heard an inhuman cry from across the dark court-yard.

"Who's that yelling his head off?" wondered Vogel.

"Anwaldt. His light's just gone on," Kopp laughed. "Seen another cockroach, I expect."

Kopp was right in part. It *was* Anwaldt shouting. But not because of a cockroach. Along the floor of his room, comically twitching their abdomens, paraded four handsome, black, desert scorpions.

BRESLAU, SATURDAY, MAY 13TH, 1933
ONE O'CLOCK IN THE MORNING

Madame le Goef, a Hungarian with an invented French name, knew how to solicit clients. She did not spend a fenig on announcements in the press or on advertisements but acted directly. Trusting her unfailing intuition, she noted about a hundred names from the Breslau telephone directory and the directory of addresses. Next a certain sumptuous prostitute with extensive connections vetted the list and it turned out that most of the names belonged to wealthy men. Apart from that, Madame drew up a list both of doctors in Breslau and of lecturers at the university and the engi-neering college. She sent all of these men discreet notes in plain-looking envelopes, advising them that a new club, where the most demanding of gentlemen could satisfy their desires, had been opened. A second wave of advertisements infiltrated men's clubs, steam baths, coffee houses and *théâtres variétés*. Amply rewarded cloakroom assistants and porters – without the knowledge of the pimps by whom they were already paid for procuring girls – slipped scented cards illustrated with an appetiz-ing Venus in black stockings and a top hat, into their guests' hands or overcoats.

In spite of the pious indignation of the press and two court cases,

Madame le Goef's club became famous. Its clients were served in various ways by the charms of thirty girls and two young men.

Nor was there any shortage of artistic performances in the salon. Artistes were recruited from among the salon staff or – as was more often the case – generously remunerated guest performances were given by dancers from the "Imperial Cabaret" or some other small theatre. Two evenings a week were designated in Oriental style (with dances – not only of the belly – by several "Egyptians" who were otherwise employed in a cabaret), two in Classical style (bacchanalia), one in bawdy German (Heidi in lace drawers), and one was set aside for special guests, who had hired the whole club for discreet rendez-vous of their own. On Mondays the establishment was closed. Before long, telephone reservations were introduced and the Prussian manor called "the little Lohe manor" in Opperau, just outside Breslau, become famous throughout the city. The capital outlay was swiftly recovered, the more so as Madame was not the only investor. The lion's share of expenses was borne by the Police Praesidium of Breslau. This institution's costs were repaid not only in material form. And so everybody was happy, most of all the occasional and regular clients. The number of the latter kept on growing. Because where else could the Professor of Oriental Studies, Otto Andreae – armed with a *khanjar* and wearing a turban – chase a defenceless houri so as to possess her on a pile of crimson cushions; where else could the Director of the Municipal Theatre, Fritz Rheinfelder, expose his fat back to the sweet cuffs of riding boots worn by a slender Amazon?

Madame understood men well and was happy if she could meet their demands. She had recently experienced such a moment of joy in finding for the Deputy Head of the Criminal Department of the Police Praesidium, Counsellor Eberhard Mock, two girls who could play chess. Madame especially liked this stocky man with his thick, black, wavy hair. The Counsellor never forgot to bring flowers for Madame and small gifts for the girls who were glad to serve him. He was level-headed and taci-turn, he loved charades, bridge, chess and curvaceous blondes. He could gratify his passions at Madame le Goef's without inhibition. He would arrive at midnight every Friday, enter by the side door and, without pausing to watch whatever was being performed on the stage, go to his favourite room where his two odalisques would be waiting for him. They would change him into a silk dressing gown, feed him caviar and give him red Rhine wine to drink. Mock would sit still, though his hands would rove over the alabaster skin of his slaves. After dinner, he would settle down with one of them to a game of chess. The other, in the meantime, would go under the table and do something known already to pre-historic peoples. The girl playing chess with Mock had been instructed that every successful move was assigned a specific erotic configuration. So, after eliminating a pawn or a bishop, whatever, Mock would get up from the table and land on the sofa with his partner where, for a few minutes, they would enact the configuration.

According to rules drawn up by himself, Mock was not allowed to satisfy his desire if either of his opponents called checkmate. It had happened once, and he had got up, given the girls each a flower and left, masking his anger and frustration behind a jester's smile. He had never allowed himself to lose concentration at the chessboard again.

After one such long session, Mock was resting on the sofa reading his reflections on human characters to the girls. This was his third passion, one which he revealed only in his favourite club. The Criminal Counsellor – a lover of ancient literature who surprised his subordinates with long Latin quotations – envied Nepos and Theophrastus and reconstructed, not without some literary pretensions, the characteristics of people he met. He based his findings both on his own observations and on police files. On average, he would put together a description of one person a month and top up existing ones with fresh facts. These descriptions and newly arising characteristics created great confusion in the girls' tired heads. Be that as it may, they sat at Mock's feet, looked into his round eyes and felt the tide of happiness rise within the client.

Indeed, Criminal Counsellor Mock *was* happy and when he left – which was usually at about three in the morning – he would give small presents to the girls and a tip to the sleepy porter. Mock's good humour was felt even by the cabby who took him along Gräbschener Strasse, quiet at this hour, to the grand tenement on Rehdigerplatz, where the Counsellor would fall asleep at his wife's side, listening to the ticking of the clock and the shouts of carters and milkmen.

Unfortunately, on the night of the 12th to 13th May, Counsellor Eberhard did not experience happiness in the arms of Madame le Goef's girls. He was just playing out an interesting Sicilian defence when Madame tapped gently on the door.

A moment later she tapped again. Mock sighed, adjusted his dressing gown, rose and opened the door. His face was expressionless, but Madame could imagine what that man felt when someone interrupted an elaborate erotic-chess manoeuvre.

"Dear Counsellor," the owner of the club spared herself what she knew would be futile apologies. "Your assistant is downstairs."

Mock thanked her politely, quickly dressed – helped by his obliging geishas, one of whom tied his tie while the other buttoned his trousers and shirt – took two small boxes of chocolates from his briefcase and said goodbye to the inconsolable chess-players. He threw a goodnight to Madame and ran downstairs, colliding forcefully with his assistant, who was leaning against the crystal shade of a lamp in the hall. The crystals clinked in warning.

"Marietta von der Malten, the Baron's daughter, has been raped and murdered," panted Max Forstner.

Mock ran down the steps into the drive, got into his black Adler, slammed the door a little too hard and lit a cigarette. Forstner sat eagerly behind the steering wheel and turned on the engine. They moved off in silence. They had crossed the bridge over the Lohe before Mock finally gathered his thoughts.

"How did you find me here?" asked the Counsellor, carefully observing the walls of the Communal Cemetery flitting past on their right. The triangular roof of the crematorium was clearly silhouetted against the sky.

"The Criminal Director Doctor Mühlhaus suggested where you might be, sir." Forstner shrugged as if he would have preferred to say: "Everyone knows where Mock is on a Friday."

"Don't permit yourself any such liberties, Forstner." Mock looked at him intently. "You are still only my assistant."

This sounded threatening, but it did not make the slightest impression on Forstner. Mock did not lower his gaze from the broad face ("small, fat, red-haired scoundrel," he was thinking) and for the nth time resolved, against his better judgment, to destroy his insolent subordinate. This was not going to be easy since Forstner had been received into the Criminal Department when the new President of Police, the fanatical Nazi, Obergruppenführer S.A. Edmund Heines, had taken over command. Mock had learned that his assistant was not only Heines' protégé but boasted of having good relations with the new Supreme President of Silesia, Helmuth Brückner, who had been imposed upon them by the Nazis shortly after they had won the elections to the Reichstag. But the counsellor had worked in the police for nearly a quarter of a century and knew that anyone could be destroyed. While he had the authority, while the Chief of the Criminal Department was the old Freemason and liberal Heinrich Mühlhaus, he could keep Forstner away from serious cases and transfer him, for example, to booking prostitutes outside the Savoy Hotel on Tauentzienplatz or checking the credentials of homosexuals beneath

8

the statue of Empress Auguste on the promenade by the School of Fine Arts. What most irritated Mock was that he did not know any of Forstner's weaknesses — his files were clean and day to day observation prompted only one, concise description: "a dumb stickler". The close bond with Heines, who was well known to be a homosexual, did provide Mock with murky suspicions, but that was not enough to bend this "mole", Gestapo agent Forstner, to his will.

They approached Sonnenplatz. The city pulsated with subcutaneous life. A tram carrying workers from the second shift at the Linke, Hofmann & Lauchhammer factory grated on the corner, gas lamps flickered. They turned right into Gartenstrasse: carts delivering potatoes and cabbages crowded by the covered market, the caretaker of the art-nouveau tenement on the corner of Theaterstrasse was repairing a lamp and cursing, two drunks were trying to accost prostitutes proudly strolling in front of the Concert House with their parasols. They passed the Kotschenreuther and Waldschmidt Car Showroom, the Silesian Landtag building and several hotels. The night sky dispersed a light, misty rain.

The Adler drew up on the far side of Main Station, on Teichäckerstrasse, opposite the public baths. They got out. Their coats and hats were soon covered with watery dust. Drizzle settled on Mock's dark stubble and Forstner's clean-shaven cheeks. Tripping over the rails, they made their way to a side track. Uniformed policemen and railwaymen stood all around, talking in raised voices. The police photographer, Helmut Ehlers, with his trademark limp, was just approaching the scene.

The old policeman, who was always sent to the most macabre crimes, came up to Mock carrying a paraffin lamp.

"Criminal Sergeant Emil Koblischke reporting," he introduced himself unnecessarily; as usual, the Counsellor knew his subordinates well. Koblischke hid his cigarette in his cupped hand and looked gravely at Mock.

"Where you and I, sir, are both to be found, things must be bad." With his eyes, he indicated a saloon carriage with the sign "BERLIN–BRESLAU". "And things in there are very bad indeed."

All three carefully stepped over the body of the prostrate rail worker in the carriage corridor. A bloated face, frozen in a mask of pain. There was no sign of blood. Koblischke grasped the corpse by the collar and sat it up; the head flopped to one side and, as the policeman pulled down the collar, Mock and Forstner leaned forward to get a better view.

"Bring that lamp nearer, Emil. I can't see a thing," Mock said.

Koblischke stood the lamp closer and turned the corpse over on to its front. He freed one arm from the uniform and shirt, then tugged hard and exposed the dead man's back and shoulders. He moved the paraffin lamp even closer. The policemen could see several red marks with blue swellings on the nape and shoulder blade. Between the shoulder blades lay three dead, flattened scorpions.

"Three insects like that can kill a man?" For the first time Forstner betrayed his ignorance.

"They're not insects, Forstner, they are arachnids." Mock did not even moderate his contempt. "Apart from which, the post-mortem is still to come."

While the policemen could be in some doubt with regard to the rail worker, the cause of death of the two women in the saloon car was only too obvious.

Mock frequently caught himself reacting to tragic news with perverse thoughts, and to a shocking sight with amusement. When his mother had died in Waldenburg, the first thought that had come to him was about orderliness: what was to be done with the old, massive divan which couldn't be lugged out either through the window or the door? At the sight of the thin, pale shins of a demented beggar cruelly beating a puppy near the old Police Praesidium on 49 Schuhbrücke, he had been seized by fool-ish laughter. So too now, when Forstner slipped on the puddle of blood which covered the floor of the saloon car, Mock burst out laughing. Koblischke did not expect such a reaction from the Counsellor. He, himself, had seen a great deal in his time, but the spectacle in the saloon car set him shaking for a second time. Forstner left the carriage, Mock began his inspection.

Seventeen-year-old Marietta von der Malten was on the floor, naked from the waist down. Her loose, thick, ash-blonde hair was saturated with blood, like a sponge. Her face was contorted as if by a sudden attack of paralysis. Garlands of intestines lay scattered at the sides of her slashed body. The torn stomach revealed remnants of undigested food. Mock caught sight of something in the abdominal cavity. Overcoming his revulsion, he leaned over the girl's body. The stench was unbearable. Mock swallowed. In the blood and mucus moved a small, vigorous scorpion.

Forstner vomited violently in the toilet. Koblischke jumped comically as something crunched under his shoe.

"*Scheisse*, there's more of them here," he shouted.

They examined the corners of the saloon car with care and killed three more scorpions. "Good thing none of them stung us." Koblischke was breathing heavily. "Otherwise we'd be prostrate like that one in the corridor."

When they had made sure that there were no more sinister creatures in the carriage, they approached the second victim, Mlle Françoise Debroux, governess to the Baron's daughter. The woman, about forty years old, was lying flung over the back of a couch. Torn stockings, varicose veins on her shins, a modest dress with a white collar, yanked up to her armpits, sparse hair freed from its spinster's bun. Her teeth biting into her swollen tongue. A curtain cord was pulled tight around her neck. Mock inspected the corpse with revulsion and, to his relief, did not see another scorpion.

11

"That's the strangest thing," Koblischke indicated the wall, lined with striped, navy-blue fabric. Writing could be seen between the carriage windows. Two lines of strange signs. The Criminal Counsellor brought his face closer to them. Again he swallowed hard.

"Yes, yes . . ." Koblischke understood him instantly. "Written in blood . . ."

Mock told the obliging Forstner that he did not wish to be driven home. He walked slowly, his coat unbuttoned. He felt the burden of his fifty years. After half an hour, he found himself among familiar houses. In the doorway of one of the tenements on Opitzstrasse, he came to a standstill and looked at his watch. Four o'clock. At this time, he would normally be coming back from his Friday "chess". Yet never had any of the exquisite sessions wearied him so much as today's experience.

Lying next to his wife, he listened to the ticking of the clock. Before falling asleep, he remembered a scene from his youth. He was staying as a twenty-year-old student on the estate of his distant family near Trebnitz and flirting with the wife of the manor steward. In the end, after many unsuccessful attempts, he had arranged a tryst with her. He was sitting on the river bank under an old oak tree, certain that the day had come when he was finally going to have his fill of her voluptuous body. Smoking a cigarette, he listened to an argument between a few country girls who were playing on the other side of the river. The cruel creatures, their voices raised, were chasing away a lame girl and calling her a cripple. The child was standing by the water and looking in Mock's direction. In her outstretched arm, she held an old doll, her darned dress rippled in the breeze, her newly polished shoes were splattered with clay. Mock realized that she reminded him of a bird with a broken wing. As he watched the girl, he all of a sudden began to cry.

Nor could he stifle his tears now. His wife muttered something in her sleep. Mock opened the window and turned his burning face to the rain.

Marietta von der Malten had been lame too and he had known her since she was a child.

BRESLAU, THAT SAME MAY 13TH, 1933
EIGHT O'CLOCK IN THE MORNING

On Saturdays, Mock would arrive at the Police Praesidium at ten in the morning. The porters, couriers and detectives would glance meaningfully at each other as, faintly smiling and heavy with sleep, the Counsellor would reply to their greetings, leaving behind him a waft of expensive eau de cologne from Welzel. But this Saturday he did not remind anyone of that self-satisfied policeman, their mild and understanding superior. He came into the building as early as eight, slamming the door behind him. He snapped open his umbrella several times, spraying droplets of rain all around. Without replying either to the porter's or to the sleepy courier's "Good morning, sir", he took the stairs at the double, caught the tip of his shoe and all but fell. Porter Handke could not believe his ears – for the first time in his experience, he heard a ripe curse from Mock's lips.

"Oh, the Counsellor's ill-disposed today," he smiled to Bender, the courier.

Mock, meantime, had entered his office, sat behind his desk, and lit a cigar. His unseeing eyes fixed on a glazed brick wall. Although aware that he was still wearing his coat and hat, he did not move. After some minutes, a knock echoed on the door and Forstner came in.

"Everybody's to be here in an hour."

"They are here already."

The Counsellor looked at his assistant with cool kindliness for the first time.

"Forstner, please arrange for me to talk to Professor Andreae from the

13

university over the telephone. And please phone Baron Olivier von der Malten's residence and ask what time the Baron would be willing to see me. Briefing here in five minutes."

It seemed to Mock that Forstner clicked his heels as he left.

The Detectives and Inspectors, titled Assistants, Secretaries and Criminal Sergeants, looked at their unshaven boss and the pale Forstner with no surprise. They knew that the latter's stomach upset was in no way due to over-indulging in his favorite dish of black pudding and onions.

"Gentlemen, you're to put aside all other cases currently in hand." Mock spoke loudly and clearly. "We are to use all means, lawful and unlawful, to find the murderer or murderers. You may use violence and you may use blackmail. I shall try to make all secret files accessible to you. Do not skimp on informers.

"Now to hard facts. Hanslik and Burck, you are to question all animal handlers, starting with suppliers of the Zoological Gardens and ending with those selling parrots and goldfish. I expect a report on Tuesday morning. Smolorz, you'll draw up a list of all private menageries in Breslau and the neighbouring regions, also a list of eccentrics who sleep with anacondas. Then you will question them all. Forstner will help you. Report on Tuesday. Helm and Friedrich, you will look through the files of all perverts and rapists in our records since the end of the war. Pay close attention to animal lovers and those who have so much as dabbled in Eastern languages. Report Monday evening. Reinhardt, you will pick twenty men, visit every brothel and question as many whores as you can. You are to ask them about any sadistic clients and those who, during orgasm, quote the Kama Sutra. Report Tuesday. Kleinfeld and Krank, your task is not easy. You are to find out who was the last to see these unfortunate victims alive. Partial reports daily at three. Gentlemen, tomorrow, Sunday, is not a day of rest."

14

Professor Andreae was stubborn. He stated categorically that he could only decipher the original text on the wallpaper itself; he did not want to hear about photographs or even the most perfect hand-written copies. Mock, who because of his – admittedly uncompleted – philological studies had great respect for manuscripts, conceded. He replaced the receiver and sent Forstner to bring the roll of fabric with mysterious verses on it from the evidence storeroom while he made his way to the Chief of the Criminal Department, Doctor Heinrich Mühlhaus, and presented him with his plan of action. The Criminal Director did not comment, did not praise, did not criticize, made no suggestion of his own. He gave the impression of a grandfather listening with an indulgent smile to the fantastical imaginings of his grandson. He smoothed his long, greyish beard, adjusted his pince-nez, puffed at his pipe and frequently closed his eyes. Mock tried to preserve this interesting image of his superior in his memory.

"Don't go to sleep on me, please, young man," Mühlhaus barked at him. "I know you're tired."

He drummed his yellow fingers on the desk: the grandfather reprimanding his grandson.

"You have to find the murderer, Eberhard. Do you know what will happen if you don't? I'm retiring in a month. And you? Instead of taking my place, which might well happen, you will be made commander of the Railway Protection Office in Silesian Manure, for example, or be sent to guard the fishponds near Lubin, Commander of the local Fisheries Police. You know von der Malten. If you don't find the murderer, he'll take his revenge. And he's got a great deal of influence still. Oh, I nearly forgot . . . watch Forstner. Thanks to him the Gestapo knows every step we take."

Mock thanked him for the counsel and went to his office. He glanced at the town moat bordered by old chestnut trees and the sun-drenched Schlossplatz where the military orchestra was marching in rehearsal for tomorrow's Spring Celebrations. The sunlight encircled Mock's head with an amber halo. He closed his eyes and again saw the shunned, crippled girl beside the river. He also saw the steward's wife approaching from afar — the object of his youthful desires.

The ringing of the phone brought him back to the Police Praesidium. He ran his fingers through his slightly greasy hair and picked up the receiver. It was Kleinfeld.

"Sir, the last person to see the victims alive was the waiter Moses Hirschberg. We've questioned him. He brought coffee to the ladies in the saloon car at midnight."

"Where was the train at the time?"

"Between Liegnitz and Breslau, past Maltsch."

"Did the train stop anywhere between Maltsch and Breslau?"

"No. It would only have waited for the green light in Breslau, just before the station."

"Thank you, Kleinfeld. Check this Hirschberg most carefully — see whether we've got anything on him."

"Yes, sir."

The telephone rang a second time.

"Counsellor, sir," Forstner's baritone resounded, "Professor Andreae recognized the alphabet as being ancient Syrian. We'll have the translation on Tuesday."

The telephone rang for the third time.

"Baron von der Malten's residence. The Baron expects you as soon as possible."

Mock discarded his first instinct — which was to give the impudent major-domo a dressing down — and assured him that he would be there shortly. He told Forstner, who had just returned from the university, to drive him to Eichen-Allee 13, where the Baron lived. The residence was besieged by journalists who, recognizing the Adler, ran towards the policemen. They avoided them without a word and, let in by the guard, entered von der Malten's domain. They were greeted in the hall by the butler Matthias.

"The Baron wishes to see only the Counsellor."

Forstner could not conceal his disappointment; Mock smiled to himself.

The Baron's study was adorned with prints full of occult symbolism. Esoteric knowledge was also the subject of numerous volumes identically bound in maroon leather. The sun, barely seeping in through the thick, green curtains, illuminated four porcelain elephants carrying a globe on their backs. In the semi-darkness shone a silver model of celestial bodies with Earth at their centre. Olivier von der Malten's voice, coming from the games room next to the library, distracted Mock from geocentric matters.

"You have no children, Eberhard, so spare yourself the condolences. Forgive this form of conversing – through the door. I don't wish you to look at me. You knew Marietta since she was a child . . ."

He broke off, and Mock thought he heard suppressed sobs. A moment later, the Baron's somewhat altered voice made itself heard again.

"Light yourself a cigar and listen carefully. First and foremost, get rid of those scribblers outside my door. Second, send for Doctor Georg Maass from Königsberg. He is as excellent a specialist on matters occult as he is on Eastern languages. He will help you find the perpetrators of this ritualistic murder . . . Yes, ritualistic. Your ears do not deceive you, Eberhard. Third, if you do find the murderer, hand him over to me. Such is my advice, my request or, if you prefer, my ultimatum. That is all. Smoke your cigar in peace. Goodbye."

The Counsellor did not say a word. He had known von der Malten since his student days and knew that any attempt at a discussion would be futile. The Baron listened only to himself; to others he issued instructions. Counsellor Eberhard Mock had long lost the habit of listening to orders because, after all, it was hard to describe the kind-hearted grumpiness of his chief, Mühlhaus, as such. Besides, Mock was not in a position to refuse – if it were not for Olivier von der Malten, he would not have earned the title of Criminal Counsellor.

BRESLAU, THAT SAME MAY 13TH, 1933
ONE O'CLOCK IN THE AFTERNOON

Mock gave Forstner instructions regarding the journalists and Doctor Maass, while he himself summoned Kleinfeld.

"Do we have anything on this Hirschberg?"

"Nothing."

"Bring him to me for questioning. At two."

He felt himself losing the self-control for which he was renowned. It seemed to him that he had sand in his eyes; his swollen tongue was covered with a sour coating of nicotine; his breathing was loud and his shirt clung to him with sweat. He waved down a taxicab and ordered to be taken to the university.

Professor Andreae had just finished his lecture on the history of the Near East. Mock walked up to him and introduced himself. The professor peered at the unshaven policeman suspiciously and invited him into his office.

"Professor, you've been lecturing at our university for thirty years now. I myself had the pleasure of listening to you when I studied classical philology years ago. But among your students there were also some who dedicated themselves entirely to Oriental Studies. Can you, perhaps, remember any who may have behaved strangely, revealed any aberrations, perversions . . . ?"

Andreae was a short, shrivelled old man with short legs and a long torso. He sat now in his enormous armchair, circling his feet in their little laced shoes. Mock half-closed his eyes and smiled to himself. He had already built a simple caricature of the professor in his mind: two vertical lines, the nose and goatee; three horizontal lines, the eyes and lips.

"The sex lives of my Oriental Studies students," — the line of Andreae's lips became even thinner — "because, as you so aptly put it, 'there were also some', don't interest me any more than does your own . . ."

The Criminal Counsellor imagined the bell on the fire-engine going down Ursulinenstrasse just then, swung within his chest. He rose and approached the professor's desk. Pressing his wrists hard against the back of the armchair he drew his face closer to the goatee.

"Listen here, you old goat, maybe you're the one who killed the girl. Did you chase her in your turban, as is your pleasure, you grotesque dwarf? Did you slash her velvet stomach with a double-edged dagger?" He moved away from the professor and sat down in his chair again. He ran his fingers through his damp hair.

"I'm sorry, but I'll have to give this text to someone else for their expert opinion. On the other hand, what *were* you doing on Friday night between eleven and one? Please — don't tell me. I know. But do you want the Dean of the Philology Department or your students to find out? There are, after all, 'also some' so inclined."

Andreae smiled.

"Fortunately there are. Counsellor, I'll translate this text as best I can. Besides, I have just remembered one student who exhibited — as you described it — certain aberrations. Baron Wilhelm von Köpperlingk."

"I don't thank you." Mock donned his hat.

Kleinfeld was waiting for him in the Police Praesidium with Moses Hirschberg, a not so tall, hunched, dark-haired man of about forty. He repeated what the Counsellor already knew from Kleinfeld's report.

"Tell me, Hirschberg, where did you work before your present employment?"

The waiter had suffered from some inflammation in his childhood which had left him with a tic: when he spoke, the right corner of his mouth was pulled a little upwards which made it look as if he were smiling idiotically or scornfully. Reciting a dozen or so moth-eaten establishments, Hirschberg did not stop smirking. The bell began to swing in Mock's chest again. He approached the questioned man and struck him with his open palm.

"Happy are you, Jew? Maybe it's you who wrote that drivel in your vile language?"

Hirschberg hid his face in his hands. The Criminal Secretary, Heinz Kleinfeld, one of the best policemen in the Criminal Department, had a father who was a rabbi. He stood, now, staring at the floor. Mock swallowed and gestured "take him away". His palm was sore. He had hit the man a little too hard.

He found his men in the briefing room. Looking at them, he gathered that he would not be hearing any valuable revelation from any of them. Hanslik and Burck had questioned twelve dealers in animals and none of them had heard of scorpions being sold. Smolorz had not come across a trace of a private menagerie, but he had acquired some interesting information. The owner of a shop selling rodents and snakes had vouchsafed that one of his regular clients, a stout, bearded man, bought poisonous reptiles and lizards. Unfortunately, the shopkeeper could not say any more about the man. Reinhardt and his men had questioned at least fifty brothel residents. One of them had stated that she knew a professor who liked to pretend he was quartering her with a sword while shouting in some foreign language. The policemen were surprised that this information seemed to make no impression on their Chief. Thanks to statements made by Detective Reinhardt's prostitutes, they drew up a list of fifteen sadists and fetishists careless enough to invite "little girls" into their own apartments. Seven of these were not at home and eight had cast-iron alibis: indignant wives, every one of whom had confirmed that their uglier halves had spent the whole of the previous night in the marital bedchamber.

Mock thanked his men and designated them similar tasks for the following day. When they had said goodbye to him, none too pleased at the prospect of a working Sunday, he said to Forstner:

"Please come and see me at ten. We'll pay a certain well-known person a visit. Then you will visit the university archives. Don't be surprised — they'll be open. One of the librarians is on special duty tomorrow. You will make a list of all those who have had anything to do with Oriental Studies: from one-term students to doctors of Persian Studies and Sanskrit specialists. *A propos*, do you know what Sanskrit is?"

Without waiting for a reply, Mock left his office. He walked along Schweidnitzer Stadtgraben towards Wertheim's Department Store. He turned left into Schweidnitzer Strasse, passed the imposing statue of Wilhelm II flanked by two allegorical figures representing State and War, made a sign of the cross at the Church of the Sacred Heart and turned into Zwingerplatz. He walked past the local state school and dropped into Otton Stiebler's coffee roasters. In the crowded room, dark with tobacco smoke and filled with a strong aroma, swarmed a fair number of aficionados of the black beverage. Mock entered the counting-room. The accountant immediately interrupted his sums, greeted the Counsellor and left, allowing him to talk freely over the telephone. Mock did not trust the police telephonists and often dealt with conversations demanding discretion from this receiver. He dialled the number of Mühlhaus' home and, introducing himself, listened to the necessary information. Then he called his wife and justified his absence from dinner on account of an enormous work load.

BRESLAU, THAT SAME MAY 13TH, 1933
HALF-PAST THREE IN THE AFTERNOON

The Bishops' Cellar in the Schlesischer Hof Hotel in Helmuth-Brückner-Strasse, in pre-Nazi times the Bischofstrasse, was famous for its exquisite soups, meat roasts and pork knuckle. The walls of the restaurant were decorated with oil paintings by the Bavarian painter, Edward von Grützner, depicting scenes from the somewhat unascetic lives of monks. Mock liked best the side room lit by a green, hazy light falling through the stained-glass window just below the ceiling. He came here very often at one time to surrender to dreams among rippling shadows, lulled by a subterranean silence, the quiet breath of the cellar. But the growing popularity of the restaurant had spoiled the sleepy atmosphere so enjoyed by the Counsellor. The shadows rippled still, but the slurping of the shop-keepers and storekeepers, as well as the yelling of the S.S. who swarmed the place of late, made the fictitious ocean waves fill Mock's imagination not with solace so much as with silt and rough seaweed.

The Criminal Counsellor was in a difficult situation. For several months now, he had observed worrying changes in the police. He knew that one of his best policemen, the Jew Heinz Kleinfeld, was regarded with disdain by many; one policeman, newly engaged by the Criminal Department, had refused outright to work with Kleinfeld, with the result that — from one day to the next — he had stopped working for the police. But that was at the beginning of January. Now Mock was not at all sure he would have thrown that Nazi out of work. Much had changed since then. On January 31st, the posts of Minister of Internal Affairs and Chief of the entire Prussian Police were taken by Hermann Göring; a month later, the new, brown-shirt Oberpräsident of Silesia, Helmuth Brückner, had moved into the impressive building of the Regierungsbezirk Breslau on Lessingplatz; and not quite two months later, the new President — shrouded in ill-repute — Edmund Heines had marched into the Police Praesidium of Breslau. A new order had come to pass. The old camp for French prisoners of war on Strehlener Chaussee in Dürrgoy had been turned into a concentration camp where the first to find themselves were Mock's close acquaintances: the former President of Breslau police, Fritz Voigt, and the former Mayor, Karl Mach. Suddenly there appeared, in the streets, bands of juveniles, drunk with a sense of their own impunity and the vilest beer from Haas. Carrying torches and in a tight cordon, they surrounded transports of arrested Jews and anti-Nazis on whom hung wooden notices with "crimes" committed against the German nation inscribed on them. From one day to the next, streets had been given the names of brown-shirt patrons. In the Police Praesidium, members of the National-Socialist German Workers' Party (NSDAP) had suddenly become active; the Gestapo had overrun in the beautiful building's west wing and all of a sudden the best men from other departments were having themselves transferred there. Heines — in defiance of Mühlhaus' protests — had settled his favourite ward, Forstner, in the Criminal Department, and Mock's particular enemy, a Counsellor Eile, had become Director of the newly created Jewish Department. No, today — in May of 1933 — Mock could not afford to react so decisively. He was in a difficult situation: he had to be loyal to von der Malten and the Masonic lodge which had facilitated his brilliant career yet, at the same time, he could not provoke the Nazis against him. What irritated him most was that he did not have any influence over the situation and his future depended on his finding the murderer of the Baron's daughter. If it turned out that it was the member of some sect – as was highly probable – Hitler's propaganda would find a convenient pretext to destroy Breslau's Freemasons and anyone connected with them, therefore also Mühlhaus and Mock. That sectarian would very readily be transformed into a Freemason by the tabloids – the *Stürmer*, for example, and the cruel felony would be depicted as a ritual murder, a settling of accounts between Breslau's three Lodges.

If the murderer turned out to be a mentally deficient pervert, Heines *et consortes* would certainly have Mock concoct an "anti-German" – Jewish or Masonic – biography for him. In both the first and the second case, the Counsellor, as an instrument in the hands of propaganda, would appear in an ambiguous light in the eyes of his protectors, the Freemasons. It was not surprising that von der Malten demanded that the murderer be given over to him; he would wreak bloody vengeance on the perpetrator while nipping any intrigue against the Lodge in the bud. Consequently, either handing over or not handing over the murderer to the Baron would mean a career in the Fisheries Police in Lubin for Mock. In the first instance, the brown-shirt newspapers, incited by Forstner, would write at length about the Masons administering justice off their own bats, in the second, Mühlhaus and his people in the Lodge would react correspondingly. Certainly, the Counsellor could break with the Lodge and become a Hitlerite, but remnants of "good taste", which twenty-four years of police service had not eradicated, protested against this course, as did his aware-ness of the end to any future career: the Lodge could avenge itself on him in a very simple way – it could inform the appropriate people about his own Masonic past.

Nicotine always clarified Mock's mind. And so it was now: a brilliant idea came to him – the perpetrator commits suicide in his own cell and a speedy funeral follows. (The Nazis will not then be able to force me to prepare the criminal's anti-German biography. I will tell them that he is already dead and I have no time to play at bureaucracy and invent protocols of interrogation. I will also be justified vis-à-vis the Lodge because even if Hitlerite newspapers concoct the appropriate *curriculum vitae* for him, I will truthfully say I had nothing to do with it.) That would save him.

A moment later, however, he grew dispirited; he had not taken into account another disagreeable eventuality: what would happen if he simply failed to find the murderer?

The waiter stood a litre, stoneware tankard of Kipke beer before him. He was on the point of asking whether, perhaps, the Counsellor needed anything else when the latter turned his unseeing eyes on him and said emphatically: "If I don't find that bastard, I'll create him myself!" Paying no attention to the surprised waiter, Mock grew thoughtful: the faces of possible murderers began to flit in front of his eyes. Feverishly he wrote several names on the napkin.

He was interrupted in this catalogue by the person he had arranged to meet. S.A.-Hauptsturmführer Walter Piontek of the Gestapo looked like a good-natured innkeeper. He squeezed Mock's small hand with his enormous, beefy paw and sat down comfortably at the table. He ordered the same as Mock – pike with spicy *crudités* of turnip. Before getting to the point the Counsellor composed a character profile of his interlocutor: an overweight Brandenburgian, bare, freckled skull pasted down with clumps of red hair, green eyes, beefy cheeks; a lover of Schubert and underage girls.

"You know everything," he said without introduction.

"Everything? No . . . I know no more than that man over there . . ." Piontek indicated a man reading a newspaper. On the first page of the *Schlesische Tageszeitung* could be seen a huge headline: *Baron daughter's death in Breslau–Berlin train. Counsellor Mock in charge of investigation.*

"Much more, I should think," Mock rounded up the last piece of crunchy pike with his fork and drank the remainder of his beer. "Off the record – I'm asking you for help, Hauptsturmführer. There is no greater expert on religious sects and secret organizations in the whole of Breslau, maybe the whole of Germany. The symbolism is clear to you. I am asking you to find an organization which uses the symbol of a scorpion. All your wisdom and advice will be welcome and most certainly reciprocated in the future. After all, the Criminal Investigation Department – and I personally – have also information at our disposal which might be of interest to you."

"Do I have to yield to the requests of higher C.I.D. officials?" Piontek smiled broadly and half-closed his eyes. "Why should I help you? Is it because my chief and yours are on first name terms and play skat every Saturday?"

"You aren't listening to me, Hauptsturmführer." Mock did not intend to lose his temper any more that day. "I am offering you something profitable: an exchange of information."

"Counsellor," Piontek devoured his pike with gusto. "My chief told me to come. I am here. I have eaten some tasty fish and carried out my chief's instructions. Everything is in order. The case is no concern of mine whatsoever. There, you see," he pointed a fat finger at the page of the paper spread out in front of him: *Counsellor Mock in charge of investigation.*

Mock bowed once again in his thoughts to his old chief. Criminal Director Mühlhaus was right – Piontek was a man who had to be stunned and made breathless. Mock knew that any attack against Piontek would involve great risk, which is why he still hesitated.

"Did your chief not ask you to help us?"

"He did not even suggest it," Piontek's lips were stretched into a smile.

Mock took a few deep breaths and felt the sweet sense of power gather within him.

"You will help us, Piontek, with all the strength at your command. You'll set every last grey cell to work. If needs be, you'll study in the library . . . And do you know why? Because it is not your chief who's asking for this, or Criminal Director Mühlhaus, or even I myself . . . You are being implored by the delightful eleven-year-old hussy, Ilsa Doblin, whom you raped in your car, paying her drunken mother generously; you are being asked by Agnes Härting, that chatterbox with bunches whom you embraced in Madame le Goef's boudoirs. You even came out quite well on the photographs then."

Piontek's broad grin never wavered.

"Give me a few days," he said.

"Of course. Please contact no-one but me. It is, after all, Counsellor Mock in charge of the investigation."

II

BRESLAU, SUNDAY, MAY 14TH, 1933
TEN O'CLOCK IN THE MORNING

Baron Wilhelm von Köpperlingk occupied the two top floors of the beautiful, art-nouveau, corner building on Uferzeile 9, not far from the Engineering College. In the doorway stood a young butler with gentle eyes and studied manners.

"The Baron is awaiting you in the games room. Please follow me."

Mock introduced himself and his assistant. The Baron was a slender and very tall man of about forty, with the slim, long fingers of a pianist. The hairdresser and the female manicurist had only just taken their leave. The Baron tried to draw the Counsellor's attention to the results of their labours by performing numerous gestures with his hands – but in vain. Because Mock was not watching the Baron's hands. He was looking around with interest at the enormous room. His attention was drawn to various details of the décor in which he could not make out any sense, detect any central idea, any predominant feature, not to mention style. Nearly every piece of furniture contradicted the purpose of its existence: the wobbly gold chair, the armchair from which grew a huge steel fist, the table with embossed Arabian ornaments rendering it impossible to stand even a glass on it. The Counsellor did not know much about art, but he was sure that the enormous paintings depicting the Lord's Passion, the *danse macabre* and orgiastic cavortings were not the work of a person in their right mind.

Forstner's attention, on the other hand, was drawn to three terrariums full of spiders and myriapods. They stood on metre-high legs by the French windows leading to a balcony. A fourth terrarium next to the blue-tiled stove was empty. It was home, usually, to a young python.

The Baron finally managed to attract the policemen's attention to his manicured hands. They noticed, with surprise, that he was using them to lovingly caress that very python, which was now wrapped around his shoulder. The servant with beautiful eyes set out the tea and shortbread on an art-nouveau plate with a stand in the shape of a ram's horns. Von Köpperlingk indicated some soft, Moorish cushions scattered on the floor to the policemen. They sat down, cross-legged. Forstner and the servant exchanged quick glances, which did not escape either Mock's or the Baron's attention.

"You have an interesting collection in the terrariums, dear Baron," Mock panted as he got up again from the floor to inspect the specimens. "I never thought myriapods could be so large."

"That's a *Scolopendra gigantea*," the Baron said with a smile. "My Sarah is thirty centimetres long and comes from Jamaica."

"It's the first time I've seen a *scolopendra*." With relish, Mock inhaled the Egyptian cigarette handed to him by the butler. "How did you bring this specimen in?"

"There's a middle-man in Breslau who – to order – imports various, all sorts of . . ."

"Vermin," Mock cut in. "Who is it?"

On a sheet of letter-paper decorated with his family crest, von Köpperlingk wrote a name and address: Isidor Friedländer, Wallstrasse 27.

"Do you also rear scorpions, Baron?" Mock did not stop watching the *scolopendra* harmoniously shift the segments of its torso.

"I used to have several at one time."

"Who imported them for you?"

"This same Friedländer."

"Why haven't you got them any more?"

"They died of homesickness for the Negev desert."

Mock suddenly rubbed his eyes in amazement. He had just noticed a porcelain pissoir secured to the wall with a gleaming metal ice-pick in the shape of a sharpened, narrow pyramid lying in it.

"Don't worry, Counsellor. That piece is only an ornament in the spirit of Duchamp; nobody uses it. Nor the ice-pick." The Baron smoothed the velvet collar of his smoking-jacket.

Mock sat down heavily on the cushions and, without looking at his host, asked:

"What made you take up Oriental Studies?"

"Melancholy, probably . . ."

"And what did you do, Baron, between eleven and one o'clock on the night before yesterday, on Friday, May 12th?" The second question was asked in the same tone.

"Am I a suspect?" Baron von Köpperlingk half-closed his eyes and got up from the cushions.

"Please answer the question!"

"Counsellor, be so good as to contact my lawyer, Doctor Lachmann." The Baron put the python back in its terrarium and stretched two long fingers which held a white visiting card towards Mock. "I'll answer all your questions in his presence."

"I assure you, Baron, I'm going to ask you that question irrespective of whether you're in the company of Doctor Lachmann or Chancellor von Hindenburg. If you have an alibi, we will save Doctor Lachmann the trouble."

The Baron mused for perhaps fifteen seconds: "I do have an alibi. I was at home. My servant, Hans, will confirm it."

"Forgive me, please, but that is no alibi. I do not trust your servant, nor any servant for that matter."

"And your assistant?"

Before he realized, the Counsellor automatically wanted to reply "not him either". He glanced at Forstner's burning cheeks and shook his head: "I don't understand. What connection do you have with my assistant?"

"Oh, we've known each other a long time . . ."

"Interesting . . . But today, by some strange coincidence, you have been hiding your acquaintanceship. I even introduced you. Why did you not want to disclose your friendship?"

"It's not a friendship. We simply know each other . . ."

Mock turned to Forstner and looked at him expectantly. Forstner's gaze was fixed intently on the carpet pattern.

"What are you trying to convince me of, Baron?" Mock was triumphant on seeing the embarrassment of both men. "That an ordinary acquaintance allows Forstner to be here with you from eleven to one at night? Ah, no doubt you're going to tell me that you were 'playing cards' or 'looking at albums' . . ."

"No, Forstner was here, at a reception . . ."

"But it must have been a singular reception, eh, Forstner? Why, it looks as if you're both embarassed by this acquaintance . . . But maybe something shameful took place at this reception?"

Mock stopped tormenting Forstner. He now knew what, until then, he had only suspected. He congratulated himself for asking the Baron about an alibi. He had no grounds for doing so at all. Marietta von der Malten and Françoise Debroux had been raped and Baron Wilhelm von Köpperlingk was a declared homosexual.

Hans with the beautiful eyes was already closing the door behind

31

them when Mock remembered something. Announced a second time by the butler, he met once more the somewhat vexed countenance of the Baron.

"Do you buy the paintings yourself or do the servants do it for you?"

"I rely on my chauffeur's tastes in that respect."

"What does he look like?"

"A well-built, bearded man with a comically receding chin."

Mock was clearly satisfied with this answer.

BRESLAU, THAT SAME MAY 14TH, 1933
NOON

Forstner did not want a lift to the university archives. He claimed he would willingly walk down the embankment along the Oder. Mock did not try to persuade him and, quietly singing an operatic couplet to himself, drove across Emperor Bridge, past the municipal gym and the park where Heinrich Göppert, the founder of the Botanical Gardens, stood on a plinth, left the Dominican Church on his right and the Main Post Office on his left and drove into beautiful Albrechtstrasse which started at the huge mass of the Hatzfeld Palace. He reached Ring and turned left into Schweidnitzer Strasse. He passed Dresdner Bank, Speier's shop where he bought his shoes, Woolworth's office block, into Karlstrasse, glanced out of the corner of his eye at the People's Theatre, past Düno's Haberdasheries and into Graupnerstrasse. An almost summer heat hung over the city, so he was not surprised by the sight of a long queue standing in front of a shop selling Italian ice-cream. After a dozen or so yards, he turned into Wallstrasse and drove up to a rather neglected tenement marked number 27. Friedländer's Pet Shop was closed on Sundays. An inquisitive caretaker soon appeared and explained to Mock that Friedländer's apartment was next door to the shop.

The door was opened by a slim, dark-haired girl, Lea Friedländer, it turned out, Isidor's daughter. She made a great impression on the Counsellor. Without even looking at his identification, she asked him into a modestly furnished apartment.

"Father will come shortly. Please wait," she stammered, clearly embarrassed by the way Mock was looking at her. Mock did not have time to avert his eyes from her curvaceous hips and breasts before Isidor Friedländer, a short, stout man, came in. He sat down in the chair opposite Mock, crossed one leg over the other and hit his knee several times with the back of his hand, causing the limb to jerk involuntarily. Mock observed him for a while, then started a series of rapid questions:

"Surname?"

"Friedländer."

"First name?"

"Isidor."

"Age."

"Sixty."

"Place of birth?"

"Goldberg."

"Education?"

"I finished Yeshivo in Lublin."

"What languages do you know?"

"Apart from German and Hebrew, a little Yiddish and a little Polish."

"How old is your daughter?"

Friedländer suddenly interrupted the experiment with his knee and looked at Mock with eyes that had practically no pupils. He panted heavily, rose and, in a bound and flash, leapt at the Counsellor who had not had time to get up. The latter suddenly found himself on the floor, crushed under Friedländer's weight. He tried to pull the gun from his pocket, but his right hand was immobilized by his opponent's shoulder.

Suddenly the pressure eased – a coarse beard prickled Mock in the neck, Friedländer's body stiffened and convulsed rhythmically.

Lea pulled her father off Mock. "Help me. We have got to lay him down on the bed."

"Please move away. I'll put him there myself."

The Counsellor felt like a teenager wanting to show off his strength. With the greatest of difficulty, he dragged the ninety kilograms on to the sofa. Lea, in the meantime, had prepared a mixture and was pouring it carefully into her father's mouth. Friedländer choked, but he swallowed the liquid. After a while, there was a steady, intermittent snoring.

"I'm twenty," Lea still avoided Mock's eyes, "and my father suffers from epilepsy. He forgot to take his medication today. The dose I gave him will enable him to function normally for two days."

Mock shook down his clothes.

"Where is your mother?"

"She died four years ago."

"Do you have any siblings?"

"No."

"Your father suffered the attack after I asked him your age. Is that a coincidence?"

"Actually I've already answered you. I'm everything to my father. If a man shows any interest in me, Father starts to get worried. And if he forgets to take his medication, he suffers an attack."

Lea raised her head and, for the first time, looked Mock in the eyes. Despite himself, he began the mating dance: precisely measured moves, lingering looks, deep timbre of voice.

"I think Father provokes these attacks on purpose." The girl would not have been able to explain why she confided in this man in particular. (Perhaps it was his ample belly.)

But the Counsellor misunderstood this small token of trust. Questions were already pressing on his lips — about a possible boyfriend, invitations to lunch or dinner — when he noticed a dark stain spread over Friedländer's trousers.

"This often happens during or after an attack." Lea quickly slipped an oilcloth under her father's thighs and buttocks. Her beige dress stretched over her hips, her slender calves were a fascinating overture to other parts. Mock glanced once more at the sleeping dealer and remembered why he had come.

"When will your father be conscious again? I'd like to ask him some questions."

"In an hour."

"Maybe you can help me. The caretaker told me that you work in your father's shop. Can one buy a scorpion there?"

"Father brought in several scorpions some time ago through a Greek company in Berlin."

"What does that mean, some time ago?"

"Three, perhaps four years ago."

"Who ordered them?"

"I don't remember. We'd have to check the invoices."

"Do you remember the name of the company?"

"No . . . I know it's in Berlin."

Mock followed her into the counting-room. As Lea was going through hefty, navy-blue files, he posed one more question:

"Has there been another policeman here apart from me in the last few days?"

"Caretaker Kempsky did say that there was somebody from the police here yesterday. We weren't home in the morning. I had taken Father for his check-up at the Jewish Hospital on Menzelstrasse."

"What's the name of your father's doctor?"

"Doctor Hermann Weinsberg. Ah, here's the invoice. Three scorpions were imported for Baron von Köpperlingk in September 1930 by the Berlin company Kekridis and Sons. May I ask you," – she looked imploringly at Mock – "to come back in an hour? Then Father will be himself again . . ."

Mock was understanding to beautiful women. He got up and put on his hat.

"Thank you, Fräulein Friedländer. I am sorry that we had to meet in such sad circumstances although no circumstances are inappropriate when one meets such a beautiful young lady."

Mock's courtly goodbye did not impress Lea in the least. She sat down heavily on the divan. Minutes passed, the clock ticked loudly. She heard a murmur coming from the next room where her father was lying and went in with a false smile.

"Oh, you've woken up so quickly, Papa. That's very good. Can I go to Regina Weiss?"

Isidor Friedländer looked at his daughter anxiously: "Please don't go . . . Don't leave me alone . . ."

Lea was thinking about her sick father, about Regina Weiss with whom she was supposed to be going to the "Deli" cinema to see Clark Gable's new film, about all the men who had undressed her with their eyes, about Doctor Weinsberg who was hopelessly in love with her, and about the squeaking of the guinea pigs in the dark, damp shop.

Someone hammered loudly on the door. Friedländer, covering the stain on his trousers with the flaps of his gabardine, went into the other room. He was shaking and stumbling. Lea put her arm around him.

"Don't be frightened, Father. It must be caretaker Kempsky."

Isidor Friedländer looked at her uneasily: "Kempsky is an utter brute, but he never hammers on the door like that."

He was right. It was not the caretaker.

Eberhard Mock was as angry on Monday morning as he was on Saturday.
He cursed his foolishness and weakness for sensuous Jewish women. If
he had acted by the book, he would have called someone from the Police
Praesidium, brought Friedländer in to Neue Graupnerstrasse on remand
and questioned him there. But he had not. He had politely agreed to Lea
Friedländer's request for an hour's delay and instead of behaving like a
proper policeman, had browsed through the newspapers in the Green Pole
Inn on Reuschenstrasse 64 for an hour, drank beer and ate the speciality
of the house – army bread with spicy, hashed meat. When he had returned
an hour later, he had found the door prised open, a terrible mess and no
sign of the tenants. The caretaker was nowhere to be seen.

Mock lit what was his twelfth cigarette of the day. He read, yet again,
the results of the autopsy and Koblischke's report. He learned no more
than he had witnessed with his own eyes. He cursed his absent-
mindedness. He had overlooked the old Criminal Sergeant's important
information: underwear belonging to the Baron's daughter had been
missing from the scene of the crime. Mock sprang to his feet and burst
into the detectives' room. Only Smolorz was there.

"Kurt!" he shouted. "Please check the alibis of all known fetishists."

The telephone rang: "Good morning," Piontek's stentorian voice
resounded. "I'd like to repay your hospitality and invite you to lunch at
Fischer's bar. At two. I've some new, interesting information on the
Marietta von der Malten case."

"Fine." Mock replaced the receiver, adding no word of courtesy.

Fischer's was crowded – as it usually was at lunchtime. The clientele was chiefly made up of policemen and uniformed Nazis who took pleasure in frequenting their idol Heines' favourite restaurant. Piontek sat sprawled at a table in the small room. The sun, its rays refracted in the aquarium under the window, caressed his bald skull with reflections of light. Between fingers as chubby as sausages rested a smoking cigarette. He was watching a miniature tuna in the aquarium and making strange noises while moving his lips exactly like the fish. Having a splendid time, he tapped on the aquarium glass.

At the sight of Mock, who had arrived five minutes earlier, he was disconcerted. He pulled himself together, rose and greeted Mock effusively. The Counsellor manifested less joy at the encounter. Piontek opened a silver cigarette case with the engraving: "To a dear Husband and Daddy on his fiftieth birthday from his wife and daughters." The musical box played, the cigarettes in blue paper gave off a sweet scent. An elderly waiter took their order and removed himself without a sound.

"I shan't conceal, Counsellor," Piontek broke the tense silence, "that all of us at the Gestapo were happy that somebody like yourself would like to work with us. Nobody knows more about the more or the less important personalities of this city than Eberhard Mock. No secret archive can be the equal of that which you have in your head."

"Ah, you overestimate me, Hauptsturmführer . . ." Mock cut him off. The waiter put down the plates of eel in dill sauce, sprinkled with glazed onions.

"I'm not suggesting you go over to the Gestapo." Piontek was not put off by Mock's indifference. "What I know about you makes me think that you would not accept such a proposal." (*But of course – and who could have told this tub of lard any such thing? Forstner, you mongrel, I'm going to destroy you.*) "But, on the other hand, you're a reasonable man. Look wisely into the future and remember: the future's going to belong to me and my people!"

Mock ate with great appetite. He wrapped the last piece of fish around his fork, submerged it in the sauce and devoured it. For several seconds, he did not take the tankard of spiced Schweidnitz beer from his lips. He wiped his mouth with his napkin and contemplated the miniature tuna.

"I believe you had something to tell me about the murder of Marietta von der Malten . . ."

Piontek was a man who never lost his self-control. He took a flat, tin box from the pocket of his jacket, opened it and offered it to Mock to whom a strange suspicion occurred: did accepting a cigar amount to accepting the proposal that he go over to the Gestapo? He pulled back his hand. Piontek's hand shook a little.

"Go on, Counsellor, have a smoke. They're really good. One mark cigars."

Mock inhaled so deeply that he felt a stabbing pain in his lungs.

"You don't want to talk about the Gestapo. So, let's talk about the C.I.D.," Piontek said jovially. "Did you know that Mühlhaus has decided to take early retirement? In a month at the latest. That's what he decided today. He told Obergruppenführer Heines, who agreed. So at the end of June there's going to be a vacancy for the post of Chief of the Criminal Department. I've heard that Heines has had some candidate from Berlin suggested to him by Nebe. Artur Nebe is an excellent policeman, but what does he know about Breslau . . . Personally I think that a better candidate would be someone who knows conditions in Breslau . . . You, for example."

"Your opinion is, no doubt, the best reference for the Prussian Minister of Internal Affairs, Göring, and the Chief of Prussian Police, Nebe." Mock tried, at all costs, to disguise with biting irony the reverie induced by the man from the Gestapo.

39

"Counsellor," Piontek surrounded himself with cigar smoke. "The two men you mentioned do not have time to waste on provincial personnel pushovers. They can simply approve the personal recommendation of the Supreme President of Silesia, Brückner. Brückner will put forward whomsoever Heines supports. And Heines communicates in all matters of personnel with my chief. Have I made myself clear?"

Mock had a great deal of experience in conversations with people such as Piontek. Nervously, he unbuttoned the collar of his shirt and wiped his forehead with a chequered handkerchief: "That lunch has somehow made me hot. Maybe we could take a walk along the promenade by the moat . . ."

Piontek glanced at the aquarium with the tuna fish. *(Could he have noticed the microphone?)* "I haven't got time for walks," he said good-naturedly. "Besides, I haven't given you the information on Fräulein von der Malten's case yet."

Mock got up, slipped on his coat and hat: "Hauptsturmführer, thank you for the excellent lunch. If you want to know my decision — and I have already made it — I'll be waiting outside."

* * *

A group of young mothers, pushing their prams near the statue of Cupid Riding Pegasus on the promenade, remarked upon the two elegantly attired men walking in front of them. The taller of the two was of a heavy build. The pale trench-coat sat tightly on his shoulders. The shorter of the two was tapping his walking stick while studying his patent leather shoes.

"Well, look at that, Marie," said the slim blonde woman quietly. "Those there must be some gentlemen."

"That's for sure," muttered the plump Marie, a scarf tied around her head. "Could be artists because why aren't they at work? Everyone works at this time, not yaps away in a park."

Marie's observations were partially accurate. In so far as Piontek and Mock were performing a work of art at that moment, it was the art of subtle blackmail, veiled threats and ingenious provocation.

"Counsellor, I know from my chief that Nebe can be stubborn and decide to place his own man as chief of Breslau's C.I.D., even in defiance of Heines or Brückner. But you can strengthen your position considerably and become the one and only, unrivalled candidate . . ."

"How?"

"Oh, it's so simple . . ." Piontek took Mock under the arm. "A successful case, loud and spectacular, would raise you to that position. Of course, a successful case plus Heines' and Brückner's support. And then even the Chief of Prussian Police, the uncompromising Nebe, will give in . . ."

Mock stopped, removed his hat and fanned himself with it for a moment. The sun glistened on the roofs of the houses on the other side of the moat. Piontek took the Counsellor by the waist and whispered in his ear:

"Yes, dear sir, success . . . And we both have no doubt that your greatest success at this moment would be capturing the murderer of Baron von der Malten's daughter."

"Hauptsturmführer, you're presuming that I want nothing more than Mühlhaus' position . . . But maybe that's not the case . . . Maybe I have other plans . . . Besides, we do not know that I will find the murderer before Mühlhaus leaves." Mock knew this sounded insincere and would not deceive Piontek. The latter leaned over to Mock's ear once more, shocking the women overtaking them.

"You've already found the murderer. It's Isidor Friedländer. He confessed last night. At our quarters, in Brown-Shirt House on Neudorfstrasse. But only I and Schmidt, my subordinate, know about it. If you so wish, Counsellor, we'll both swear it was you who forced Friedländer to confess at the Police Praesidium." Piontek grasped Mock's small hand

and folded it into a fist. "There, you're holding your career in the palm of your hand."

BRESLAU, TUESDAY, MAY 16TH, 1933
TWO O'CLOCK IN THE MORNING

Mock woke with a stifled cry. The duvet pressed down on his chest as if it weighed a hundred kilograms. His nightshirt, soaked in sweat, was twisted around his limbs. He threw the duvet violently aside, got up, went to his study, lit the lamp with a green shade on his desk and set out his chess set. In vain, he wanted to chase away the nightmare of his bad conscience. The dream he'd had a moment ago re-appeared before his eyes: the lame girl was looking straight at him. Despite the river separating them, he clearly saw her eyes full of passion and hatred. He also saw the steward's wife heading towards him. She approached with a swaying gait. He looked with surprise at her face covered in a rash. She sat down, hitched her dress up high and spread her legs. From her thighs and stomach grew syphilitic cauliflowers.

The Counsellor threw the window wide open and returned to the safety of the green circle of light. He knew he would not be able to sleep before the morning. Both women in the dream had faces he knew well: the girl, that of Marietta von der Malten; the syphilitic Phaedre, Françoise Debroux.

* * *

Schlesische Tageszeitung of May 19th, 1933

Page 1: Counsellor Eberhard Mock of Breslau's Criminal Police, after several days of investigation, apprehended the felon who killed the Baron's daughter, Marietta von der Malten, her governess, Françoise Debroux, and the conductor of the saloon car, Franz Repell. It turned out to be the sixty-year-old, mentally sick dealer, Isidor F. Further details on p.3.

Page 3: Isidor F. murdered the Baron's 17-year-old daughter and her guardian, 42-year-old Françoise Debroux in an exceptionally brutal manner. He raped both women, then quartered them. Prior to that, he took the life of the carriage conductor. Stunning the victim, he slipped three scorpions under his shirt which fatally stung the unfortunate man. The perpetrator of the crime decorated the carriage with writing in a Coptic tongue: 'Both for the poor, and for the rich – death and vermin.'

The epileptic Isidor F. had long been treated by Doctor Weinsberg from the Jewish Hospital. Here is the doctor's opinion: 'Following an attack of epilepsy, the sick man would remain in a state of unconsciousness for a long time, although giving the impression of being fully aware. After an attack of epilepsy, the schizophrenia which plagued him ever since he was a small child would re-appear. He would then be unpredictable; he would shout in strange tongues, and have horrifying, apocalyptic visions. In such a state, he was capable of anything.'

The accused is being held in a place known only to the police. The trial will take place within a few days.

Völkischer Beobachter of May 20th, 1933

Page 1: The abominable Jew defiled and quartered two German women. Prior to that, he killed a German railwayman in a perfidious manner. That blood cries out, demands vengeance!

Berliner Morgenpost of May 21st, 1933

Page 2: This last night, the vampire of Breslau, Isidor Friedländer, committed suicide in his cell. He killed himself in a manner as macabre as that in which he killed his victims: he bit through his veins . . .

Breslauer Zeitung of July 2nd, 1933

Extract from an interview with Criminal Director Eberhard Mock, the new Chief of the Criminal Police in the Police Praesidium of Breslau, page 3:

"Where did Friedländer know Coptic from?"

"He learned Semitic languages at the Talmud High School in Lublin.

"The murderer expressed the Coptic text in the ancient Syrian alphabet. This is a difficult task even for an eminent Semitist, but for the average graduate of a Jewish high school – unfeasible . . .

"After an attack of epilepsy, the accused would have apocalyptic visions, speak in various languages, apparently unknown to him, fall into a trance. Dangerous schizophrenia, from which he suffered ever since childhood, would then re-appear. He revealed more than natural abilities, skills in resolving tasks which were, in fact, impossible to resolve."

"One last question. Can the people of Breslau now sleep in peace?"

"The inhabitants of such a large city as Breslau face various dangers more frequently than people in the provinces. We will counteract these threats. If, God forbid, other criminals manifest themselves, I will most certainly apprehend them."

III

Herbert Anwaldt opened his eyes and then immediately shut them. He had the vain hope that when he opened them again all around would turn out to be a dismal mirage. It was a futile hope: the drunkard's den where he found himself was an unshakeable reality, pure realism. In Anwaldt's head, a small gramophone replayed the refrain he had heard yesterday, over and over again – Marlene Dietrich's *"Ich bin von Kopf bis Fuß auf Liebe eingestellt . . ."*

He moved his head several times. The dull ache slowly spread beneath the vault of his skull; cigarette fumes filled his eye sockets. Anwaldt screwed up his eyes. The pain had become intense and unremitting. In his throat nestled a thick, burning mass tasting of vomit and sweet wine. He swallowed it – through the dry pipeline of his gullet pressed a red-hot bullet. He did not want to drink; he wanted to die.

He opened his eyes and sat up on the bed. The brittle bones of his temples crunched as if squeezed by a vice. He looked around and concluded that he was seeing this interior for the first time. Next to him lay a drunken woman in a dirty, slippery petticoat. At the table slept a man in a vest; his massive hand, with its tattoo of an anchor, caressingly

46

crushed a fallen bottle against the wet oilcloth. On the window, a paraffin lamp was dying. A light streak of dawn filtered into the room.

Anwaldt glanced at the wrist on which he wore a watch. The watch was no longer there. Oh yes, yesterday, overcome with pity, he had offered it to a beggar. A persistent thought stung him: how to get out of the place. This was not going to be easy. He could not see his clothes anywhere. Although he had no shortage of extravagant ideas, he was not wont to go out into the street wearing nothing but his underpants. He noted with relief that, true to a habit which he had acquired at the orphanage, he had tied his shoes together and hung them around his neck.

He picked himself up from the bed and almost fell. His legs slid apart on the wet floor, his arms waved about frantically and found support: the left on a child's metal bed, the right on a stool where someone had spilt the contents of an ashtray.

Hammers continued to bang within his head, his lungs pumped fiercely, his throat emitted a rasping sound. Anwaldt struggled with himself for a moment — he wanted to lie beside the drunken nymph, but when he looked at her and smelt the odour of rotten teeth and putrid gums, he put the idea firmly aside. In the corner, he espied his creased suit. As swiftly as he could, he dressed in the darkness of the stairwell, dragged himself out into the street and remembered its name: Weserstrasse. He did not know how he had got there. He whistled at a passing droschka†. Criminal Assistant Herbert Anwaldt had been drinking for what was already the fifth day. With short intervals, he had been drinking for six months.

† A horse-drawn cab.

Criminal Commissioner Heinrich von Grappersdorff was exploding with rage. He thumped the table with his fist and screamed blue murder. It seemed to Anwaldt that the snow-white, round collar of his superior's shirt would snap over the distended, bull-like neck. He was not especially perturbed by the screaming. Firstly, because any thoughts getting through to his mind were muffled by the thick filter of a hangover; secondly, because he knew that the "old ox from Stettin" had not fallen into a genuine fury yet.

"Look at yourself, Anwaldt." Von Grapperdorff grasped the Assistant under the armpits and stood him in front of a mirror mounted in an engraved frame. The gesture gave Anwaldt pleasure, as if it were a coarse masculine caress. He saw, in his reflection, the slim, unshaven face of an auburn-haired man which undeniably betrayed the five-day binge. The whites of his eyes, shot with blood, were lost in their swollen sockets, from the dry lips stuck out flakes of sharp skin, the hair clung to a deeply furrowed brow.

Von Grappersdorff took his hands from Anwaldt and wiped them with revulsion. He stood behind his desk and once more assumed the stance of Thunderer.

"You're thirty and look as if you were forty. You've sunk to the very bottom like the worst whore! And all because of some rag with the face of an innocent. Soon any Berlin thug will buy you out for a tankard of beer! And I don't want any corruptible whores here!" He drew in a breath and roared: "I'm throwing you out, Schnappswald! Reason: five days' unauthorised leave."

The Commissioner sat down behind his desk and lit a cigar. Blowing clouds of smoke, he did not take his eyes off what used to be his best employee. The filter of a hangover had stopped working. Anwaldt realized that he would soon be left without a pension and would only be able to dream of alcohol. This thought had the necessary effect. He looked pleadingly at his superior, who suddenly started reading a report from the previous day. After a long while, he sternly said:

"I am dismissing you from the Berlin police. As of tomorrow, you start work at the Breslau Police Praesidium. A certain very important person there wants to entrust you with a rather difficult mission. So? Do you accept my proposition or are you going to beg on Kurfürstendamm? If the local boys let you in on a cushy job . . ."

Anwaldt tried not to burst into tears. He did not think about the Commissioner's proposition so much as about holding back his tears. This time von Grappersdorff's fury was genuine.

"Are you going to Breslau or aren't you, you wine-sodden tramp?"

Anwaldt nodded. The Commissioner calmed down immediately.

"We'll meet on Friedrichstrasse this evening at eight, on platform three. I'll give you a few essential details then. Here are fifty marks to clean yourself up. Pay me back when you're settled in Breslau."

BERLIN, THAT SAME JULY 5TH, 1934
EIGHT O'CLOCK IN THE EVENING

Anwaldt arrived punctually. He was clean, shaven and — most importantly — sober. He was dressed in a new, lightweight, pale-beige suit and matching tie. He carried a tattered briefcase and an umbrella. His hat, somewhat askew, made him look like an American actor whose name von Grappersdorff did not know.

"Well. Now, that's more like it." The Commissioner approached his former employee and sniffed. "Breathe out!"

Anwaldt did as he was told.

"Not a single beer?" Von Grappersdorff was incredulous.

"Not even a beer."

The Commissioner took him by the arm and they began to walk along the platform. The engine was expelling clouds of steam.

"Listen carefully. I don't know what it is you've got to do in Breslau, but the task is very difficult and dangerous. The bonus you'll receive will allow you not to work for the rest of your life. Then you'll be able to drink yourself to death, but during your stay in Breslau, not a drop . . . Understood?" Von Grappersdorff laughed heartily. "I must admit, I advised Mühlhaus, my old friend from Breslau, against this. But he insisted. I don't know why. Maybe he heard that you used to be good from somewhere. But, to the point. You've got the entire carriage to yourself. Have a good time. And here's a going-away present from your colleagues. It'll help with the hangover."

He wagged his finger. A shapely brown-haired woman in a playful hat came up to them. She handed Anwaldt a piece of paper: "I'm a present from your colleagues. Take care and drop in to Berlin again from time to time."

Anwaldt looked around and behind the ice-cream and lemonade stall on the platform he saw his laughing colleagues pulling silly faces and making rude gestures. He was embarrassed. The girl, not in the least.

BRESLAU, FRIDAY, JULY 6TH, 1934
HALF-PAST FIVE IN THE AFTERNOON

Criminal Director Eberhard Mock was getting ready to leave for Zoppot, where he intended to spend a two-week holiday. The train was leaving in two hours so it was not surprising that an indescribable mess reigned in his apartment. Mock's wife felt like a fish in water. The short and corpulent blonde was giving the servants brief instructions in a loud voice. Mock sat in an armchair, bored and listening to the radio. He was in the process of searching for a different wavelength when the telephone rang.

"The Baron von der Malten's residence here," he heard the butler Matthias' voice. "The Baron is expecting you, Criminal Director, just as soon as is possible."

Without ceasing to search for his wavelength on the radio, the Criminal Director said in a calm voice:

"Listen here, you lackey, if the Baron wants to see me then let him take the trouble 'just as soon as is possible' himself because I'm just about to leave on holiday."

"I was expecting just such a reaction, Eberhard." Eberhard heard the deep and cold voice of the Baron over the receiver. "I foresaw it and, since I have respect for time, I have placed a visiting card with a telephone number on it next to the receiver. It cost me a lot of trouble to get hold of it. If you don't come here straight away, I'll dial the number. Do you want to know who I'll be connected to?"

Mock was suddenly no longer interested in the martial music transmitted over the radio. He ran his finger along the top of the radio set and muttered: "I'll be there directly."

A quarter of an hour later he was on Eichen-Allee. Without a word of greeting, he passed the old butler, who was standing – straight as an arrow – in the doorway, and growled: "I know how to find the Baron's study!"

His host was in the open door, dressed in a long, piqué dressing gown and slippers of pale leather. Beneath the unbuttoned collar of his shirt was a silk neckerchief. He was smiling, but his eyes were extremely mournful. The slim, furrowed face was aflame.

"It's a great honour for us that your Excellency has deigned to trouble himself to come and see us," he contorted his face in a joker's grin. All of a sudden he grew serious. "Come inside, sit down, have a smoke and don't ask any questions!"

51

"I'll ask one." Mock was clearly angry. "Who were you going to phone?"

"I'll start with that. If you hadn't come, I'd have phoned Udo von Woyrsch, Chief of the S.S. in Breslau. He's a nobleman from an excellent family, somehow even connected to the von der Maltens by marriage. He would most certainly have helped me get through to the new Head of the Gestapo, Erich Kraus. Did you know . . . von Woyrsch has been in an excellent mood for a week now. He drew his knife during 'the night of the long knives' too, and destroyed the despised enemy: Helmuth Brückner, Hans Paul von Heydenbreck and other S.S.-men. Oh my, and what a terrible thing met our dear rake and conqueror of boys' hearts, Edmund Heines! The S.S. killed him in beautiful Bavarian Bad Wiessee. They dragged him out of not just anybody's bed, but that of the Chief of the S.A., Ernst Röhm himself, who not long after, shared his loved one's fate . . . And what happened to our beloved, hearty Piontek that he had to go and hang himself in his own garden? Apparently they showed his darling wife a few photographs where old Walter, dressed in a spherical cap, was performing what the ancients used to call lesbian love, with a nine-year-old girl. If he hadn't done away with himself, our brown-shirt cubs from Neudorfstrasse would have dealt with him."

The Baron, a dedicated lover of Homer, adored retardation. This time the retardation was actually an introduction.

"I'll ask you a brief and succinct question: do you want Kraus to see the documents I keep and which prove irrefutably that the Chief of the Criminal Department used to be a Freemason? Answer 'yes' or 'no'. Did you know that the Chief of the Gestapo of barely a few days feverishly wants to prove himself so as to show his principals in Berlin that their decision had been correct. We have in the Gestapo now a man who is more of a Hitlerite than Hitler himself. Do you want the Hitler of Breslau to find out the whole truth about your career?"

Mock began to wriggle in his chair. The choice cigar suddenly took on a sour after-taste. He had known somewhat earlier about the planned attack on Röhm and his Silesian followers, but he had, with particular relish, forbidden his men to intervene in any way. "Let them kill themselves, the swine," he had told the one and only man in the police whom he trusted. And he, himself, had gladly supplied the S.S. with a number of compromising photographs. He had wanted to greet the fall of Piontek, Heines and Brückner with champagne, but as he was raising a solitary toast his arm suddenly stiffened. He had realized that the thugs had executed a purge among themselves but that they continued to rule. And that after the few bad specimens, even worse might follow. He had anticipated correctly: Erich Kraus was the worst of all the Hitlerites he had known.

"Don't answer, you little shoemaker from Waldenburg, you little hustler, you mediocrity! Even your interpretations of Horace had the finesse of a shoemaker's hoof. *Ne ultra crepidam.*† You did not heed the warning and lied at our door. For your career. You left the Lodge. You secretly served the Gestapo. Don't ask how I know all this . . . Of course, you also did this for your career. But it is my daughter who served your career best. You remember – the same one who, limping, would run to meet you. You remember how much she liked you? 'Dear Herr Ebi' . . . she'd cry when she saw you."

Mock got up abruptly.

"What do you want? I've already handed you the murderer. Speak, as you promised, 'briefly and succinctly' and spare yourself this Ciceronian performance!"

Von der Malten did not say a word, but walked up to his desk and took a tin Wiener Chocolate box from a drawer. He opened it and slipped it under Mock's nose. A scorpion was pinned to the red velvet. Next to it lay

† *Watch your hooves, shoemaker*, i.e. mind your own business (Latin).

a little blue card with the Coptic verses about death which he already knew. Underneath was added in German: 'Your pain is still too small.' I found this in my study."

Mock looked at the geocentric model of Earth and said far more calmly now:

"There is no lack of psychopaths. In our city, too. And most certainly among your servants — who could get into such a well-guarded residence?"

The Baron was toying with a paper-knife. Suddenly, he turned his eyes to the window. "Do you want to see in order to believe? Do you really want to look at my daughter's *dessous*? I've put it away. It was in this box next to the scorpion and this letter."

Mock did, indeed, remember that Marietta's underwear was missing from the scene of the crime. He had even told one of his men to check on all fetishists on this very account.

Von der Malten put the knife aside and said in a voice trembling with rage:

"I finished off that 'murderer' in the cellar, the man you delivered to me . . . That old, demented Jew . . . There's only one man I hate more than you: the real murderer. You're going to put all that's within your power, Mock, to work and find that murderer. No . . . no . . . not you personally. Somebody else will be heading the new investigation. Someone from the outside, whom no gang from Breslau will ensnare. Besides, you've already caught the murderer . . . How would that be? You looking for him again? You might even lose your position and your medal . . ."

The Baron leaned across the desk and their faces came within a few centimetres of each other. Stale breath enveloped Mock.

"Are you going to help me or am I to ruin your career? Are you going to do everything I tell you or am I to call von Woyrsch and Kraus?"

"I'll help you, but I don't know how. What am I to do?" he replied without hesitation.

"That's your first intelligent question." Anger still trembled in the Baron's voice. "Come into the drawing-room. I'll introduce you to somebody."

*   *   *

As the Baron opened the door to the drawing-room, two men sitting at a side table immediately stood up. The not too tall man with curly, dark hair looked like a teenager caught by his parents in the act of looking through pornographic illustrations. The younger, slim, auburn-haired man, had the same expression of weariness and satisfaction in his eyes as Mock saw in his own on Saturday mornings.

"Criminal Director," the Baron addressed Mock. "Let me introduce Doctor Georg Maass from Königsberg and Criminal Assistant of the Berlin Police, Herbert Anwaldt. Doctor Maass is a fellow at the University of Königsberg and an eminent Semitologist and historian; Assistant Anwaldt a specialist in crimes of a sexual nature. Dear gentlemen, this is Chief of the Criminal Department of the Police Praesidium in Breslau, Criminal Director Eberhard Mock.

The men nodded to each other, after which – following the Baron's example – they sat down. The host continued ceremoniously:

"In keeping with his courteous assurance, the Criminal Director will give you any help you need. Files and libraries stand open to you. The Criminal Director has kindly agreed to employ – as of tomorrow – Assistant Anwaldt in the establishment under his command as Official in Charge of Special Affairs. Am I right, Criminal Director?" – Mock, astounded by his implied "courtesy", nodded – "Assistant Anwaldt, having access to all files and information, will commence a highly secret investigation into my daughter's murder. Have I omitted anything, Criminal Director?"

"No, you have omitted nothing, Baron," confirmed Mock, wondering how he would assuage his wife's anger when she found out that she would be spending the first days of her holiday alone.

BRESLAU, SATURDAY, JULY 7TH, 1934
EIGHT O'CLOCK IN THE MORNING

A uniform heat prevailed over Breslau. The hollow in which Breslau lay roasted in streaks of burning air. Sellers of lemonade sat under parasols on street corners, in shops and other places rented out for the purpose. They did not have to advertise their goods. All were employing helpers who supplied them with buckets of ice from the stores. Fanning itself incessantly, the sweaty crowd filled the cafés and pastry shops on elegant Gartenstrasse. Musicians, soaked in sweat, played Sunday marches and waltzes on Liebichshöhe where, under the spread of chestnut and plane trees, the weary middle class breathed the dusty air. Squares and parks were peopled with old folk playing skat and angry nursemaids trying to calm over-heated children. Older pupils, who had not yet left for the holidays, had long forgotten about *sine* or about Hermann and Dorothea and were organizing swimming competitions on Bürgerwerder. The lumpenproletariat from the little, poor, dirty streets around Ring and Blücherplatz drank tankfuls of beer and, by morning, lay sprawled in doorways and gutters. Youngsters arranged hunts for rats which were rummaging among the dustbins in unusually large swarms. Damp bedclothes hung dolefully from windows. Breslau gasped under the weight of the heat. The manufacturers and sellers of ice-cream and lemonade rubbed their hands. The breweries worked at full steam. Herbert Anwaldt was beginning his investigation.

* * *

56

The policemen sat in the briefing room without their jackets, their collars loosened. The sole exception was Mock's deputy, Max Forstner, who — although sweating in his rather too tight suit and stiff collar — did not allow himself even the appearance of informality. He was not much liked. The reason for this antipathy lay in the conceit and malice which he dealt out to his subordinates in small yet virulent doses. Here he would criticize someone's cut of hat as being unfashionable, there pick on someone's badly shaven stubble or stained tie, or dispute yet other trivialities, which — according to him — spoke ill of a policeman's image. But this morning the heat deprived him of any arguments in all eventual dispute regarding his subordinates' wardrobe.

The door opened and Mock came in, alongside him a slim, auburn-haired man of about thirty. The new policeman looked like a man who could not get enough sleep. He was stifling his yawns, but his eyes betrayed him with their tears. Forstner grimaced at the sight of the pale beige suit.

Mock, as usual, started by lighting a cigarette, an action repeated after their superior by almost all the men.

"Good morning, gentlemen. This is our new colleague, Criminal Assistant Herbert Anwaldt, who until recently was working with the Berlin Police. Assistant Anwaldt, as of today, is employed as Official in Charge of Special Affairs in our Criminal Department and is heading an investigation. He is responsible solely to me for its progress and results. Please execute his requests scrupulously. For the length of this investigation, Criminal Assistant Anwaldt is, in keeping with my decision, as good as your superior. This does not, of course, include Forstner." Mock extinguished his cigarette and remained silent for a moment; his men knew that the most important item of the briefing was about to follow. "Gentlemen, if Assistant Anwaldt's instructions momentarily deter you from your existing cases, leave those aside. Our new colleague's case is, at the moment, of prime importance. That's all, please return to your duties."

* * *

Anwaldt looked around Mock's office with curiosity. Try as he might, he could not find anything in this room that might express any individuality, that might bear any mark of the person occupying it. Everything had its place and was clean to the point of sterility. The Director suddenly unsettled the balance of all this paraphernalia — he removed his jacket and threw it across the back of his chair. Between the blue braces with their singular pattern (naked female bodies entwined in an embrace) proudly protruded a rather prominent belly. Anwaldt, pleased to finally discern a man of flesh and blood, smiled. Mock did not notice; he had just asked for two cups of strong tea over the phone.

"Apparently, it's excellent for quenching thirst when it's so hot. We'll see . . ."

He passed Anwaldt a box of cigars. Unhurriedly and methodically, he cut the tip of one with a small pair of tweezers. Mock's assistant, Dietmar Krank, laid a jug and some cups on the desk.

"Where would you like to start, Anwaldt?"

"Criminal Director, I have a suggestion . . ."

"Forget the formal address. We're not as ceremonious as the Baron."

"Of course, as you wish. I spent last night reading the case files. I'd like to know what you think of the following reasoning: somebody made a scapegoat of Friedländer, *ergo* somebody wants to hide the real perpetrator. Perhaps it's precisely that somebody who is the murderer. I have to find the person or persons who framed Friedländer, meaning — in other words — those who planted him for you to devour. So I'll start with Baron von Köpperlingk because he pointed you to Friedländer." Anwaldt smiled surreptitiously. "But, by the way, how could you have believed that a sixty-year-old – within half an hour – managed to kill a railway man, then have intercourse twice, which – one may surmise – the victims did not make easy. Then kill both women, write some squiggles on the wall, thereafter jump out of the window and dissolve into the mist. Show me a twenty-year-old who could perform such a feat."

"My dear man," Mock laughed. He liked Anwaldt's naïve enthusiasm. "Exceptional, superhuman powers can occur quite often in epileptics, after a fit, too. All such behaviour is the result of mysterious hormones, which Friedländer's physician, Doctor Weinsberg, elaborated to me in detail. I've no reason not to trust him."

"Exactly so. You trust him. But I do not trust anyone. I have to see that doctor. Perhaps somebody told him to tell you about the extraordinary gifts of epileptics, dervishes' trances and other such . . ." Anwaldt could not find the word, "other such nonsense."

Mock slowly drank his tea.

"You're very categorical, young man."

Anwaldt drank half a cup in one go. He wanted, at all costs, to show the Director how confident he felt in matters such as these. And it was precisely self-confidence that he lacked. He was behaving, right now, like a little boy who has wet his bed in the night and, on waking in the morning, does not know what to do with himself. (I was chosen. I am the chosen one. I will earn masses of money.) He finished what remained of his tea.

"I'd like a transcript of Friedländer's interrogation, please," he tried to give his voice a hard edge.

"What do you need a transcript for?" Mock's tone was no longer playful. "You've been working in the police for years and you know that sometimes the person being interrogated needs to be appropriately pressurized. The transcript has been touched up. It's better that I tell you what happened. I'm the one who questioned him after all." He looked out of the window and started to invent fluently. "I asked about an alibi. He didn't have one. I had to strike him. *(The man from the Gestapo, Konrad, forced him to talk in short order, no doubt. He has his methods.)* When I asked about the strange writing with which he filled thick notebooks, he laughed that it was a message to his brothers who were going to avenge him. *(I have heard that Konrad slashes through tendons with a razor.)* I had to be far more persuasive. I told them to fetch his daughter. That did the trick. He calmed down immediately and confessed he was guilty. That's all. *(Poor girl . . . What to do? I had no choice but to hand her over to Piontek . . . He got her addicted to morphine and packed her into bed with various high-ranking types.)*"

"And you believed a madman?" Anwaldt's eyes opened wide in astonishment. "Whom you subjected to blackmail like that?"

Mock was sincerely amused. He assumed Mühlhaus' attitude in face of Anwaldt – a kind-hearted grandfather stroking the head of a fantasizing grandson.

"Isn't that enough for you?" A sarcastic smile spread over his lips. "Here I have a madman and epileptic who, as the doctor states, can perform miracles shortly after a fit; no alibi, strange writing in notebooks. If you, having such evidence, continued to look for the murderer, you'd never finish your investigation. But maybe you were equally discerning in Berlin and old von Grappersdorff finally sent you off into the country?"

"Director, sir, did all this really convince you?"

Mock consciously gave slow vent to his irritation. He adored the feeling: to control waves of emotion and to give them free reign at any moment.

"Are you running an investigation or drawing up a psychological profile of my person?" he shouted. But he had played it wrong; he had not scared Anwaldt in the least. Mock did not know that shouting did not work on him. He had heard it all too often in childhood.

"Sorry," said the Assistant. "I didn't mean to offend you."

"Look, my son," Mock spread himself comfortably in his chair, toying with his wedding ring and, in his thoughts, constructing his own keen profile of Anwaldt. "If I had such thin skin, I wouldn't have been able to work for what's coming up to twenty-five years in the police." He immediately realized that Anwaldt was pretending to be humble. This intrigued him to such an extent that he decided to join in this subtle game.

"You didn't have to apologize. This way you revealed your weakness. I'll give you some good advice: always hide your own weak points, expose those of others. That way you ensnare others. Do you know what it means, 'to have something on somebody' or 'to hold someone in a vice'? That 'vice' might, for example, be gambling; or it might be harmoniously built ephebes; or again, Jewish origins. By tightening that vice, I have triumphed an infinite number of times."

"Can you now use my weakness against me? Can you catch me in 'the grips of anxiety'?"

"But why should I?"

Anwaldt ceased being humble. This conversation was giving him a great deal of pleasure. He felt like the representative of a rare scientific discipline, who suddenly meets another demon of the science in a train and is trying not to count the stations passing by inexorably.

"Why? Because I've renewed an investigation which you concluded with such incredible success. (From what I know, the investigation advanced your career prodigiously.)"

"Then run the investigation and don't perform psychological vivisections on me!" Mock had decided to lose his temper a little again.

Anwaldt fanned himself for a while with a copy of the *Breslauer Zeitung*. Finally, he risked: "And so I am. Starting with you."

Mock's whole-hearted laughter resounded in the room. Anwaldt timidly chimed in. Forstner was listening at the door – in vain.

"I like you, son," Mock finished his tea. "If you have any problems, call me any time, night or day. I've got a 'vice' for almost everybody in this city."

"But not yet one for me?" Anwaldt was putting the elegant visiting card away in his wallet.

Mock got up, giving the sign that he considered the conversation over. "And that's why I still like you."

BRESLAU, THAT SAME JULY 7TH, 1934
FIVE O'CLOCK IN THE AFTERNOON

Apart from the kitchen, Mock's study was the only room in his five-roomed apartment on Rehdigerplatz 1 to have north-facing windows. Only here was it possible to enjoy a pleasant coolness in the summer. The Director had just finished eating lunch, brought to him from the Grajecka restaurant across the courtyard. He sat at his desk and drank cold Haselbach beer which he had taken from the larder a short while ago. As usual after a meal, he was smoking and reading a book picked at random from his bookshelf. This time he had picked the work of a banned author: *The Psychopathology of Everyday Life* by Sigmund Freud. He was reading the paragraph about slips of the tongue and slowly falling into much-desired sleep when it came to him that he had called Anwaldt "my son" that day. It was a slip of the tongue which, in Mock's speech, was highly unusual. He considered himself to be a very reserved man and, under Freud's influence, he believed it was precisely slips of the tongue which disclosed our hidden needs and desires. His greatest dream was to father a son. He had divorced his first wife after four years of marriage when she had betrayed him with a servant because she could no longer

62

tolerate his increasingly brutal accusations of barrenness. Later, he had had many lovers. If one of them had only become pregnant, he would have married her without any hesitation whatsoever. Unfortunately, the succession of lovers all left the gloomy neurotic, found someone else and created more or less happy herds. They all had children. Mock, then forty, still did not believe in his infertility and continued to search for a mother for his son. Finally he found a former medical student whose family had disowned her because of her illegitimate child. The girl was expelled from university and became the mistress of a certain rich fence. Mock was questioning her regarding a case in which the fence was involved. A few days later, Inga Martens moved into an apartment on Zwingerstrasse which Mock had rented for her, and the fence – after the policeman had caught him in a "vice" – very willingly moved to Liegnitz and forgot about his lover. Mock was happy. He would come to Inga every morning for breakfast after intensive sessions at the swimming pool next door to her house. After three months, his happiness reached it zenith: Inga was pregnant. Mock made the decision to marry a second time; he had come to believe the old Latin saying – "*amor omnia vincit*". After a few months, Inga moved out of Zwingerstrasse and gave birth to the second child of her lecturer, Doctor Karl Meissner who, in the meantime, had got a divorce and married her. Mock, for his part, had lost his faith in love. He stopped living an illusion and married a rich, childless Danish woman, his second and last wife.

The Director's reminiscences were interrupted by the phone ringing. He was glad to hear Anwaldt's voice.

"I'm taking advantage of your kind permission and calling. I have a problem with Weinsberg. He's called Winkler now and is pretending not to know anything about Friedländer. He did not want to talk and almost set his dogs on me. Do you have 'something' on him?"

Mock considered for a full minute.

"I think so, but I can't talk about it over the phone. Please come here in an hour. Rehdigerplatz 1, apartment 6."

He replaced the receiver and dialled Forstner's number. He asked him two questions and listened to the exhaustive replies. A moment later, the telephone began to ring again. Erich Kraus' voice combined within itself two contrary intonations: the Chief of the Gestapo was at once asking and ordering.

"Mock, who is this Anwaldt, and what's he doing here?"

Eberhard could not abide this arrogant tone. Walter Piontek had always humbly asked for information even though he knew that Mock could not refuse him, whereas Kraus brutally demanded it. Although he had worked in Breslau for only a week, the latter was already sincerely loathed by many for this lack of tact. "A *parvenu* from Frankenstein and a fanatic," – whispered Breslau's aristocrats, both those of blood and those of spirit.

"Well, have you fallen asleep over there?"

"Anwaldt is an Abwehr agent," Mock had been prepared for questions about his new assistant. He knew that giving the true answer would be very dangerous for the Berliner. This reply also protected Anwaldt since the Head of Breslau's Abwehr, the Silesian aristocrat, Rainer von Hardenburg, detested Kraus. "He's uncovering Polish Intelligence in Breslau."

"Why do you need him? Why haven't you gone on holiday as planned?"

"A personal matter kept me here."

"What?"

Kraus valued, above all, military marches and a stable family life. Mock felt revulsion for this man who, precisely and methodically, washed his hands of the blood of prisoners he himself had tortured in order later to sit down to a family meal. On the second day of office, Kraus had battered to death a married prisoner who had refused to reveal where he met with his lover, an employee of the Polish Consulate. He later boasted to the entire Police Praesidium that he hated marital infidelity.

Mock drew in some air and hesitated:

"I stayed back because of a girlfriend . . . But I ask you to be discreet . . . You know what it's like . . ."

"Psh," snorted Kraus. "I do *not* know what it's like."

The receiver was slammed down with force. Mock approached the window and stared at the dusty chestnut tree whose leaves were not ruffled by the slightest breeze. The water carrier was selling his life-giving liquid to the residents of the block, children chased each other and shouted on the playground belonging to the Jewish Community School and raised clouds of dust. Mock was somewhat irritated. He wanted a rest, but here they were not giving him any peace even after working hours. He set out the chessboard on his desk and reached for *Chess Traps* by Überbrand. When the combinations had absorbed him to such an extent that he had forgotten about the heat and his own tiredness, the doorbell rang. *(Dammit, that must be Anwaldt. I hope he plays chess.)*

Anwaldt was an enthusiast of the game. So it is not surprising that he and Mock sat at the chessboard until dawn, drinking coffee and lemonade. Mock, who ascribed prognostic meanings to the simplest of actions, wagered that the result of the last game would prophesy the success of Anwaldt's investigation. They played out the sixth and last game between two and four o'clock. It ended in a draw.

BRESLAU, SUNDAY, JULY 8TH, 1934
NINE O'CLOCK IN THE MORNING

Mock's black Adler drove up to the shabby tenement on Zietenstrasse where Anwaldt lived. The Assistant heard the sound of the horn just as he was coming downstairs. The men shook hands. Mock drove along Seydlitzstrasse, passed the enormous Busch Circus building, turned left, crossed Sonnenplatz and stopped in front of the Nazi printers on Sonnenstrasse. He got out and shortly returned with a small bundle under his arm. He turned sharply and accelerated so as to move the hot, stagnant air in the car at least a little. He was short of sleep and silent. They drove under the viaduct and found themselves on the long and beautiful Gabitzstrasse. Anwaldt watched the churches go by with interest as Mock knowingly told him to whom they were dedicated: first the small Jesuit chapel as if joined to the neighbouring tenement, then the new church of Christ the King, and the recent St Charles Boromeus with its stylized medieval outline. Mock drove fast, overtaking trams from as many as four different lines. He passed the municipal cemetery, cut across Menzelstrasse, Kürassier Allee and parked in front of the brick barracks of the guardsmen on Gabitzstrasse. Here, in the modern tenement, number 158, a large comfortable apartment was occupied by Doctor Hermann Winkler, until recently Weinsberg. The Friedländer case had changed his life auspiciously. The good angel of this transformation was Hauptsturmführer Walter Piontek. The start of their acquaintance had not been encouraging. One evening in May of '33, Piontek had crashed into his old apartment, cruelly abused him and then, in a sweet voice, presented his alternative: either he would convincingly declare in the newspapers that Friedländer changed into Frankenstein's monster after epileptic fits, or he would die. When the doctor hesitated, Piontek added that if he accepted his proposition, it would significantly boost his finances. So Weinsberg had said "yes" and his life had indeed changed. Thanks to Piontek, he acquired a new identity and, every month, a sum of money flowed into his account at "Eichborn and Co." business enterprise, which – although not very large – pleased the exceptionally frugal doctor. Unfortunately, this *dolce vita* had not lasted long. A few days ago, Winkler had learned about

Piontek's death from the newspapers. That same day, the Gestapo had paid him a visit and retracted the agreement negotiated with the generous Hauptsturmführer. When he had tried to protest, one of the Gestapo, an overweight savage, acting — so he claimed — on the instructions of his boss, broke the fingers of Winkler's left hand. After that visit, the doctor had bought himself two fully grown Great Danes, repudiated the Gestapo's remuneration and tried to make himself invisible.

Mock and Anwaldt drew back when, behind Winkler's door, the dogs began to bark and howl.

"Who's there?" they heard through the minimal opening in the door.

Mock restricted himself to showing his identification — every word would have been drowned by the racket coming from the dogs. Winkler, with difficulty, calmed the hounds, tied them on a leash and invited his unwelcome guests into the drawing-room. There, as if on command, they lit cigarettes and looked around the room which appeared more like an office than a drawing-room. Winkler, a man of middling height, red-haired and about fifty, was a classic example of the pedantic bachelor. Instead of glasses and carafes, on the side-board stood canvas-bound files. Each of them had the name of a patient neatly written on its spine. The thought occurred to Anwaldt that this modern block of a house would collapse sooner than any of the files would change their place. Mock broke the silence.

"The dogs, are they for your protection?" he asked with a smile, indicating the Danes huddled on the floor and observing the strangers with mistrust. Winkler had tied them to the heavy oak table.

"Yes," the doctor retorted dryly, wrapping his bathrobe around him. "What brings you here this Sunday morning?"

Mock ignored the question. He smiled amicably.

"To protect you . . . Yes, yes . . . From whom? Perhaps from those who broke your fingers?"

The doctor was perturbed and, with his good hand, reached for a cigarette. Anwaldt gave him a light. The way in which he inhaled showed that this was one of the few cigarettes in his life.

"What do you want?"

"What do you want? What brings you here?" Mock mimicked Winkler. Suddenly, he approached within safe distance and yelled:

"I'm the one who's asking questions here, Weinsberg!"

The doctor just about managed to pacify the dogs which, growling, threw themselves at the policeman, almost bringing down the table to which they were tied. Mock sat down, waited a moment and continued calmly now:

"I'm not going to ask you any questions, Weinsberg. I'm only going to present you with our demands. Please make all your notes and materials concerning Isidor Friedländer accessible to us."

The doctor started to tremble despite the almost physical waves of heat which flooded the sunny room.

"I haven't got them any more. I handed everything over to Hauptsturmführer Walter Piontek."

Mock studied him. After a minute, he knew Weinsberg was lying. He was glancing at his bandaged hand a little too often. This could only have signified either "these men are going to start breaking my fingers, too" or "oh God, what'll happen if the Gestapo return and demand those materials?" Mock took the second possibility to be closer to the truth. He placed the small bundle from the printers on the table. Winkler tore the parcel open and started to flick through the yet unstitched brochure. His bony finger slid along one of the pages. He turned pale.

"Yes, Winkler, you're on the list. This is only a proof as yet. I can get in touch with the editor of that brochure and get your new, or even old, name removed. Am I to do that, Weinsberg?"

* * *

The temperature in the car was even a few degrees higher than outside, meaning it was about 35°C. Anwaldt threw his jacket and a large cardboard box covered with green paper on to the back seat. He opened the box. In it were copies of notes, articles and one primitively pressed gramophone record. The writing on the lid of the box read: "The case of I. Friedländer's prognostic epilepsy."

Mock wiped the sweat from his brow and anticipated Anwaldt's question:

"It's a list of doctors, nurses, paramedics, midwives and other of Hippocrates' servants of Jewish descent. It's to appear shortly."

Anwaldt looked at one of the last names: Doctor Hermann Winkler, Gabitzstrasse 158. "Are you in a position to have it removed?"

"I'm not even going to try." Mock followed two girls walking beneath the red wall of the barracks with his eyes. His pale jacket was darkened at the armpits by two stains. "Do you think I'm going to risk contention with the Chief of the S.S., Udo von Woyrsch, and the Chief of Gestapo, Erich Kraus, for one quack who prattled nonsense in the papers?"

He saw the clear sarcasm in Anwaldt's eyes: "Well, admit it, that nonsense did you no harm in your career."

IV

Anwaldt sat in the police laboratory, studying Weinsberg's materials, and grew increasingly convinced that the paranormal did exist. He remembered Sister Elisabeth from the orphanage. That petite and unassuming person with a prepossessing smile had drawn unexplained, alarming incidents to the orphanage. It had been during her stay in the institution — never before nor after — that processions of silent people in pyjamas would march during the night, that the cast-iron coverings of the cisterns in the toilets would fall with a crash, a dark figure would sit at the piano in the clubroom, and the telephone would ring every day at the same time. After Sister Elisabeth had left, albeit at her own request, the mysterious incidents had come to a stop.

From Weinsberg's — alias Winkler's — notes, it appeared that Friedländer differed from Sister Elisabeth in that he did not conjure up events and situations but foresaw them. In his state following an epileptic fit, he would shout five or six words, repeating them over and over like a monotonous refrain. Doctor Weinsberg recorded twenty-five such cases, of which he noted down twenty-three, and recorded two on a gramophone record. He analysed the material in detail and presented his results in the

Twentieth Annual of the *Zeitschrift für Parapsychologie und Metaphysik*. His article was entitled "The Tanathological Predictions of Isidor F.". Anwaldt had an off-print of the article in front of him. He read the methodological introduction cursorily and immersed himself in Weinsberg's arguments:

It has been stated beyond all doubt, that the words shouted by the patient come from Ancient Hebrew. This is the conclusion reached by the Berlin Semitist, Prof. Arnold Schorr, after three months of analysis. His linguistic expertise establishes it to be irrefutably so. We have included it in our materials and can render it accessible to those who might be interested. The sick man's prophetic messages can be divided into two: a name written in code and the circumstances of its bearer's death. After three years of research, I have managed to decipher twenty-three of the twenty-five messages. It is very difficult to solve the last two, even though they have been recorded on gramophone record. The messages which I have understood can be divided into those which have concurred with reality (ten) and those which refer to a person still living (thirteen). It must be emphasized that the majority of Isidor F.'s predictions concern people unknown to him personally, and this has been confirmed by the daughter. These persons are connected in two ways: 1 – all lived or are living in Breslau; 2 – all died a tragic death.

The *condicio sine qua non*† of understanding the whole message is to fish out and decipher the name contained within it. It is expressed in two ways: either by the sound, or the Hebrew meaning of the word. The Hebr. *geled* "skin", for example, we deciphered as being Gold (similar sound, the same consonants *gld*). It must be pointed out, however, that the patient could have expressed this name in a different

† Necessary condition (Latin).

"semantic" way. Indeed, Gold meaning "gold" could be coded synonymically in the Hebr. *zahaw*. This is the second way, where the name is hidden in the meaning and not in the sound of the Hebrew word. This can be seen, for example, in the Hebr. *hamad* – "helmet", which clearly points to the German name Helm, which means nothing else but precisely "helmet". Certain distortions were inevitable here, e.g. the Hebr. *sair* means "goat" (*Bock*), but the prophecy referred to a deceased bearing the name Beck. The most interesting and also the most satisfying to decipher was the Hebr. *jawal adama* – "river", "field" (Germ. *Fluss*, *Feld*). It seemed, therefore, that the name should be identified as Feldfluss or Flussfeld.

When I looked through the official list of deaths, I came across the name Rheinfelder, the circumstances of death: beating with an army belt. In a word, Rhein is "the Rhine", "river". From Rheinfeld to Rheinfelder is but a short distance. Here is the full roll of prophecies referring to persons deceased (I hold the list of those living in my records, but am not publishing it so as not to provoke any unnecessary, strong emotions).

Hebrew words	Names	Details concerning death in prophecy	Actual state of affairs
charon – divine flame *srefa* – charred remains *geled* – skin	*geled* = Gold	divine flame charred remains synagogue	Abraham Gold, cantor, died during a fire in synagogue.
lavan – white *mayim* – water *pe* – lips *nefesh* – breath *shemesh* – sun	*white* = Weiss	water, lips breath, sun	Regine Weiss, drowned in bathing resort.

aw – cloud *esh* – fire *bina* – reason *er* – giving witness *bazar* – dispersed *atsanim* – bones	*bina-er* = Wiener	cloud, fire chariot, dispersed bones	*Moritz Wiener,* *died in an air* *accident.*
romach – spear *shaa* – murmur *gulgolet* – skull *merkav* – cart *hen-ruach* – behold breath *pasak* – split	*hen-ruach* = Heinrich	spear, skull, murmur, cart, split	*Richard* *Heinrich, died* *hit by a car* *carrying pipes.* *One of them* *split his skull.*
kamma – how large *pasak* – divided *parash* – horse *akev* – hoof *hazer* – yard	*kamma pasak* = Kempsky	horse, hoof, yard	*Heinz Kempsky,* *died kicked in* *the head by a* *horse in the* *yard.*
ganna – garden *tsafir* – goat *chira* – wasp *zeninim* – sting *zara* – to pollinate	goat = Bock ~ Beck	garden, wasps, stings, to pollinate	*Friedrich Beck,* *died in his* *garden stung in* *the throat by a* *wasp.*
chebel – loop *safak* – spewed *chemer* – wine	helmet = Helm	loop, spewed up, wine, excrement	*Reinhard Helm,* *alcoholic, hung* *himself in the* *toilet which he*

afer – helmet *galal* – excrement			*fouled with his vomit.*
ish – man *or* – fire *shelach* – bullet *nebel* – harp *machol* – dance *keli* – weapon	*man* = Mann	bullet, harp, dance, fire, weapon	*Luise Mann,* *variety artiste,* *was shot on* *stage.*
yaval – river *adama* – field *mr'w hi* – to whip *barshel* – iron *aluf* – ox	*river* = the Rhein = Rhein field = Feld, therefore Rheinfelder	to whip, iron, ox	*Fritz Rheinfelder* *(he was fat –* *hence "ox"), was* *beaten with the* *buckle of an* *army belt.*
eben – stone *gag* – roof *silla* – street *meri* – resistance *kardom* – axe *nas* – quickly flew away	*meri kardom* = Marquardt	stone, roof, street, quickly flew away	*Hans* *Marquardt, was* *pushed out of* *the window of a* *skyscraper.*

From the examples mentioned above, it is clear that patient F.'s prophecies can really only be understood after the death of the person they specify. Let us, for example, look at example 2. There are several possible interpretations. The person mentioned in the prophecy could equally well have been called Weisswasser ("white water") – there are fifteen families of that name in Breslau. And then some Weisswasser could have been struck by angina ("lips", "breath") while sunbathing ("sun"). The deceased could also have been called Sonnemund ("lips", "sun") — three families in Breslau. Foretold death: choking ("breath") on vodka (one of Danzig's vodkas is called *Silberwasser*, "silver water").

I guarantee that I could also interpret the remaining cases in numerous ways. That is why we are not publishing the list which has not, so to speak, been validated by death. Let us simply say that it includes eighty-three names and various circumstances of tragic death.

Does such a variety of interpretations disqualify Isidor F.'s prophecies? Not in the least. The complex and gloomy forecasts of my patient divest the person of any possible defence. It is impossible to imagine a more spiteful and cruel fatalism — because here we would be publishing a list of eighty-three people of whom thirteen are yet to die tragically. And thirteen do, indeed, die — or maybe twelve, or maybe ten! But suddenly, after some time, we go through the death certificates and find a few deceased who were not on the list but to whom Isidor F.'s prophecies did apply. A person mentioned in his prophecies falls prey to harpies of the dark forces, is a helpless puppet whose proud declarations of independence are shattered by the stern sound of Hebrew consonants, and whose *missa defunctorum*† is only the derisive laughter of a self-satisfied demiurge.

After this pathetic note followed dreary and learned proofs comparing Friedländer to clairvoyants and various mediums who prophesy in a trance. Anwaldt read Weinsberg's article to the end with far less attention and started studying the eighty-three interpretations which, held together by brass paperclips, formed a clearly noticeable wad among the other materials and notes. He soon became bored with it. For dessert, he left himself the audio prophecies, sensing that they had something to do with the death of the Baron's daughter. He set up the gramophone and surren-

† Mass for the Dead (Latin).

dered himself to listening to the mysterious messages. What he was doing was irrational for, at secondary school, Anwaldt notoriously used to miss extra-curricular lessons in Biblical language and might now as well be listening to an audition in Quechuan with as much understanding. But the hoarse sounds induced in him the same state of morbid unease and fascination as had overcome him when he had first seen the flowing letters of Greek. Friedländer emitted sounds similar to choking. The sounds once purred, once hissed, once a wave forced from the lungs practically ripped the tense larynx. After twenty minutes of this relentless refrain, the sounds broke off.

Anwaldt was thirsty. For a while, he drove away the thought of a frothy tankard of beer. He got up, put all the materials — except the gramophone record — into the cardboard box, and went to the old store of office supplies which, now equipped with a desk and telephone, served the Official for Special Affairs as an office. He telephoned Doctor Georg Maass and arranged a meeting with him. Then he made his way to Mock's office with the list of gramophone names and his impressions. On the way, he passed Forstner, who had just left his superior. Anwaldt was surprised to see him there on a Sunday. He had a mind to joke about the heavy police work, but Forstner passed him without a word and ran briskly down the stairs. (*That's how someone looks who Mock has caught in a vice.*) He was wrong. Forstner had been held in a vice all along. Mock only tightened it from time to time. That is what he had done a moment ago.

BRESLAU, THAT SAME JULY 8TH, 1934
HALF-PAST TWO IN THE AFTERNOON

Standartenführer S.S. Erich Kraus kept professional and private matters neatly apart. He dedicated far fewer hours to the latter, of course, but it was time strictly measured out — Sunday, for example, was held to be a day of rest. Following his post-prandial siesta, it was his habit to talk to his four sons between four and five o'clock. The boys would sit at a huge round table and relate to their father the progress they were making in their work, the ideological activities of the Hitlerjugend and the resolutions which they had regularly to make in the Führer's name. Kraus would pace up and down the room, comment good-naturedly on what he heard, and pretend not to notice the surreptitious glances at their watches and the suppressed yawns.

But he was not permitted the freedom to spend his first Sunday in Breslau in a purely private capacity. The taste of his lunch was spoiled by the sour thought of General-Major Rainer von Hardenburg, the chief of Breslau's Anwehr. He loathed this stiff, monocled aristocrat with all his might – he, the son of a bricklayer and alcoholic. Kraus swallowed a delicious schnitzel with onions and felt his gastric juices rise. Furious, he got up from the table, threw his napkin down in a rage, walked through to his study and, for the umpteenth time that day, phoned Forstner. Instead of exhaustive information about Anwaldt, he heard half a minute of a long, intermittent ringing tone. *(Where has that son-of-a-bitch gone?)* He dialled Mock's number, but when the Director of Police picked up the telephone, Kraus threw down the receiver. *(I won't learn any more from that obsequious prat than he's already told me.)* The helplessness he experienced in the face of von Hardenburg, whom he had already known in Berlin, was somehow comprehensible to Kraus: in the face of Mock, it was almost contemptible – which is why it so wounded his *amour propre.*

He paced around the table like a rabid beast. Suddenly, he stood still and hit his forehead with an open palm. *(This heat, damn it, is killing me. I can't think any more.)* He sat down comfortably in his armchair next to his telephone. First Hans Hoffmann, then Mock. In a dry tone, he gave both one and the other a number of instructions. The tone of his voice

77

shifted towards the end of his conversation with Mock, from the cold tone of a superior, to the yelling of a madman.

Mock had decided that he would leave for Zoppot that evening. He had made that decision after his visit to Winkler. Kraus' phone call tore him from his afternoon nap. The man from the Gestapo quietly reminded Mock of his dependence on the secret police and demanded a written report on Anwaldt's work for the Abwehr. Mock calmly refused. He said that he was due some rest and was leaving for Zoppot that evening.

"And what about your girlfriend?"

"Oh, those girlfriends . . . Here one minute, gone the next. You know what they're like . . ."

"I do *not* know what they're like!"

BRESLAU, THAT SAME JULY 8TH, 1934
THREE O'CLOCK IN THE AFTERNOON

Hans Hoffmann had been a secret agent for the police since time immemorial. He had served the Emperor, the Republic police, and now the Gestapo. He put his considerable professional success down to his warm-hearted appearance: a slender figure, small moustache, carefully combed, thin hair, honey-coloured, kind, laughing eyes. Who would have thought that this sympathetic, elderly gentleman was one of the most valued of secret agents?

Anwaldt and Maass, who paid no attention to the neat old man sitting on the neighbouring bench, certainly did not suspect. Maass in particular was unconcerned about the presence of other strollers and pontificated loudly, somewhat irritating Anwaldt not only by his squeaky voice but, above all, by the drastic contents of his confessions which were mostly focussed on a woman's body and the rapture it entailed.

"Just look, Herbert — indeed, I may call you that, may I not?" Maass went so far as to smack his lips when he saw a young and shapely blonde strolling with an older woman. "How wonderfully that thin dress clings to the girl's thighs. She's probably not wearing a petticoat . . ."

Anwaldt started to be amused by this satyr's airs. He took Maass by the arm and they began to walk along Liebichshöhe. Above them rose a tower, crowned with a statue of the winged Roman goddess of victory. Spurting fountains refreshed the air to a certain extent. The crowd milled around on the pseudo-baroque terraces. The little old man ambled just behind them, smoking a cigarette in an amber cigarette holder.

"My dear man," Anwaldt, too, allowed himself a degree of familiarity. "Is it true that women become pushy in summer?"

"How do you know?"

"From Hezjod. I'd like to verify a twenty-seven-century-old belief with a specialist. The poet claims that in summer they are *mahlotatai de gynaikes, aphaurotatoi de toi andres*." Anwaldt quoted in Greek an extract from Hezjod's *The Works and Days*.[†]

Maass paid no attention to Anwaldt's sarcastic tone. He was interested in knowing where the Police Assistant had learned his Greek.

"My secondary school teacher of Classical languages was good, that's all," Anwaldt said.

After this brief *entre'acte*, Maass returned to the main topic of his interest.

"Secondary school, you say . . . Did you know, my dear Herbert, that the schoolgirls of today are pretty well acquainted with the facts of life? I spent a blissful afternoon with one in Königsberg recently. Have you read the Kama Sutra? Have you heard anything about swallowing the mango fruit? Imagine that this seemingly innocent girl was able to force my steed into obedience when it was just on the point of tearing out of control. I didn't give her private tuition in Sanskrit for nothing . . ."

[†] "Women are most excited, men most sleepy" (Greek).

This mention of a lascivious schoolgirl irritated Anwaldt a great deal. He removed his jacket and unbuttoned his collar. He thought intensively about frothy tankards of beer; about the slight buzz after the first, the dizziness after the second, the tremor of the tongue after the third, the clarity of mind after the fourth, the euphoria after the fifth . . . He looked at the small man with curly, dark hair and a sparse beard and interrupted his pontification none too politely:

"Doctor Maass, please listen to this record. They'll lend you a gramophone from the police laboratory. Should you have any problems with the translation, please contact me. Professor Andreae and one Hermann Winkler are at your disposition. The texts have probably been recorded in the Hebrew language."

"I don't know if it's of any interest to you," Maass, offended, looked at Anwaldt, "but the third edition of Hebrew grammar — of which I am author — has just been published. I manage quite well in this language and have no need of impostors such as Andreae. Winkler, on the other hand, I do not know and do not wish to know."

He turned away abruptly and hid the record under his jacket: "I bid you goodbye. Please come to me tomorrow for the translation of these texts. I think I should manage it," he added in a wounded tone.

Anwaldt did not pay any attention to Maass' acerbity. He was feverishly trying to remember something the latter had said and which he had been wanting to ask for several minutes now. Nervously, he chased away the visions of frothy tankards and tried not to hear the shouts of children running about on the pathways. The leaves of the splendid plane trees formed a dome beneath which clung a suspension of dust, thick from the heat. Anwaldt felt a stream of sweat run down between his shoulder blades. He glanced at Maass, who was plainly waiting for an apology, and croaked through his dry throat:

"Doctor Maass, why did you call Professor Andreae an impostor?"

Maass had obviously forgotten about the offence because he became markedly revitalized:

"Would you believe that this moron discovered several new Coptic inscriptions? He worked them out, and then — on the basis of them — modified Coptic grammar. This would have been a wonderful discovery if it wasn't for the fact that these 'discoveries' had been laboriously composed by himself. He had simply needed a subject for his post-doctoral thesis. I disclosed this fraud in the *Semitische Forschungen*. Do you know what arguments I put forward?"

"I'm sorry, Maass, but I'm in a bit of a hurry. I'll willingly get acquainted with this fascinating puzzle when I have a free moment. Anyway, I take it that you and Andreae are not friends. Am I right?"

Maass did not hear the question. He had dug his insatiable gaze into the generous curves of a girl walking past in school uniform. It did not go unnoticed by the elderly man who was blowing the cigarette butt out of his amber cigarette holder.

BRESLAU, THAT SAME JULY 8TH, 1934
HALF-PAST THREE IN THE AFTERNOON

Forstner drank what was his third schnapps within a quarter of an hour and ate a hot frankfurter topped with a white hat of horseradish. The large dose of alcohol calmed him. He sat, gloomily, in a discreet alcove separated from the rest of the room by a maroon curtain, and tried, with the help of strong drink, to loosen the vice which Mock had tightened over his head an hour ago. It was all the more difficult in that the pincers of the vice were manipulated by two mighty and despised powers: Eberhard Mock and Erich Kraus. On leaving his apartment on Kaiser-Wilhelm-Strasse, he had heard the persistent ringing of the telephone. He knew it was Kraus calling for information about Anwaldt's mission. Standing on the scorching pavement at the 2 and 17 tram stop, he brooded over his own helplessness, Mock, Kraus and, above all, Baron von Köpperlingk. He cursed the wild orgies in the Baron's palace and gardens at Kanth, during which naked teenage nymphs and curly-haired cupids invited guests to drink ambrosia, and the pool swarmed with naked dancers, male and female. Forstner had felt safe under the wing of the omnipotent Piontek, all the more so as his chief had still remained ignorant as to the private life and contacts of his assistant. He had not been worried about Mock, although he knew from Piontek that, after Baron von Köpperlingk's unfortunate remark, the Counsellor had been acquiring ever more information about him. He had been lulled and entirely anaesthetised by his spectacular promotion to the position of Deputy Chief of the Criminal Department. When, during "the night of the long knives", Heines, Piontek and all the top people of Breslau's S.A. fell, Forstner — previously an employee of the Criminal Department — had been spared; but he had lost the ground under his feet. He had become entirely dependent on Mock. One word whispered into Kraus' ear about Forstner's contacts would plunge him into inexistence, following in the footsteps of his protectors. As a homosexual, he could be certain of the double cruelty of Kraus. His very first day in office, the new Chief of Gestapo had announced that "if he were to find a queer within his department, he would end up like Heines". Even if he did not make good his threat when confronted with Forstner, who was, after all, a policeman from a different department, he would most assuredly withdraw his support. And then Mock would devour him with wild relish.

Forstner tried to calm his nerves with a fourth, significantly smaller, schnapps. He put a splodge of horseradish and fat left by the frankfurter on a roll, swallowed it and grimaced. He had realized that it was Mock, not Kraus, who was squeezing the vice with doubled force. He had decided to suspend his co-operation with the Gestapo for the length of

Anwaldt's secret investigation. His silence vis-à-vis Kraus could be justified by the exceptional secrecy of the investigation. If, however, he were to incur Mock's displeasure by refusing to co-operate, disaster was unavoidable.

Separating the truth from probability in this way, Forstner heaved a sigh of some relief. He wrote Mock's informal instructions into his notebook: "to draw up a detailed dossier on Baron Olivier von der Malten's servants." Then he raised his frosted glass high and drank it down in one go.

BRESLAU, THAT SAME JULY 8TH, 1934
QUARTER TO FOUR IN THE AFTERNOON

Anwaldt sat on tram 18 contemplating with great interest the unusual cabled bridge he was just crossing. The tram rumbled over the bridge; red-brick buildings and a church wrapped in old chestnut trees flitted by on the right, solid tenements on the left. The tram stopped in a very busy square. Anwaldt counted the stops. He was to alight at the next one. The tram moved away and quickly gathered speed. Anwaldt prayed for it to go even faster. The reason for his supplications was an enormous wasp which had begun its mad dance around the Assistant's head. At first, he had tried at all costs to keep calm, and moved his head as little as possible, once to the right, once to the left. These moves greatly intrigued the insect, which had taken a clear liking to Anwaldt's nose. *(I remember: the sticky jar of cherry juice in the delicatessen store in Berlin, angry wasps stinging little Herbert, the shopkeeper's laughter, the reek of onion peelings applied to the stings.)* He lost control and flapped his arms. He felt he had struck the wasp. With a slight flick, it fell to the tram floor. He was about to squash it with his shoe when the tram suddenly braked and the policeman tumbled on to a corpulent lady. The wasp started up with a buzz and sat on Anwaldt's hand, who, instead of a sting, felt the hard blow of a newspaper, then heard a distinctive crunch. He looked with gratitude at his saviour – a not very tall, old man of endearing appearance, who had just stamped on the assailant. Anwaldt thanked him politely *(Where do I know this old man from?)* and got off at the tram stop. Following Mock's instructions, he crossed to the other side and made his way between some official buildings. On one of them, he read the sign: UNIVERSITY CLINIC. He turned left. The buildings were burning in the heat, the cellars stank of rat poison. He reached the river, leaned against the barrier and removed his jacket. He was disorientated – he had obviously made a mistake – and waited for someone who could show him the way to Hansastrasse. A fat servant, lugging an enormous bucket full of ashes, approached the barrier. Slowly, unworried by the presence of a witness, she started to spill them on to the grassy embankment. Suddenly, a gust of wind picked up – the harbinger of a storm. The grey dust of ashes swirled around the bucket and blew right into the face and on to the neck and shoulders of the furious Anwaldt. The policeman showered the contrite wench with a volley of vulgar abuse and went off to look for a tap with clean water. He did not find one, however, and confined himself to blowing the ashes off his shirt and wiping them from his face with a handkerchief.

The adventure with the wasp and with the ashes, his unfamiliarity with Breslau all made Anwaldt late for his meeting with Lea Friedländer. When finally he got to Hansastrasse and found the Fatamorgana Studio of Photography and Film, it was four-fifteen. Pink curtains were drawn across the window front, a brass sign ENTRANCE FROM THE YARD was nailed to the door. Anwaldt obeyed the instruction. He knocked for a long time; it was several minutes before the door was opened by a red-haired servant. In a strong foreign accent, she informed him that "Fräulein Susanne" did not admit clients who arrived late. Anwaldt was too irritated to try subtle persuasion. Without ceremony, he moved the girl aside and sat in the not very large waiting room.

"Please tell Fräulein Friedländer that I'm a special client." He calmly lit a cigarette. The servant left, clearly amused. Anwaldt opened all the doors except for the one behind which the girl had disappeared. The first led to a bathroom lined with pale blue tiles. His attention was drawn to a bath of unparalleled size which stood on a high pedestal, and a bidet. Having looked at the unusual sanitary equipment, Anwaldt entered the large front room where the film studio "Fatamorgana" was located. The centre was taken up by an enormous divan strewn with gold and crimson cushions. Spotlights and several wicker paravents, hung with elegant, lace underwear, were arranged all around. There could not be the slightest doubt as to the nature of the films shot here. He heard a rustling, turned and saw a tall, dark-haired girl standing in the door, wearing nothing but stockings and a see-through peignoir. She rested her hands on her hips, parting her garment. In this way, Anwaldt became acquainted with most of the beautiful secrets of her body.

"You're half an hour late. So we haven't got much time," she spoke slowly, drawing out the syllables. She walked over to the large bed, gently swaying her hips. She gave the impression that crossing these two metres was beyond her strength. She sat down heavily and, with a slender hand, made an inviting gesture. Anwaldt approached quite cautiously. She pulled him firmly towards her. It seemed she would never finish the simple action of unbuttoning his trousers. He interrupted these manipulations, leaned over a little and took her tiny face in his hands. She looked at him with surprise. Her pupils had dissolved, entirely covering her irises. The shadows of the semi-darkness outlined Lea's face – pale and sick. She tossed her head in order to sever the gentle embrace. The peignoir slipped from her shoulder to reveal fresh prick marks. Anwaldt felt the cigarette burn his lips. He quickly spat it out, straight into a large porcelain bowl. The butt hissed in a residue of water. Anwaldt removed his jacket and hat and sat down in the armchair opposite Lea. Rays of the setting sun penetrated the pink curtains and danced on the wall.

"Fräulein Friedländer, I'd like to talk with you about your father. Only a few questions . . ."

Lea's head fell forward. She rested her elbows on her thighs as if she were falling into a sleep.

"What do you need this for? Who are you?" Anwaldt guessed rather than heard the questions.

"My name's Herbert Anwaldt and I'm a private detective. I'm leading the investigation into Marietta von der Malten's death. I know that your father was forced into confessing his guilt. I also know Weinsberg's alias Winkler's nonsense . . ."

He broke off. His parched throat was refusing to obey. He walked up to a sink mounted in the corner of the studio and took a moment to drink water straight from the tap. Then he sat in the armchair again. The water he had just drunk evaporated through his skin. He wiped a wave of sweat with the surface of his hand and asked the first question:

"Someone framed your father. Maybe the murderer himself. Tell me, who could have wanted to make your father the murderer?"

Lea brushed the hair languidly away from her forehead. She said nothing.

"Mock, most certainly," he answered himself. "Thanks to finding the 'murderer', he got a promotion. But it really is difficult to suspect the Director of such naivety. Or maybe those who murdered the Baron's daughter are the ones who pointed us to him? Baron von Köpperlingk? No, that's impossible for natural reasons. No homosexual is capable of raping two women within a quarter of an hour. Besides, he spoke the truth when he told us about your shop as a place where scorpions could be bought, so all this does not look like being construed in advance. To put it briefly, your father was slipped under Mock's nose by someone who knew that the Baron had once bought scorpions from you and also knew about your father's mental illness. That someone found the perfect scapegoat in your father. Who could have known about the scorpions and your father's madness? Think! Did anybody apart from Mock come to see you and ask your father about an alibi? A private detective like myself, perhaps?"

Lea Friedländer turned to lie on her side and rested her head on her bent arm. A cigarette smoked in the corner of her mouth.

"If I tell you, you'll die," she laughed quietly. "Funny. I can deal out death sentences."

She fell back and closed her eyes, the cigarette slipped out of the painted lips and rolled across the bed. Anwaldt threw it into the porcelain bowl. He was on the point of getting up from the divan when Lea threw her arms around his neck. Like it or not, he lay down next to her. Both lay on their stomachs, close to each other, Anwaldt's cheek touching her smooth shoulder. Lea put the man's arm on her back and whispered in his ear:

"You'll die. But now you're my client. So do your bit. Time is running out . . ."

For Lea Friedländer, time had indeed run out. Anwaldt turned the inert girl and pulled her eyelids open. The eyes slipped away into the cranial vault. For a moment, he struggled with the desire that was overcoming him. He gained control of himself, however, removed his tie and unbuttoned his shirt to the waist. Cooling himself a little in this way, he went into the hall and then into the only other room he had not yet inspected: a drawing-room full of furniture under black covers. A pleasant coolness prevailed – the windows gave on to the yard. A door led to the kitchen. No sign of the servant girl. Everywhere were piles of dirty dishes, beer and lemonade bottles. (*What does the servant do in this house? Probably makes films with her mistress . . .)* He took one of the clean tankards and half filled it with water. Tankard in hand, he entered the windowless room which ended this untypical suite of connecting rooms. *(Larder? Servant's room?)* Practically the whole surface was occupied by an iron bed, a decorative escritoire and a dressing-table with an intricately twisted lamp. On the escritoire stood some dozen books bound in faded green cloth. The titles were printed on the spines in silver. One of them did not have a title and this was the one which interested Anwaldt. He opened it: a notebook half full of large, rounded writing. On the title page, meticulously calligraphed, was written: "Lea Friedländer. Diary". He removed his shoes, made himself comfortable on the bed and immersed himself in reading. This was not a typical diary but rather memories of childhood and youth, recently noted.

Anwaldt compared his imagination to a revolving stage. Often the scene he was reading would appear in front of his eyes with intense reality. In this way, while he had been reading Gustav Nachtigal's memoirs recently, he had felt the scorching desert sands under his feet and the stench of camels and Tibbu guides assaulted his nostrils. As soon as he tore his eyes away from the book, the curtain would fall, the imagined sets evaporate. When he returned to the book, the appropriate scenery would return, the Sahara sun would burn.

Now, too, he saw what he was reading about: the park and the sun penetrating through the leaves. The sun was refracted in the lace of dresses worn by young mothers, next to whom ran little girls. The girls looked their mothers in the eyes and snuggled their heads under their arms. Beside them strolled a beautiful girl with an overweight father who minced beside her and soundlessly cursed the men greedily observing his daughter. Anwaldt made himself more comfortable. His eyes rested on a painting hanging on the wall; then he returned to the pages of the diary.

Now he saw a dark yard. A little girl had fallen from the outdoor clothes horse and was calling: "Mummy!" The father came up and hugged her, his lips smelling of familiar tobacco. The father's handkerchief smudged the tears on her cheeks.

He heard a noise in the kitchen. He looked out. A large, black cat was majestically strolling along the sill. Anwaldt, reassured, returned to his reading.

The set he was now visiting was a little blurred. Thick greenery filled the picture with vivid patches. A forest. The leaves of trees hung over the heads of two little beings holding each other by the hand and walking tentatively along a path. Sick beings, crooked, distorted, choked by the dark greenery of the forest, the damp moss, the touch of coarse grasses. This was not his imagination — Anwaldt was staring into the painting which hung above the bed. He read the plate attached to it: "Chaim Soutine. Exiled children".

He rested his burning cheek on the headrest and glanced at his watch. It was almost seven. He dragged himself up with difficulty and went to the atelier.

Lea Friedländer had pulled herself out of her drugged sleep and was lying on the divan with her legs spread wide.

"Have you paid?" she sent him a forced smile.

He took a twenty-mark note from his wallet. The girl stretched herself so that her joints cracked. She moved her head a few times and quietly squeaked.

"Please don't go yet . . ." she looked at him pleadingly, black shadows blossomed under her eyes. "I don't feel well . . ."

Anwaldt buttoned up his shirt, fastened his tie and put on his jacket. He fanned himself for a while with his hat.

"Do you remember what we spoke about, the questions I asked you? Who are you warning me against?"

"Please don't torture me! Please come the day after tomorrow, at the same time . . ." She pulled her knees up to her chin in the helpless gesture of a little girl. She was trying to control the trembling which shook her.

"And if I don't learn anything the day after tomorrow? How am I to know you won't fill yourself with some filth?"

"You don't have a way out . . ." Suddenly Lea threw herself forward and clung to him with her whole body. "The day after tomorrow . . . The day after tomorrow . . . I beg you . . ." *(Lips smelling of familiar tobacco, the warm underarm of a mother, exiled children.)* Their embrace was reflected in the mirrored wall of the atelier. He saw his face. Tears, of which he had not been aware, had dug two furrows in the ash deposited on his cheeks by an unfavourable wind.

BRESLAU, THAT SAME JULY 8TH, 1934
A QUARTER-PAST SEVEN IN THE EVENING

Mock's chauffeur, Heinz Staub, braked gently and parked the Adler on the approach to Main Station. He turned and looked questioningly at his boss.

"Wait a moment, please, Heinz. We're not getting out yet." Mock took an envelope from his wallet. He spread out a letter, covered in tiny, uneven writing. He read carefully yet again:

Dear Herr Anwaldt!

I would like you to be quite clear at the start of your investigation about the course which my own took. I state that I never believed Friedländer to be guilty. Nor did the Gestapo believe it. Yet both I and the Gestapo greatly needed Friedländer to be the murderer. Accusation of the Jew helped me in my career, the Gestapo used it in their propaganda. It is the Gestapo who turned

Friedländer into a scapegoat. I would, however, like to argue with your reasoning here: "He who framed Friedländer is the murderer". It is not the Gestapo who is behind the Baron's daughter's death. Indeed, the late Hauptsturmführer S.A. Walter Piontek eagerly made use of the track suggested by Baron Wilhelm von Köpperlingk (who, by the by, has many friends in the Gestapo), but it would be nonsense to state that the secret police committed this crime so as to destroy an unknown dealer and then use the whole case for the purposes of propaganda. The Gestapo would rather have carried out some obvious provocation so as to widely justify their planned pogrom of the Jews. Here the most fitting person would be one of Hitler's dignitaries, and not the Baron's daughter.

The fact that the Gestapo is not behind the crime does not, however, mean that men from this institution will be pleased with an investigation into the matter. If somebody finds the true murderers, then the entire propaganda will be turned into a laughing stock by the English and French newspapers. I warn you against these people – they are ruthless and capable of forcing anyone into giving up an investigation. If, God forbid, you ever find yourself at the Gestapo, please stubbornly state that you are an agent of the Abwehr uncovering the Polish Intelligence network in Breslau.

This letter is proof of trust on my part. The best proof on your part would be to destroy it.

Yours respectfully,
Eberhard Mock

P.S. I'm leaving for my holiday in Zoppot. During my absence, the official car is at your disposal.

Mock slipped the letter into the envelope, sealed it and handed it to the chauffeur. He got out of the car and tried to breathe. The burning air shocked his lungs. The pavement and the walls of the station reflected the heat of the stifling day. Somewhere far beyond the city, the faint announcement of a storm was departing. The Chief of Police wiped his brow with a handkerchief and made towards the entrance, ignoring the flirtatious smiles of prostitutes. Heinz Staub dragged two suitcases behind him. As Mock was nearing the platform, someone quickly walked up to him and took him by the elbow. Despite the heat, Baron von der Malten was dressed in an elegant, worsted suit with silver stripes.

"May I walk you to your train, Eberhard?"

Mock nodded, but he could not control his face: it expressed a mixture of amazement and aversion. Von der Malten did not notice this and walked beside Mock in silence. He tried to delay *ad infinitum* the question which he had to ask Mock. They stopped in front of a first-class carriage. The chauffeur carried the heavy suitcases into a compartment; the conductor signalled to the passengers to board the train. The Baron clasped Mock's face in both hands and pulled it towards himself as if he wanted to kiss him but instead of a kiss he posed a question, then immediately covered his ears so as not to hear an affirmative reply.

"Eberhard, have you told Anwaldt that I killed that luckless Friedländer?"

Mock triumphed. Heinz Staub stepped down from the carriage, informing them that the train was about to leave; Mock smiled; the Baron squeezed his eyes shut and covered his ears; the conductor made polite requests; the police dignitary tore the Baron's hands from his ears.

"I haven't told him yet . . ."

"I beg of you, don't!"

The conductor grew impatient; Staub insisted; the Baron looked at Mock with imploring fury; Mock smiled. Clouds of steam spurted from

92

under the engine; Mock entered his compartment and shouted through the window:

"I won't tell him if you let me know why it's so important to you."

The train moved slowly away. The conductor slammed the door; Staub waved goodbye; von der Malten clung on to the window and pronounced four words in a booming voice. Mock fell back on to the sofa cushions, amazed. The Baron jumped away from the window. The train gathered speed. The conductor nodded menacingly. Staub walked down the stairs. A beggar pulled at the sleeve of the Baron's jacket ("the respected gentleman nearly fell under the train"). The Baron stood erect, all but brushing the train. And Mock sat motionless in his compartment, repeating to himself over and over that what he had heard was not just a Freudian illusion.

BRESLAU, THAT SAME JULY 8TH, 1934
A QUARTER TO EIGHT IN THE EVENING

Maass sat in his three-roomed apartment on Tauentzienstrasse 14, listening to the crackling gramophone record and reconstructing the Hebrew words by ear. He dipped his nib in the round-bellied inkpot with enthusiasm and marked the paper with strange, slanting signs. He was lost in his work. He could not allow himself any hesitation, any doubt. The doorbell painfully tore his attention away from the Biblical language. He turned off the light, deciding not to open, then heard the grating of a key in the lock. (*The inquisitive owner of this tenement no doubt. He thinks I'm not at home and wants to snoop around a bit.*) He got up and made his way furiously to the hall, where – he supposed – he would see the cunning hypochondriac with whom he had already managed to argue on the first day about rent. Maass, to be sure, did not pay a fenig towards the rent from his own pocket but had accused the landlord of extortion on principle.

93

The men he did see were no more to his taste. Next to the terrified owner, three men in S.S. uniform stood in the hall. All three were baring their teeth at him. But Maass was in no mood to smile.

BRESLAU, THAT SAME JULY 8TH, 1934
EIGHT O'CLOCK IN THE EVENING

Returning home in a droschka, Anwaldt lay on the seat and anxiously regarded the tops of the tenements. He thought the parallel lines of the roofs opposite met and merged over him in an undulating ceiling. He closed his eyes and, for a while, repeated in his thoughts: "*I am normal, there is nothing wrong with me.*" As if to negate this creed, Chaim Soutine's painting of "Exiled Children" swam before his eyes. A boy in short trousers was pointing something out to a little girl with a deformed leg. She could barely walk and held tightly to her companion's hand. The yellow path cut the blue-black of the azure vault in the distance and met the teasing greenery of the forest. On the meadow burst red ulcers of flowers.

Anwaldt instantly opened his eyes and saw the enormous, bearded, weather-beaten face of the cabby looking suspiciously at his passenger.

"We're on Zietenstrasse."

Anwaldt slapped the cabby gruffly on the shoulder. (*"I am normal, there is nothing wrong with me."*) He grinned broadly:

"And do you have a good brothel in this town? But it's got to be, you know, first rate. Wenches with backsides the size of a horse. That's the kind I like."

The cabby narrowed his eye, retrieved a small visiting card from his breast pocket and handed it to the passenger: "Here the respected gentleman will find all the dames he wants."

Anwaldt paid and went to Kahlert's corner restaurant. He ordered the

94

elderly waiter to bring him a menu and, without even looking at it, pointed randomly to an item. He wrote his address on a napkin and handed it to the polite head waiter.

At home, he found no shelter from the heat. He closed the south-west-facing window and promised himself to open it only late into the night. He undressed to his long johns and lay down on the carpet. He did not close his eyes – Soutine's painting might otherwise have floated in again. The knocking on the door was insistent. The waiter passed him a plate covered with a silver lid and left after receiving his tip. Anwaldt went into the kitchen and turned on the light. He leaned against the wall and groped for the bottle of lemonade which he had bought the previous day. His diaphragm jerked, he felt his throat cramp up: his gaze fixed on a large cockroach which, alarmed by the current of air, disappeared as fast as it could somewhere under the iron sink. Anwaldt slammed the kitchen door. He sat at the table in his room and swallowed half the bottle of lemonade, imagining it to be vodka.

A quarter of an hour passed before the image of the cockroach vanished from his eyes. He glanced at his supper. Spinach and fried egg. He quickly covered the plate so as to chase away yet another image: brown panelling of the orphanage dining-room, nausea, the pain in his nose as it was being squeezed, the sticky gunge of spinach being tipped down his throat with an aluminium spoon.

As if playing a game with himself, he uncovered his plate again and started to rummage thoughtlessly in his food with a fork. He split the thin coating of the yolk. It spilt over, flooding the egg white. Anwaldt recre-ated a familiar landscape with his fork: the slippery path of the yolk meandering through the greasy greenery of spinach. He rested his head against the edge of the table, his arms hung languidly; even before he fell into a sleep, the landscape from Soutine's painting returned. He was holding Erna by the hand. The whiteness of the girl's skin contrasted vividly with the navy blue of her school uniform. A white, sailor's collar covered the small shoulders. They were walking along a narrow path in a dark corridor of trees. She rested her head on his shoulder. He stopped and began kissing her. He was holding Lea Friedländer in his arms. A meadow: kindly beetles crawling up grass stalks. She was feverishly unbuttoning his clothes. Sister Dorothea from the orphanage was shouting: you've shit yourself again, look how nice it is to clean up your shit. Scorching sand pours on to torn skin. Scorching desert sand is settling on the stone floor. Into the ruined tomb peers a hairy goat. Hoof marks on the sand. Wind blows sand into zigzag gaps in the wall. From the ceiling tumble small, restless scorpions. They surround him and raise their poisonous abdomens. Eberhard Mock throws aside his Bedouin headgear. The sinister creatures crunch under his sandals. Two scorpions, which he had not noticed, dance on Anwaldt's belly.

The sleeping man shouted and thumped himself in the stomach. In the closed window hung a red moon. The policeman staggered to the window and opened it as wide as he could. He threw the sheets on the carpet and lay on the pallet, soon soaked in sweat.

Breslau's night was merciless.

V

The morning proved a little cooler. Anwaldt went into the kitchen and inspected it closely: no trace of cockroaches. He knew that, during the day, they hide in various gaps, cracks in the walls, behind skirting-boards. He drank a bottle of warm lemonade. Not worrying about the sweat which had coated his skin, he began a series of swift moves. With a few drags of his razor, he tore away the hard stubble, then poured a jug of cold water over himself, put on clean underwear and a shirt, sat down in the old, tattered armchair and attacked the mucous membrane of his stomach with nicotine.

Two letters lay under his door. He read Mock's warnings with emotion and burnt the letter over the ashtray. He was pleased with the news from Maass: the learned man dryly informed him that he had translated Friedländer's cries and was expecting Anwaldt at ten in his apartment on Tauentzienstrasse 14. He studied a map of Breslau and soon found the street. Carried away, he burnt that letter too. He felt an enormous surge of energy. He had not forgotten anything; he gathered the plate with his smeared supper from the table, threw its contents into the toilet on the half-landing, returned the crockery to the restaurant where he consumed a light breakfast, then sat down behind the steering-wheel of the black, gleaming Adler which Mock's chauffeur had parked outside the building for him. As the car pulled away from the shade, a wave of hot air poured in. The sky was white; the sun barely penetrated the mush which hung heavily over Breslau. So as not to lose his way, Anwaldt followed the map: first Grübschener Strasse, then – on Sonnenplatz – he turned left into little Telegraphstrasse, passed by the Telegraph Office, the Hellenistic mansion of the Museum of Fine Arts, and parked the car on Agnesstrasse, in the shade of the synagogue.

Bank Allgemeine Deutsche Credit-Anstalt was housed in Tauentzienstrasse 14. The residential part of the building was reached from the yard. The caretaker politely allowed the new tenant's – Doctor Maass' – guest to pass. The policeman's irritation, provoked by the heat, increased when he found himself in the spacious, comfortable *en suite* apartment rented out for Maass by the Baron. Anwaldt was accustomed to difficult conditions. He could not, however, suppress his irritation when he compared this beautiful apartment to his cockroach-infested hole with its toilet on the landing.

Maass did not even pretend to be happy at seeing his guest. He sat him behind the desk and threw down a few sheets of paper covered in regular, legible writing. He himself strode around the room drawing on his cigarette greedily as if he had not smoked for months. Anwaldt swept his eyes over the elegant desk and the luxurious objects on it (the pad of green leather, the ornamental sand-box, the fanciful, round-bellied inkstand, the brass paper-press in the shape of a woman's leg), and found it hard to hold back the bitterness of envy. Maass paced the room, clearly excited. Thirst was drying out Anwaldt's throat. A wasp furiously pounded between the window panes. The policeman glanced at Maass' bulging cheeks, folded the sheets, and put them away in his wallet.

"Goodbye, doctor. I'll examine this in my study," he emphasized the word "my" and made to leave. Maass leapt towards him, waving his arms.

"But, my dear Herbert, you're on edge . . . It is the heat . . . Please, do read my expert opinion here . . . And forgive my vanity, but I'd like to know what you think of my translation right away. Please do ask questions and give me your comments . . . You're an intelligent man . . . I implore you . . ."

Maass circled around his guest, pulling out cigarettes, cigars and his hissing cigarette lighter in turn. Anwaldt thanked him for the cigar and, not caring how strong it was, inhaled several times, then began to study Friedländer's apocalyptic outbursts. He looked cursorily through a detailed description of the method used and comments on Semitic vowels and concentrated on the translation of the prophecies. The first of them read: *raam* – "noise"; *chavura* – "wound"; *makak* – "to spread/melt, to fester"; *arar* – "ruin"; *shamayim* – "sky"; and the second: *yeladim* – "children"; *akrabbim* – "scorpions"; *sevacha* – "grille"; *amotz* – "white". Further on, Maass shared his doubts: "Due to the unclear recording, the last word of the second prophecy can be understood as being either *chol* (10 – תֹל) – 'sand' or *chul* (IV – תֹל) – 'to wriggle, dance, fall'."

Anwaldt relaxed, the wasp flew out through the open gap in the casement window. Maass' hypothesis was as follows: ". . . it seems that the person indicated by Friedländer in the first prophecy will die of a festering wound (*death, wound, to fester*), caused by the collapse of a building (*ruin*). The key to this person's identity lies in the word (*shamayim* – 'sky'). The future victim may be somebody whose name is composed of the sounds *sh, a, m, a, y, i, m*, e.g. Scheim or somebody with the name Himmel, Himmler or such like.

"We believe that the second prophecy has already been fulfilled. It concerns – in our opinion – Marietta von der Malten (child, white shore

— that's the name given to the island of Malta), murdered in a saloon carriage furnished in checks (grille). In her abdominal cavity were found wriggling scorpions."

The detective did not want to show what a great impression this expertise had made on him. He diligently stubbed out his cigar and stood up.

"Do you really have no comments?" Maass' vanity demanded praise. He glanced stealthily at his watch. Anwaldt was reminded of an incident in the orphanage: he exhausted his tutor urging him to look at the tower of bricks built by little Herbert.

"Doctor Maass, your analysis is so precise and convincing that it's hard to find any questions. I thank you very much," he held out his hand in farewell. Maass seemed not to notice.

"My dear Herbert," he squeaked sweetly. "Perhaps you'd like a cold beer?"

Anwaldt considered this for a moment (Dear Sir, please look at my tower. "I haven't got any time . . .")

"I don't drink alcohol, but I'd love some cold lemonade or soda water."

"Of course," Maass brightened up. Going out to the kitchen, he glanced at his watch again. Out of professional habit, Anwaldt looked over the desk more carefully than he had the first time. *(Why does he want to keep me here at all costs?)* Under the paperweight, lay an open, elegant, heather-coloured envelope with a coat-of-arms printed on it. He opened it without hesitation and pulled out a hard, black card, folded in two. Inside, beautifully written in silver ink, appeared:

I cordially invite you to a masked ball this evening (i.e. Monday, July 9th) at seven. It will take place at my residence, Uferzeile 9. Ladies must dress as Eve. Gentlemen are also welcome to dress as Adam.
    Wilhelm Baron von Köpperlingk.

Anwaldt noticed Maass' shadow as the latter was leaving the kitchen. He quickly replaced the invitation under the weight. He accepted the thick, hexagonal glass with a smile, emptied it in one mighty draught and tried to understand what he had just read. Maass' falsetto did not penetrate his swirling thoughts although the Semitist, with great animation and paying no heed to his listener's want of concentration, was describing the scientific dispute with Professor Andreae. When he got to the point of discussing matters of grammar, the front door bell rang. Maass looked at his watch and sprang to the hall. Through the open study door, Anwaldt caught sight of a schoolgirl. (*Holidays, the heat, and she's in uniform. Apparently the idiotic rules of wearing a uniform all the year round are still in force.*) They whispered for a moment, then Maass landed her a racy slap on the backside. The girl giggled. (*Ah, that is why he kept me here. He wanted to demonstrate that his claim about debauched schoolgirls was not unfounded.*) He could not control his curiosity and left the study. He felt his stomach suddenly cramp up and a sweetish taste gather in his mouth. Before him stood the schoolgirl Erna.

"Allow me – Assistant Anwaldt, Fräulein Elsa von Herfen, my pupil. I give the young lady private tuition in Latin," Maass emitted ever higher tones. "Fräulein Elsa, this is Criminal Assistant Anwaldt, my good friend and colleague."

The policeman all but fainted at the sight of the girl's intensely green eyes.

"I think we know each other . . ." he whispered, leaning against the door frame.

The girl's alto had nothing in common with Erna's quiet, melodious voice, and the large mole on the surface of the girl's hand nothing with Erna's alabaster skin. He realized that he had a double in front of him.

"I'm sorry . . ." he sighed with relief. "You look very much like a friend

101

of mine in Berlin. Dear Doctor, you've already made yourself very much at home in Breslau. You've been here barely four days and you've already acquired a pupil . . . And what a pupil . . . I won't disturb you. Goodbye."

Before he closed the door on Anwaldt, Maass made an obscene gesture: he joined the thumb and index finger of his left hand and slipped the index finger of his right hand in and out of the circle several times. Anwaldt snorted with contempt and ran down a few steps. Then he went upstairs and stopped above the Semitist's apartment, on the half-landing beside a stained-glass window which ran the whole height of the building scattering coloured "dancing coins" across the stairwell. He rested his elbow on an alcove where a small copy of the Venus de Milo was concealed.

He envied Maass and that envy had eclipsed his suspicions for a moment. He reluctantly greeted the reappearing memories, knowing that, although unpleasant, they would help kill the time. He had decided to wait for Elsa von Herfen so as to see what Maass' seductive charm was worth.

Somehow a memory managed to drift to him. It was November 23rd, 1921. He was to be sexually initiated that day. He was the only one in his dormitory not to have known a woman. His friend Josef had promised to arrange everything. The young, stout, orphanage cook had allowed herself to be invited by the three wards to a small storeroom where the gym equipment, used sheets and towels were kept. Two bottles of wine had helped. She had arranged her sweaty body on a gym mat. The first had been Josef. The second turn had been drawn by fat Hannes. Anwaldt had waited patiently for his go. When Hannes had dragged himself off the cook, she had smiled mischievously at Anwaldt:

"Not you. I've had enough."

The boy had returned to his dormitory and lost the desire to know women. Fate, however, had not let him wait for long. The nineteen-year-old prime pupil found himself employed as private tutor to the daughter of a rich industrialist. He disclosed the secret components of Greek to the seventeen-year-old, somewhat capricious girl, while she willingly repaid him by disclosing the secrets of her body. Anwaldt fell head over heads in love. When, after half a year of hard but very pleasant work, he asked her father for his remuneration, the latter, surprised, retorted that he had already handed over the remuneration through his daughter who, in her daddy's presence, robustly confirmed the fact. The industrialist reacted appropriately. Two of his servants kicked the beaten-up "foul swindler" out of the manor.

It looked as though Anwaldt had lost all illusions. Unfortunately, he regained them yet again thanks to another schoolgirl, the poor, beautiful Erna Stange from a good working-class family in the Wedding district of Berlin. The thirty-year-old, having a career in the police ahead of him, thought about getting married. Erna's father, an honest and hardened railwayman, had tears in his eyes as he watched the proposal. Anwaldt tried for a loan from the police coffers. He was waiting for Erna's final exams and thinking about a place to live. After three months, he stopped thinking about anything but alcohol.

He did not believe in the disinterested passion of schoolgirls. That is why he did not quite believe in what he had seen a moment ago. A beautiful girl giving herself to an ugly creature.

The door to the apartment grated. Maass, eyes closed, was kissing his pupil. He gave the girl a hard slap on the backside once again and snapped the lock. Anwaldt heard the clatter of shoes on the stairs. He descended cautiously. The heels clattered through the gate. A flirtatious "goodbye" reached the shaggy ears of the caretaker. He, too, said goodbye to the caretaker, but he did not leave in a hurry. He emerged a little and observed: the girl was getting into a black Mercedes, the bearded chauffeur removed his hat, bowed and slowly pulled away. Anwaldt quickly ran to his Adler. He moved off with a roar, furious to see he was losing the Mercedes from sight. He accelerated and almost ran over an elderly gentleman in a top hat who was crossing the street. In two minutes, he found himself at a safe distance from the Mercedes, which was following a route known to Anwaldt: Sonnenplatz and Grübschener Strasse. Both cars plunged into the stream of cars, droschkas and a few carts. Anwaldt saw only the neck and head of the chauffeur. *(She's tired. Evidently lying on the back seat.)* They kept going straight. Anwaldt watched the names of the streets: they were still driving along Grübschener Strasse. Past the cemetery wall, above which protruded a smooth tympanum. *(The crematorium, no doubt; there's one like that in Berlin.)* The followed car suddenly accelerated and vanished from Anwaldt's view. The policeman put his foot down and leapt over a bridge across a small river. On the left, a sign with the name "Breslau" flitted past. He turned into the first street on his left and found himself in a shady, beautiful alley along which ran villas and small houses concealed among lime and chestnut trees. The Mercedes was standing in front of a corner manor. Anwaldt turned right, into a small side street, and turned off his engine. He knew from experience that following someone in a car was less effective than doing so on foot. He got out of the Adler and carefully approached the crossroads. Peering out, he caught sight of the Mercedes as it turned back. In seconds, the car had disappeared, turned right and driven back towards Breslau. He had not the slightest doubt: the chauffeur was alone. He jotted down the number plate and went up to the manor from which the Mercedes had driven away. It was a stylish, neo-Gothic building. The closed shutters appeared very mysterious. A sign was visible over the entrance: NADŚLEŻAŃSKI MANOR.

"All brothels are asleep at this hour," he muttered to himself, looking at his watch. He was proud of his photographic memory. He took the visiting card handed to him the previous day by the cabby from his wallet. He compared the address on the card to the one on the building. They tallied: Schellwitzstrasse. *(This place just outside Breslau must be Opperau, as on the card.)*

He pressed the bell at the gate to the drive for a long time. Finally, a man with the build of a heavyweight boxer appeared in the driveway. He walked up to the wicket gate and forestalled Anwaldt's questions:

"Our club opens at seven."

"I'm from the police. Criminal Department. I'd like to ask the man in charge a few questions."

"Anyone could say that. I don't know you and I know everyone from the Criminal Investigation Department. Besides, everyone from C.I.D. knows that the boss is a woman not a man . . ."

"Here's my identification."

"It says 'Berlin Police'. And we in Opperau belong to Breslau."

Anwaldt cursed his own absent-mindedness. His Breslau identification had been waiting for him in the personnel department since Saturday. He had forgotten about it. The "boxer" was looking at him with swollen eyes, detached. Anwaldt stood in a puddle of sun and counted the decorative railings.

"Either you open this gate, you pig, or I phone my chief's deputy, Max Forstner," he said in a raised voice. "Do you want your boss to be in trouble because of you?"

The gorilla was short of sleep and hung over. Slowly, he neared the fence:

"Clear out or . . ." he strained to think of something that would sound threatening, but Anwaldt had already noticed that the wicket gate was not properly closed. He threw himself at it with all his weight. The iron grille hit the gorilla plumb in the middle of his face. Finding himself on the property, Anwaldt jumped aside to avoid being stained with the blood

105

spurting profusely from the guard's nose. The man quickly recovered from the surprise of the blow. He took a swing and Anwaldt lost his breath: a mighty fist had hit him in the carotid artery. Stifling his cough, he dodged a second blow at the last moment. The guard's fist whammed with full force into the iron fence. The gorilla stood for a few seconds examining his injured hand in disbelief. Immediately, the policeman was behind his back and took a swing with his leg as if to kick a ball. The aim was accurate – the pointed tip of his shoe hit the crotch. A second, accurate blow to the temple was decisive. The guard swayed at the gate like a drunk and tried, somehow, to remain upright. Out of the corner of his eye, Anwaldt noticed men running out of the manor. He did not reach for his gun; he knew he had left it in the car.

"Hold it!" a woman's authoritative voice held back the three guards hurrying to punish adequately the man who had made mincemeat of their colleague. They stopped obediently. A stout woman was standing in the window of the first floor and examined Anwaldt. "Who are you?" she called in what was clearly a foreign accent.

Not only did the battered guard not maintain a vertical position, but he lay flat out on the ground, his good hand on his stomach. Anwaldt felt sorry for the man, who had been abused simply because he had been scrupulously performing his duty. He looked up and shouted back:

"Criminal Assistant Herbert Anwaldt."

Madame le Goef was angry but not to such a degree as to lose control:

"You're lying. You threaten to call Forstner. He not boss of C.I.D."

"Firstly, please do not be too familiar with me," he smiled, listening to this peculiar German. "Secondly, my chief is Criminal Director Eberhard Mock, but I cannot telephone him. He's away on holiday."

"Please, sir. Come in." Madame knew that Anwaldt was not lying. The previous day, Mock had cancelled his weekly game of chess because of the trip. Besides, she was mortally afraid of Mock and would have opened up even to a burglar if he had entered with Mock's name on his lips.

Anwaldt did not look at the set faces of the guards he passed. He entered the hall and admitted to himself that this sanctuary of Aphrodite was, in its interior décor, second to none in Berlin. He could say the same of the owner's study. He sat down casually, in the open window. The shoes of the guard being dragged back by his colleagues scraped along the driveway. Anwaldt removed his jacket, cleared his throat and rubbed the bruise on his neck.

"A black Mercedes drove up to your salon shortly before I arrived and a girl wearing a school uniform got out. I want to see her."

Madame picked up the telephone and uttered a few words (probably in Hungarian).

"She'll be here presently. She's having her bath now."

"Presently" turned out to be a very short moment. Anwaldt had no time to treat his eyes to the splendid reproduction of Goya's *Naked Maya* before Erna's double was standing in the door. The school uniform had been replaced by pink tulle.

"Erna . . ." He covered this slip of the tongue with a sarcastic tone. "Sorry, Elsa . . . Which school do you go to?"

"I work here," she squeaked.

"Ah, here," he aped her. "So *cui bono*[†] are you learning Latin?"

The girl remained silent, having modestly lowered her eyes. Anwaldt turned all of a sudden to the owner of the brothel:

"What are you still doing here? Please leave."

Madame did so without a word, winking meaningfully to the girl. Anwaldt sat down behind the desk and listened for a while to the sounds of summer in the garden.

"What are you doing with Maass?"

[†] To what good? (Latin).

"Shall I show you?" (*Erna had looked at him like that when he had stepped into Klaus Schmetterling's bachelor apartment. They had had their eye on this inconspicuous apartment in the Berlin district of Charlottenburg for a long time. They knew that the banker, Schmetterling, had a taste for underage girls. The raid was a success.*)

"No. You don't have to show me," he said in a weary tone. "Who hired you? Who's the bearded chauffeur's employer?"

The girl stopped smiling.

"I don't know. This bearded guy came along and said some sucker likes schoolgirls. What's it to me? He paid a lot. He drives me there and back. Oh, he's supposed to be taking me to some big party today. I think it's going to be at his boss'. I'll tell you all about it when I get back."

Anwaldt had questioned numerous prostitutes in the past and was sure that the girl was telling the truth.

"Sit down!" he showed her a chair. "You're going to be carrying out assignments for me now. This evening, at the reception, you're to make sure that all the windows – especially the ones to the balcony – are at least ajar. Understand? Then I'll have another assignment for you. My name's Herbert Anwaldt. As of today, you work for me or you end up in the gutter! I'll throw you to the mercy of the worst pimps in town!"

He was aware that he did not have to say this. (*Every whore's greatest fear is a policeman.*) He heard the grating of his own vocal cords.

"Bring me something cold to drink! Lemonade would be best!"

Once she had left, he leaned his head out of the window. Unfortunately, the heat could not burn away his memories. (*"You know her, don't you, Anwaldt?" He kicked the door to the room furiously. Banker Schmetterling shielded his eyes from the glare of the flashes as he tried to pull the eiderdown over his head.*)

"Here's your lemonade," the girl smiled flirtatiously at the handsome policeman. "Do you have any special tasks for me? I'll willingly do them . . ." (*Schmetterling's body was immobilized. United in a love embrace. The fat body shook, the supple one writhed. Indissoluble* coitus *joined the fat banker to Anwaldt's fiancée, beautiful as a dream – Erna Stange.*)

The policeman got up and approached the smiling Erna Stange. The green eyes covered over with a thin film of tears as he slapped her with full force. Descending the stairs, he heard her muffled sobs. In his head murmured Samuel Coleridge's maxim: "When a man takes his thoughts to be people and objects, he is a madman. That precisely is the definition of a madman."

BRESLAU, THAT SAME JULY 9TH, 1934
ONE O'CLOCK IN THE AFTERNOON

Anwaldt sat in his office in the Police Praesidium, savouring the coolness which reigned there and waiting for a telephone call from the Criminal Sergeant, Kurt Smolorz, the only man, according to Mock, that he could trust. The small window just below the ceiling faced north, and looked out on one of the five interior yards of the police building. He laid his head on the table. The deep sleep lasted perhaps a quarter of an hour. It was interrupted by Smolorz, who appeared in person.

"Here are the dinner jacket and mask," the red-haired, portly man smiled amicably. "And now for some important news: the black Mercedes with the number plate you gave us belongs to Baron Wilhelm von Köpperlingk."

"Thank you. Mock didn't overestimate you. But where on earth did you get hold of that?" he pointed to the black, velvet mask.

In reply, Smolorz put a finger to his lips and retreated from the room. Anwaldt lit a cigar and leaned back in his chair. Wrapping his hands behind his neck, he stretched his whole body several times. Everything

109

was coming together into a uniform whole. Baron von Köpperlingk had fulfilled Maass' sweetest dream when he had sent him the beautiful schoolgirl. "How did he know about it?" he noted on a piece of paper. *(Not important. Maass does nothing to hide his predilections. He was loud enough expressing them in the park yesterday.)* "What for?" the nib squeaked on the paper once more. *(So as to control Maass and, indirectly, my investigation.)* "Why?" the successive question appeared on the squared paper. He set his memory to work and summoned a few lines from Mock's letter before his eyes: ". . . the late Hauptsturmführer S.A. Walter Piontek eagerly made use of the track suggested by Baron Wilhelm von Köpperlingk (who, by the by, has many friends in the Gestapo) . . . If somebody finds the true murderers, then the entire propaganda will be turned into a laughing stock by the English and French newspapers. I warn you against these people – they are ruthless and capable of forcing anyone into giving up an investigation."

Anwaldt felt a wave of pride surge though him. He pulled the mask over his face.

"If the Gestapo gets to know the reason for my investigation, it'll certainly put an end to it – for fear of being ridiculed by France and England," he muttered, walking up to the small mirror on the wall. "Yet I think there are some people within the Gestapo who will want to put a stop to it for an entirely different reason."

The velvet mask covered two-thirds of his face. He pulled a joker's expression and clapped his hands.

"Maybe I'll meet them at the Baron's ball," he said aloud. "Time for the ball, Assistant Anwaldt!"

With no difficulty, but at the cost of a five-mark note, Anwaldt convinced the caretaker of tenement Uferzeile 9 that he wanted to make a few sketches of the Zoological Gardens in the evening glow. He opened the door to the attic with the key given him and climbed the wobbly ladder to the gently sloping roof. The roof he was now intending to climb rose three metres higher. From his backpack, he pulled out some thick rope with a steel, three-forked hook knotted to its end. Some ten minutes went by before the hook finally fastened on to something. Anwaldt climbed to the higher roof, not without effort. As soon as he got here, he threw off the dirty drill trousers and long apron under which his dinner jacket and patent leather shoes were disguised. He checked that he had his cigarettes and looked about him. He quickly found what he was looking for: a slightly rusty ventilation outlet covered with a small triangular shelter. He affixed the hook to it and very slowly, taking care so as not to get dirty, lowered himself a few metres down the rope. Two minutes later, his feet were touching the stone balustrade of the balcony. He stood there for a fair while, panting. When he had cooled a little, he looked into the lit window and realized that the windows of two rooms gave on to the balcony. A moment later, one of his eyes found itself in the light. He observed what was happening in the room attentively. On the floor lay the taut bodies of two females and two males. Half a minute passed before he understood this complicated configuration. Nearby, on the sofa, a man wearing only a mask spread himself while two girls in school uniform knelt on either side of him. Worried by a strange sound, Anwaldt moved to the other window. It was the hiss of a whip: two girls in long boots and black uniform were flogging a scrawny blond lad handcuffed to the gleaming door of a tiled stove. The man yelled as the iron tips of the large whips lacerated his bruised body.

Both windows were wide open. The air, saturated with the scent of incense, quivered from the more or less fake moans of women. Anwaldt entered the first room by the balcony door. As he had correctly supposed, none of those present paid any attention to him. He, on the other hand, examined them all carefully. He easily recognized Maass' receding chin and the "schoolgirl's" hand with its mole. He went out into the hall and closed the door gently behind him. Several niches had been fashioned out in the spacious corridor where small marble columns stood. Moved by a chameleon's instinct, he removed his dinner jacket and shirt and hung them on one of the columns. The soft sound of stringed instruments drifted up from below. He recognized Haydn's "Emperor Quartet".

He descended the stairs and saw three pairs of doors wide open. He stood in one of them and looked around. The glass partition walls of three enormous rooms had been drawn aside to form a huge hall thirty metres long, forty wide. The entire floor was taken up by wooden tables laden with fruit, glasses and bottles in ice buckets, and by umpteen low two-seater sofas and chaise-longues occupied by naked, slow-moving bodies. The Baron was conducting the quartet with a peculiar baton – a human tibia. The beautiful-eyed servant, dressed only in an Indian sash which covered his genitalia, was pouring generous measures of wine into tall glasses. This Ganimede interrupted his activity for a moment and graciously circulated among the guests, scattering rose petals. He was making sure that each of the guests was happy and was very surprised to see a tall dark-haired man stand in the doorway then quickly sit on a chaise-longue from which a female couple had just rolled away. He danced up to Anwaldt and asked melodiously:

"Does the respected gentleman desire anything?"

"Yes. I just went to the toilet for a moment and my partner disappeared."

Ganimede frowned and sung:

112

"No problem. We'll get you a new one."

The stench of manure drifted in from the Zoological Gardens; from time to time, the roar of animals irritated by the heat rose towards the sky. The Oder surrendered the remains of its moisture to the dry air.

The Baron threw the tibia aside and began a striptease. The instrumentalists, in wild passion, hit their bows against taut strings. The Baron, completely naked, fixed a great red beard to his face and donned the tiered hat of Nebuchadnezzar. Some of the orgiasts were growing weak and slipping on their own sweat. Other couples, trios and quartets were trying in vain to surprise each other with ingenious caresses. Anwaldt glanced above the bodies and met the intent gaze of Nebuchadnezzar who had, in the meantime, donned a heavy golden cloak. *(I look like a cockroach on a white carpet lying here alone, wearing trousers, among naked people. None of them are alone. It's not surprising that that prick is looking at me like that.)* Nebuchadnezzar stared, the string instruments turned into percussion, women moaned in feigned rapture, men writhed in forced ecstasy.

Anwaldt writhed under the Baron's attentive gaze. He decided to accept the invitation of two lesbians who had been calling him to them for a long time. Suddenly Ganimede appeared, leading a somewhat intoxicated blonde in a velvet mask. Nebuchadnezzar ceased to be interested in him. The girl squatted by Anwaldt's sofa. He closed his eyes. *(Let me get something out of this orgy, too.)* Unfortunately, his expectations were not fulfilled; instead of the girl's delicate hands and lips, he felt hard, calloused fingers press him forcefully to the sofa. A huge, dark man with an aquiline nose was leaning his hands against Anwaldt's biceps and ramming him into the sofa. The Baron's servant was holding Anwaldt's dinner jacket and a handful of black invitations to the ball. The assailant opened his mouth, breathing garlic and tobacco:

"How did you get in here? Show your invitation!"

113

Anwaldt had heard a similar accent before when interrogating a Turkish restaurateur in Berlin who had been mixed up in opium smuggling. Now he lay paralysed, not so much by the strong hold, as by the sight of the strange tattoo on the assailant's left hand. With the steel grip, the muscle between the index finger and the thumb bulged large and round, quivering at the slightest movement. The muscle's quivering set a neatly tattooed scorpion in motion. The assailant wanted to immobilize his victim yet more, but as he threw his leg over the sofa in order to straddle the policeman, the latter quickly flexed his knee and hit the garlic lover in a tender spot. The man, under the stress of pain, tore his arm from Anwaldt's shoulder who, partially regaining his freedom of movement, struck his opponent in the face with his forehead. The tattooed man lost his balance and fell off the sofa. The policeman ran towards the exit. Nobody was interested in the fight; the quartet continued to perform its crazed rondo as more and more ever-weaker people lay strewn across the wet dance floor.

The only obstacle Anwaldt had to overcome was Ganimede, who had slipped out of the hall earlier on and was in the process of locking the front door. Anwaldt aimed a strong kick at his armpit, a second thumped his ribs. The servant, however, managed to lock the door and push the key through the letterbox. The key clattered on the other side, on the stairwell floor. A third blow, in the head, deprived Ganimede of consciousness. Anwaldt, unable to escape by the door, made his way towards the first floor of the apartment by the internal stairs. He heard the heavy breathing of the foreigner behind him. The blast of a shot being fired tore the air and even mildly alarmed the orgiasts, who were resting after their great efforts. The policeman felt a pain in his ear and hot blood on his neck. (*Godammit, I haven't got my gun again; it spoiled the cut of my jacket.*) He bent over and snatched one of the heavy rods pressing the purple carpet to the stairs. Out of the corner of his eye, he noticed that his assailant was preparing to shoot again. But the blast came only once Anwaldt was on the first floor. The bullet chipped a marble column and ricocheted a moment or two in the stone niche. The policeman threw himself towards a door from which protruded a large key. He turned it and leapt out on to the stairwell. The chasing man was close by. Bullets hit the ceramic tiles covering the walls. Anwaldt ran down blindly. A floor below, by the main entrance to the apartment, stood a late arrival. From behind the black mask escaped stiff, red hair. Alarmed by the shots, he held a revolver in his hand. He saw Anwaldt and shouted "Stop or I'll shoot!" The policeman squatted, took a swing and threw the rod. The metal bar hit the red-head in the brow. As the man slipped to the floor, he fired two shots into the ceiling. Plaster and dust rained down. Anwaldt picked up the rod and, with a bound, flew over the banister. He found himself on the next landing. The building shook with gunfire. He ran, tripped and fell, until finally he reached the last landing. He backed away abruptly: four men, armed with huge shovels for sweeping snow, were climbing the stairs. Anwaldt guessed that the caretaker had joined the hunt with three of his colleagues. He turned and opened the window to the yard, jumped headlong and fell straight on to a wagon. Splinters from rough planks dug into his body; piercing pain twisted his ankle. Limping, he scrambled across the yard. The evil eyes of the windows flared up – he was as visible as on an open palm. The blast of shots shook the empty well of the yard. He ran under the walls of the building and tried to get into one of the houses by a back door. All, as luck would have it, were bolted. The chase was close. Anwaldt stumbled down the stairs leading to the cellar of another house. If that door too proved to be locked, the men pursuing him would corner him in the concrete rectangle. But the door gave way. Anwaldt bolted himself from the inside just as the first assailant arrived at the door. The smell of rotten potatoes, fermenting wine and rat droppings was, for him, the sweetest of smells. He slid down the wall, grazing his back against raw brick. He put his hand to his ear. A sharp shudder shook him, drops of thick blood streamed down his neck again. His twisted ankle pulsated with warm pain. On his forehead, at the hairline where the assailant had cut the skin with his teeth, a cloying jelly had congealed. Knowing that before his persecutors had surrounded that block several minutes would have gone by, he tried to get out of the cellar's labyrinth.

He walked in absolute darkness, groping his way, frightening a few rats and wrapping his face in rolls of cobweb. He lost all sense of time and was being overcome by sleep when a distant reflection effectively over-powered his drowsiness. He easily identified the light of a street lamp penetrating a dusty window. He opened the window and, after a few unsuccessful attempts, managed to get outside, tearing the skin on his stomach and ribs in the process. He closed the window behind him and looked around. Thick bushes, from behind which came the patter of several people's feet running here and there, separated him from the pavement and street. He lay supine on the lawn, panting. *(I have to wait a few hours.)* He looked around and found the ideal hiding-place. The balcony of the first-floor apartment was overgrown with wild vine hanging to the ground. Anwaldt crawled in and felt consciousness slip away.

The dampness of the earth and the surrounding silence woke him. Taking cover between the trees and benches of the promenade along the Oder, he crept to the car parked outside the Engineering College. He could scarcely drive. He was sore and lacerated. Climbing up to his floor, he clung to the banister. He did not turn on the light in his kitchen so as not to see the cockroaches. He drank a glass of water in one draught, threw his torn trousers down in the hall, opened the window in his room and collapsed on to the tangled sheets.

116

On waking, Anwaldt could not lift his ear from the pillow. The congealed blood formed a strong adhesive. He sat up in bed with difficulty. His hair, plastered with blood, bristled stiffly on the crown of his head. His entire torso was grazed and covered with bruises. His heel ached; his swollen ankle was turning purple. Hopping on one leg, he made his way to the telephone and called Baron von der Malten.

A quarter of an hour later, the Baron's personal physician, Doctor Lanzmann, arrived at Anwaldt's apartment. After a further quarter of an hour, they were at von der Malten's residence. After four hours, the patient, Anwaldt — having slept well, his head and torn ear dressed, his sprained ankle immobilized in bamboo splints, and yellow stains all over his body — was smoking a long, choice *Ahnuri Shu* Przedecki cigar and relating the previous night's events to his employer. When the Baron — having heard him through — went out to his study, Anwaldt phoned the Police Praesidium and asked Kurt Smolorz to prepare all the material on Baron von Köpperlingk for six that evening. Then he got through to Professor Andreae and arranged to meet him for a talk.

Baron von der Malten's chauffeur helped him downstairs and into the car. They moved off. Anwaldt asked, with interest, about practically every building, every street. The chauffeur answered patiently:

"We're driving along Hohenzollernstrasse . . . On the left is the water tower . . . On the right, St John's Church . . . Yes, I agree, it's beautiful. Recently built . . . Here's the roundabout. Reichspräsidentenplatz. This is still Hohenzollernstrasse . . . Yes, and now we're coming on to Gabitzstrasse. Yes? . . . You know these parts? We'll go under the viaduct and we'll be on your Zietenstrasse . . ."

The drive in the car gave Anwaldt the most enormous pleasure. *(A beautiful city.)* Unfortunately, his Adler had been burning in the high sun since morning and when he heaved himself in behind the steering-wheel, sweat poured down his shirt and jacket. He opened the windows, threw his hat on the back seat and pulled away with a screech of tyres, longing to cool himself by the current of air. With no success – his lungs filled with dry dust. As if this torment were not enough, Anwaldt lit a cigarette, drying his mouth out completely.

Following the instructions given by von der Malten's chauffeur, he arrived at the College of Oriental Studies at Schmiedebrücke 35 without any problems. Professor Andreae was waiting for him. He listened closely as Anwaldt imitated the way yesterday's assailant spoke. Although the lines the policeman repeated several times were short – (*"How did you get in here? Show your invitation!"*) – the professor had no doubts. The German-speaking foreigner at the Baron's ball was most certainly a Turk. Pleased with his linguistic intuition, Anwaldt bade the professor farewell and drove on to the Police Praesidium.

In the entrance, he met Forstner. They exchanged glances and easily recognized each other: Anwaldt's bandaged head and Forstner's cut eyebrow. They greeted each other with feigned indifference.

"I see you didn't spend last night at the Salvation Army on Blücherplatz," laughed Smolorz, greeting Anwaldt.

"It's nothing. I had a slight accident." He glanced at the desk: Baron von Köpperlingk's file lay there. "Not very thick."

"The thicker one's probably in the Gestapo archives. You have to have special connections to get in there. I haven't got any . . ." He wiped his sweaty forehead with a chequered handkerchief.

"Thank you, Smolorz. Ah . . ." Anwaldt rubbed his nose nervously. "I'd be most grateful if you'd prepare a list of all the Turks who have lived in Breslau over the last eighteen months by tomorrow. Is there a Turkish Consulate here?"

"Yes, on Neudorfstrasse."

"They're bound to help you. Thank you, you're free to go."

Anwaldt was left alone in his cool office. He rested his forehead on the slippery, green surface of the desk and felt he was reaching the lowest point of the sinusoid — the critical point of his good and bad moods. He became painfully conscious of the fact that he reacted differently to other people: the furiously burning world outside released, in him, energy and action, the pleasant coolness of the office, surrender and resignation. (*Each one's a microcosmos connected to the movement of the universe; I'm not. I'm different from them. Haven't I been told that ever since childhood? I'm an isolated mini-universe where multi-directional gravitation rules and welds everything into heavy, concentrated blocks.*)

He abruptly got up, slipped his shirt off and leaned over the basin. Hissing with pain, he washed his neck and armpits then sat in his chair and allowed the water to run down his wounded torso in narrow streams. He wiped his face and hands on his vest. (*Be active! Do something!*) He picked up the receiver and instructed the runner to buy some cigarettes and lemonade, then closed his eyes and easily mastered the chaotic images. He tore them from himself and set them in order: "Scorpions in Marietta von der Malten's belly. A scorpion on the Turk's hand. The Turk killed Marietta." This observation pleased Anwaldt with its self-evidence yet the prospect of ineffective work gave him cold feet. (*The Turk killed the Baron's daughter; the Turk guards Baron von Köpperlingk's house; the Baron is protected by the Gestapo; ergo, the Turk has something to do with the Gestapo; ergo, the Gestapo is mixed up in the Baron's daughter's murder; ergo, I'm as weak and helpless as a child in the face of the Gestapo.*)

A knock on the door. A kn-o-ck. The runner brought in an armful of bottles and two packets of strong Bergmann Privat cigarettes. The cigarette weakened him for a moment. He drank a bottle of the lemonade in one go, closed his eyes and again the thought-images became thought-sentences. *(Lea Friedländer knows who pointed her father out to Mock and made a scapegoat of him. It could be someone from the Gestapo. If she's going to be afraid to tell me, I'll force her. I'll withhold the morphine, terrorize her with the needle. She'll do anything I say!)* He rejected the erotic vision "she'll do anything I say" and got up from his desk. *(Be active!)* He paced the room and voiced his doubts out loud:

"Where are you going to make her talk? In a cell. What cell? Here, in the Police Praesidium. What've you got Smolorz for? Great — you lock a doll like that up in a cell and all the screws and policemen are going to know about it within an hour. And most certainly the Gestapo."

In moments of greatest discouragement, Anwaldt always turned his thoughts to entirely different matters. And so it was now: he engaged himself in studying the Baron's file. He found several photographs of an orgy in some garden and a list of names unknown to him — names of those present at the parties. None betrayed Turkish descent. There was very little on the host himself. The ordinary life story of an educated Prussian aristocrat and a few official notes from the Baron's meetings with Hauptsturmführer S.A. Walter Piontek.

He buttoned his shirt and tightened his tie. He went downstairs slowly to the archives, picking up his Breslau police identification on the way. *(Be active!)* In the basement of the Police Praesidium, he met with bitter disappointment. On the orders of Doctor Engel — who was executing the duties of Police President — Piontek's files had been transferred to the Gestapo archives. Anwaldt barely managed to get to his office: pain was shooting through his swollen heel, his wounds and abrasions burning. He sat down behind his desk and, in a hoarse voice, asked Mock, who was sunbathing on a Zoppot beach:

"When are you coming back, Eberhard? If you were here you'd extract Piontek's and Baron von Köpperlingk's files from the Gestapo . . . You'd find a safe place where we could subject Lea to a morphine detox . . . You'd

surely find a vice in your memory for that crazy Baron . . . When are you finally coming back?"

Longing for Mock was longing for the Baron's money, for tropical islands, for slaves with skin like silk . . . (*You've built a fine tower, Herbert, with those bricks. Be active, force Lea to speak yourself, can't you? You've built a fine tower, Herbert.*)

VI

On the main road which lay at the end of Hansastrasse, Anwaldt found a small restaurant. Out of professional habit, he noted the owner's name and the address: Paul Seidel, Tiergartenstrasse 33. There he ate three hot sausages immersed in a mash of boiled peas and drank two bottles of Deinart mineral water.

Ten minutes later and feeling somewhat heavy, he stood outside Fatamorgana Studio of Photography and Film. He thumped for some time − loudly and stubbornly − on the closed door. *(No doubt she's topped herself up with morphine again. But it's the last time.)* The old caretaker shuffled out of the gate on to the pavement.

"I haven't seen Fräulein Susanne going out anywhere. Her servant left an hour ago . . ." he muttered, inspecting Anwaldt's identification.

The policeman removed his jacket and resigned himself to the trickles of sweat: he did not even attempt to wipe them off with a handkerchief. He sat down on a stone bench in the yard next to a dozing pensioner in a perforated hat. One window-vent in Lea's apartment, he noticed, was not quite closed. He barely managed to climb on to the sill − his swollen heel was aching and his stomach lay heavily. Slipping his hand inside, he

122

turned the brass handle and, for a moment, struggled with the tangling curtain netting and rampant ferns standing on the window sill. He felt at home in this apartment and took off his jacket, waistcoat and tie, hung all this on the back of a chair and set off in search of Lea. He made towards the studio where, so he thought, he would find her lying, intoxicated. But, before he got there, he turned to the bathroom: the peas and sausages were sending out strong physiological messages.

Lea Friedländer was in the bathroom, her legs hanging over the toilet bowl, her thighs and shins smeared with faeces. She was naked. The thick cable wrapped around her neck was attached to the overflow pipe just below the ceiling and the corpse's back was touching the wall. The painted crimson lips revealed gums and teeth from between which protruded a blue, swollen tongue.

Anwaldt threw up the contents of his stomach into the bidet. He then sat on the edge of the bath and tried to collect his thoughts. In no more than a few minutes, he was sure Lea had not committed suicide. There was no stool in the bathroom, nothing from which she could have kicked herself off. She could not have rebounded from the toilet bowl because she was not tall enough. She would have had to tie the loop on the thick drain-pipe below the ceiling and then, holding on to it with one hand, place the loop around her neck. *(Such a feat would have been hard for an acrobat let alone a morphine addict whom half a dozen men must have shagged that day. It looks as if someone very strong strangled Lea, hung the rope in the bathroom, lifted the girl and slipped her neck through the loop. Except that he forgot about the chair which would have made the trick credible.)*

Suddenly, he heard the curtain flutter in the window through which he had climbed. A draught. *(There must be another window open in this apartment.)*

In the door, stood a huge, dark man. He took a rapid swipe. Anwaldt jumped aside, treading on the silk petticoat lying on the floor. His right leg slid back; the entire weight of his body rested on his swollen left foot; it was more than he could take. The left leg gave way under him; Anwaldt bent forward in front of the Turk. The latter clasped his hands and gave a blow from below — to the chin. The policeman collapsed backwards into the enormous bathtub. Before he realized what had happened, he saw the assailant's face over him and an enormous fist armed with a knuckle-duster. The punch in his solar plexus took his breath away. A cough, wheezing, a blurred image, wheezing, wheezing, night, wheezing, night, night.

BRESLAU, THAT SAME JULY 10TH, 1934
EIGHT O'CLOCK IN THE EVENING

The icy water restored Anwaldt's consciousness. He was sitting, quite naked, in a windowless cell, tied to a chair. Two men in black, unbuttoned S.S. uniforms were observing him. The shorter of the two twisted his long, intelligent face in a grimace reminiscent of a smile. He reminded Anwaldt of his secondary school maths teacher who used to pull similar faces when one of his pupils could not solve a problem. (*I warn you against these people — they are ruthless and capable of forcing anyone into giving up an investigation. If, God forbid, you ever find yourself at the Gestapo, please stubbornly state that you are an agent of the Abwehr uncovering the Polish Intelligence network in Breslau.*)

The man from the Gestapo walked around the cell, where the stench of sweat was almost palpable.

"Bad, Anwaldt, isn't it?" he clearly expected an answer.

"Yes . . ." the tortured man gasped. His tongue caught the jagged remains of his front tooth.

"Everybody's bad in this city." He circled the chair. "Yeees, Anwaldt.

124

So what are you doing here . . . in this Babylon? What brought you here?"

The man in uniform lit a cigarette and put the flaming match to the prisoner's crown. Anwaldt flung himself about; the stink of burning hair was suffocating. The second torturer, a sweaty, fat man, threw a wet rag over his head, extinguishing the fire. The relief was short-lived. That same Gestapo man squeezed the prisoner's nose with one hand while, with the other, he shoved the rag into his mouth.

"What's your assignment in Breslau, Berliner?" the muffled voice repeated. "Enough, Konrad."

Freed of the stinking gag, Anwaldt fell into a long fit of coughing. The slim Gestapo man waited patiently for an answer. Not getting one, he looked at his helper.

"Herr Anwaldt doesn't want to answer, Konrad. He evidently feels safe. He thinks he's protected. But who's protecting him?" he spread his hands. "Criminal Director Eberhard Mock, perhaps? But Mock isn't here. Do you see Mock anywhere, Konrad?"

"No, I don't, Herr Standartenführer."

The slim man bowed his head and uttered in a pleading voice:

"I know, I know, Konrad. Your methods are foolproof. No secret remains, no name blotted from memory, when you question your patients. Allow me to cure this patient. May I?"

"Of course, Herr Standartenfuhrer."

The smiling Konrad left the cell. The Standartenführer opened an old, tattered briefcase and took out a litre bottle and a half-litre jar. He poured the contents of the bottle — some kind of suspension — over Anwaldt's head. The prisoner tasted something sweet on his tongue.

"It's water with honey, you know, Anwaldt," the torturer reached for the jar. "And this? You know what this is? Alright, alright . . . I'll satisfy your curiosity." He shook the jar several times. A low buzzing of insects emanated from it. Anwaldt looked: two hornets were furiously jumping on each other and thrashing against the sides of the jar.

"Oh dear, what awful monsters . . ." the man from Gestapo lamented. Suddenly, he took a swing and smashed the jar against the wall. Before the disorientated hornets had found their wings in the small cell, the prisoner was alone.

Anwaldt had never imagined that these enormous insects gave off the same sound with their wings as small birds. The hornets first threw themselves at the wire-encased light bulb but, after a moment, changed direction. They made strange convulsive movements in the fusty air and with every shudder fell lower. Soon, they found themselves in the vicinity of Anwaldt's head where they were drawn by the smell of honey. The prisoner tried to use his imagination to escape the cell. He succeeded. *(He was walking along a beach washed by gentle waves, rippled by a fresh breeze. His feet sank into the warm sand. Suddenly, a wind arose, the sand grew white-hot, the waves — instead of licking the beach — roared and lashed out at Anwaldt in raging froth.)*

His imagination refused to obey. He felt a slight current of air near his lips which were stuck together by the honey and water. He opened his eyes and saw a hornet which clearly had its eye on his lips. He blew at it with all his strength. The hornet, propelled by the rush of air, settled on the cell wall. Meanwhile, the second insect had started to circle his head. Anwaldt moved abruptly with his chair and flung his head from side to side. The hornet sat on one of his collar bones and dug its sting into his skin. The prisoner pressed it down with his chin and felt a searing pain. A blue, pulsating swelling merged the jaw with the collar bone. The squashed insect contorted its black and yellow body on the floor. The other hornet broke away from the wall and made to attack — stubbornly towards the lips. Anwaldt tilted his head and the insect, instead of landing on the lips, found itself on the edge of an eye socket. The pain and swelling spilt over the entire eye. Anwaldt jerked his head and, together with the chair, tumbled on to the concrete. Darkness flooded the left eye. Then the right.

A bucket of ice-cold water restored his consciousness. The Standartenführer dismissed the helper with his hand. He grabbed the chair by the backrest and, without the least difficulty, returned Anwaldt to a vertical position.

"You've got fighting spirit," he looked at the prisoner's swollen face with concern. "Two hornets attacked you and you killed them both."

The policeman's skin was painfully taut over the hard spheres of swelling. The hornets were still twitching on the rough floor.

"Tell me, Anwaldt, is that enough? Or do you want me to ask those aggressive creatures for help again? Do you know, I'm even more frightened of them than you are. Tell me, Anwaldt, is that enough?"

The prisoner affirmed with a nod. The fat torturer entered the cell and placed a chair in front of the officer. The latter sat astride it, rested his elbows on its back and looked amicably at his victim.

"Who are you working for?"

"The Abwehr."

"Your mission?"

"To uncover the Polish spy network."

"Why did they bring you in all the way from Berlin? Isn't there anybody good enough in Breslau?"

"I don't know. I received orders."

Anwaldt heard a stranger's voice coming from his own vocal cords. Every word was accompanied by pain in his throat and facial muscles stiff between the lumps made by the stings on his eye and jaw.

"Untie me, please," he whispered.

The Standartenführer observed him without a word. A warmer emotion flickered in his intelligent eye.

"Uncovering Polish Intelligence. And what have Baron von Köpperlingk and Baron von der Malten to do with it?"

"The man I was following was present at Baron von Köpperlingk's ball. But von der Malten has got nothing to do with the matter."

"What's the man's name?"

Anwaldt was taken in by the torturer's friendly expression. He filled his lungs with air and whispered:

"I can't tell you . . ."

The man in uniform laughed silently for a while then began a strange monologue. He asked questions in a deep voice then answered himself in a trembling falsetto:

"Who beat you up at the Baron's ball? Some swine, officer. Are you afraid of the swine? Yes, officer. But you're not afraid of hornets? Oh, I am, officer. How come? After all, you did kill two! Without even using your hands! Oh, I see, Anwaldt, two's not enough for you . . . You can have more . . ."

The man from Gestapo finished his bass-falsetto medley and deliberately stamped his cigarette into the swelling on Anwaldt's collar bone.

A stranger's voice practically tore apart Anwaldt's swollen throat. He lay on the floor, yelling. One minute. Two. The Standartenführer called: "Konrad!" A bucket of cold water silenced the prisoner. The torturer lit a new cigarette and blew on its tip. Anwaldt stared at the glow in horror.

"Name of the suspect?"

"Paweł Krystek."

The Gestapo man got up and left. After five minutes, he entered the cell in the company of the Turk whom Anwaldt knew.

"You're lying, you fool. There was nobody by that name at the Baron's, was there?" he turned to the Turk who, having put on his glasses, was going through a wad of black and silver invitations. He shook his head as he did so, confirming, in his oriental manner, the words of the Gestapo man, who was greedily inhaling the last of his cigarette.

"You've wasted my time and are making a mockery of my methods. You've hurt my feelings. You've annoyed me," he sighed and sniffed a couple of times. "Please take care of him. Maybe you'll be more effective."

The Turk got two bottles of honey diluted in a small amount of water from the briefcase and slowly — both at the same time — poured them on the prisoner's head, shoulders and stomach, particularly abundantly covering the lower abdomen and genitalia. Anwaldt started to yell. Gibberish emerged from his larynx, but the Turk understood: "I'll talk!" The Turk took a jar from the briefcase and shoved it under the prisoner's eyes. Some dozen hornets were stinging each other and contorting their thick abdomens.

"I'll talk!"

The Turk held the jar in his outstretched hand. Over the concrete floor.

"I'll talk!"

The Turk dropped the jar.

"I'll talk!"

The jar neared the floor. Urine spattered all around. The jar landed on the stone floor. Anwaldt had lost control over his bladder. He was losing consciousness. The jar did not shatter. It only hit the concrete with a dull thud.

The Turk moved away from the unconscious prisoner with revulsion as fat Konrad appeared. He untied Anwaldt from the chair and grabbed him under the arms. His legs dragged through the puddle. The Standartenführer barked:

"Wash that piss off him and take him to Oswitzer Wald." He closed the door behind Konrad and looked at the Turk. "Why do you look so surprised, Erkin?"

"But you had his back up against the wall, Standartenführer Kraus. He was all ready to sing."

"You're too hot-headed, Erkin." Kraus observed the hornets thrashing around in the jar of thick Jena glass. "Did you take a good look at him? He's got to have a rest now. I know men like him. He'll start singing such nonsense that it'll take us a week to check it out. And I can't keep him here that long. Mock is still very strong and is on very good terms with the Abwehr. Apart from that, Anwaldt's mine. If he decides to leave, my people in Berlin will get him. If he stays here, I'll invite him for another talk. In the first and second instance, it's enough for him to see an ordinary bee and he'll start singing. Erkin, as of today, to that man you and I are demons who will never leave his side . . ."

BRESLAU, WEDNESDAY, JULY 11TH, 1934
THREE O'CLOCK IN THE MORNING

A damp shroud of dew fell over the world. It pearled on the grasses, trees and the naked body of a man. On touching the burning skin, it immediately evaporated. The policeman woke up. For the first time in many days, he experienced a cool shudder. He just about managed to get up and, dragging his swollen leg, bumped against the trees and emerged on a gravel alley. He was making his way towards a dark building whose angular shadow contrasted with the brightening sky when the glare of headlights lashed him. By the building stood a car, its lights painfully carved Anwaldt's nakedness out of the darkness. He heard the cry "Stop!", a woman's muffled laughter, the sound of gravel crunching under the shoes of approaching men. He touched his aching neck, a coarse eiderdown rubbed against his wounded body. He opened his eyes in the soothing glow of a bedside lamp. The wise eyes of Doctor Abraham Lanzmann, Baron von der Malten's personal physician, were observing him from behind thick lenses.

"Where am I?" the faint effort of a smile appeared on his lips. It amused him to think that this was the first time his loss of memory was not due to alcohol.

"You're in your apartment," Doctor Lanzmann was short of sleep and serious. "You were brought in by some policemen who were patrolling the so-called Swedish Bastion in Oswitzer Wald. A lot of girls gather there in the summer. And where they are, there's always something shady going on. But to the point. You were barely conscious. You persistently repeated your name, Mock's name, the Baron's and your address. The policemen did not want to leave what they suspected was their drunk colleague and brought you home. From here, they phoned the Baron. I've got to leave you now. The Baron has asked me to pass this sum on to you," his fingers caressed an envelope lying on the table. "Here's some ointment for your swellings and cuts. You'll find instructions about what the medication is for and how to take it on each bottle and phial. I managed to find quite a bit in my first-aid cabinet at home – considering the unusual time of day. Goodbye. I'll come back at about midday, when you've had some sleep."

Doctor Lanzmann's eyelids closed over his wise eyes, Anwaldt's over his swollen ones. He could not fall asleep. The walls, reflecting the day's heat, bothered him. With a few moves, he rolled off the bed on to the dirty carpet. Crawling on all fours, he reached the sill, pulled the heavy curtains apart and opened the window. He fell on his knees and slowly reached the bed. He lay on the eiderdown and mopped himself with a linen shawl, avoiding the swellings – volcanoes of pain. As soon as he opened his eyes, swarms of hornets flew in. When he closed the windows against them, the walls of the tenement stifled him with a burning breath, and cockroaches crawled out from the holes – some looking like scorpions. In a word, he could not fall asleep with the window closed and could not sleep with open eyes.

It was a little cooler in the morning. He fell asleep for two hours. When he woke, he saw four people sitting at his bedside. The Baron was talking quietly to Doctor Lanzmann. Seeing that the sick man was awake, he nodded to two orderlies standing by the wall. The two men grasped the policeman under the arms, carried him to the kitchen and put him in a huge tub of luke-warm water. One washed Anwaldt's sore body, the other removed his dark stubble with a razor. After a while, Anwaldt was lying in bed again, on a clean, starched sheet and exposing his wounded limbs to the effects of Doctor Lanzmann's ointments and balsams. The Baron patiently waited with his questions until the medic had finished. Anwaldt talked for about half an hour, stopping and stumbling. He had no control over his loose syntax. The Baron listened with seeming indifference. At one moment, the policeman broke off in mid-word and fell asleep. He dreamt of snow-capped peaks, icy expanses, freezing gusts of the Arctic: the wind blew and dried his skin; where was the wind coming from? the wind? He opened his eyes and in the dark setting sun saw a boy fanning him with a folded newspaper.

"Who are you?" he could barely move his bandaged jaw.

"Helmut Steiner, the Baron's kitchen boy. I'm to look after you until Doctor Lanzmann comes in tomorrow to examine you."

"What's the time?"

"Seven in the evening."

Anwaldt tried to walk around the room. He could barely put his weight on the swollen heel. He made out his beige suit on the chair, cleaned and pressed. He quickly pulled on his underpants and looked around for some cigarettes.

"Go to the restaurant on the corner and bring me some pork knuckle and cabbage, and beer. Buy some cigarettes, too." He realized with rage

132

that his cigarette case and watch had been stolen at the Gestapo. While the boy was absent, he washed himself at the kitchen sink and, exhausted, sat down at the table, trying not to catch sight of himself in the mirror. Shortly, a steaming plate stood in front of him, the quivering fat of pork knuckle bathing in a portion of young cabbage. He devoured everything in a matter of minutes. When he looked at the round-bellied bottle of Kipke beer – droplets of water streaming down its cool neck, a white, porcelain hat secured by a nickel-plated clasp in its mouth – he remembered his resolution of total abstinence. He burst out in derisive laughter and poured half a bottle of beer down his throat. He lit a cigarette and inhaled greedily.

"I told you to buy pork knuckle and beer, didn't I?"

"Yes."

"Did I clearly say 'beer'?"

"Yes."

"Just imagine, I said that automatically. And did you know that when we speak automatically, it's not us speaking but someone else speaking through us. So that when I told you to buy some beer it wasn't me telling you but someone else. Do you understand?"

"Who, for example?" the baffled boy grew interested.

"God!" roared Anwaldt with laughter then laughed until pain almost drilled his head asunder. He fastened on to the bottle neck and, after a moment, put it aside, empty. He dressed awkwardly. He barely squeezed his hat on to his bandaged head. Hopping on one leg, he mastered the spiral staircase and found himself on a street inundated by the setting sun.

VII

Eberhard Mock strolled along Zoppot pier, rejecting the thought of the approaching lunch with distaste. He was not hungry because he had drunk several tankards of beer between meals, interspersed with bites of hot frankfurter sausages. On top of that, for the sake of lunch, he had to relinquish watching the girls stroll by the casino, their lazy bodies provocatively taut under the slippery silk of dresses and swim suits. Mock shook his head and tried once more to chase away a nagging thought which stubbornly drew him towards that distant city suffocating in the hollow of stagnant air, towards those tight, crowded quarters of tenements and dark wells of yards, towards monumental buildings enclosed in the classicistic white of sandstone or neo-Gothic red of bricks, towards islands weighed down by churches and wrapped in the embrace of the dirty green snake of the Oder, towards residences and palaces concealed by greenery, where the "gentleman" betrays the "lady" with reciprocity and the servants merge with the panelling of the walls. The persistent thought drew Mock to the city where someone throws scorpions into the bellies of girls as beautiful as a dream and dispirited men with dirty pasts lead investigations which will always end in defeat. He knew what to call his thoughts: the qualms of conscience.

Filled with beer, sausages and heavy thoughts, Mock entered the Spa House where he was renting a so-called junker's apartment with his wife. He was greeted in the restaurant by the beseeching eyes of his wife, standing next to two old ladies who did not leave her side for an instant. Mock realized that he was not wearing a tie and turned back to go to their apartment and repair this *faux pas*. As he was crossing the hotel hall he caught sight out of the corner of his eye of a tall man in dark clothes getting up and making his way towards him. Mock instinctively halted. The man stood in his path and, pressing his hat to his chest, bowed politely.

"Oh, it's you Hermann," Mock looked carefully at Baron von der Malten's chauffeur's face, grey with fatigue.

Hermann Wuttke bowed once more and handed Mock an envelope with the Baron's golden initials. Mock read the letter three times, put it neatly back in its envelope and muttered to the chauffeur:

"Wait for me here."

Shortly afterwards, he entered the restaurant, travel-bag in hand. He neared the table, glared at by the two ladies and followed by the distressful gaze of his wife. She was clenching her teeth so as to swallow the bitter taste of disappointment. She knew that their holiday together was coming to an end — yet one more unsuccessful rational attempt to save their marriage. He did not need to have his travel-bag with him for her to know that, in a moment, he would be leaving the health resort of which he had dreamt for years. It was enough for her to look into his eyes: hazy, melancholic and cruel — as always.

BRESLAU, THURSDAY, JULY 12TH, 1934
TEN O'CLOCK IN THE EVENING

After a two-hour walk through the city centre (Ring and the dark streets around Blücherplatz peopled with rogues and prostitutes), Anwaldt sat in

Orlich's beerhouse, Orwi, on Gartenstrasse not far from the Operetta, looking through the menu. There was a variety of coffee, cocoa, a vast choice of liqueurs and Kipke beer. But there was also something he particularly wanted. He folded the menu and the waiter was at his side. He ordered cognac and a siphon of Deinart mineral water, lit a cigarette and looked around. Soft chairs surrounded dark tables in fours, landscapes of the Riesengebirge hung over wainscotting covered in wood, green velvet discreetly veiled booths and small rooms, nickel taps poured streams of frothy beer into pot-bellied tankards. Laughter, loud conversation and the abundant fumes of aromatic tobacco filled the restaurant. Anwaldt listened attentively to customers' conversations and tried to guess their professions. As he easily gathered, they were mainly small manufacturers and owners of large craft enterprises selling their wares in their own stores adjacent to their workshops. Nor was there a lack of agents, petty officials and students wearing the insignia of their societies. Colourfully dressed women sauntered through the place, smiling. But, for reasons unknown to him, they avoided Anwaldt's table. He only realized why when he glanced at the marble table top: on to a napkin embroidered with Trebnitz flowers had crawled a black scorpion. It was moving its crooked abdomen dartingly, directing its venomous sting upwards, defending itself in this way against the hornet which was trying to attack it.

The policeman closed his eyes and tried to get a hold on his imagination. Warily, his hand groped for the familiar shape of the bottle which had found itself on to his table a moment ago. He uncorked it, raised it to his lips. His lips and throat burnt pleasurably with the molten gold. He opened his eyes: the monsters had vanished from the table. He wanted to laugh now at his anxieties. With an indulgent smile, he looked at the packet of Salem cigarettes with its illustration of a large wasp. He filled the balloon of thin glass and drank it in a single draught; he inhaled his cigarette. The alcohol, fortified with a hefty dose of nicotine, infiltrated his blood. The siphon bubbled amicably. Anwaldt began to listen to conversations at the neighbouring tables.

"Don't worry, Herr Schultze . . . Isn't there enough evil in this world to contend with? Really, Herr Schultze . . ." some elderly gentleman with a bowler hat glued to the crown of his head was mumbling. "I tell you: neither the day, nor the hour . . . And that's the truth . . . Because take that last incident, for instance. The tram was turning into Gartenstrasse from Teichstrasse near the Hirschlik bakery . . . And, let me tell you, he went and hit a droschka going to the station . . . The rascal cabby survived, but the woman and child were killed . . . That's how that swine sent . . . into the next world . . . Nobody knows the day nor the hour . . . Neither you, nor I, nor this one here or that one there . . . Hey, you who's been beaten up, what are you staring at?"

Anwaldt lowered his eyes. The agitated siphon hissed. He lifted the tablecloth and saw two coupling hornets, abdomens interlocked. Swiftly, he smoothed down the tablecloth which changed into a sheet. The sheet used to cover Banker Schmetterling clenched in a painful knot with the beautiful schoolgirl, Erna.

He drank two glasses of cognac on the trot and glanced over to the side, avoiding the eyes of the fat drunkard who was revealing the secret wisdom of life to Herr Schultze.

"What? Under the statue of Battle and Victory on Königsplatz? They go there, you say? Servants and nursemaids on the whole? You're right, that is an exceptional situation. You don't have to woo or strut . . . All they want from you is what you want from them . . ." a thin student was drinking Beaujolais straight from the bottle and becoming more and more excited. "Yes. It's a clear situation. You approach, smile and take her home. You don't waste your money or lose your honour. Eh, what competition are soldiers . . . Excuse me, but do I know you?"

"No. I was lost in thought . . ." Anwaldt said. (*I'd like to talk to someone. Or play chess. Yes, chess. As at the orphanage once. Karl — he was one keen chess-player. We would place a cardboard suitcase between the beds and put the chessboard on it. Once, when we were playing, the drunk tutor came into the dormitory.)* Anwaldt clearly heard the clatter of chess pieces scattering now and felt the kicks dealt by the tutor to both the suitcase and their bodies hiding under the beds.

Two glasses, two gulps, two hopes.

"Herr Schultze, it's good that they threw those professors out of work. No Jew's agoing to teach German children . . . Agoing to fu . . . fu . . . Agoing to foul . . ."

The hiss of gaslight, the impatient hiss of the siphon: another drink!

"Oh, those Polish students! They know next to nothing! And what demands! What manners! And it's a good thing they've been taught some sense at the Gestapo. They're in a German city, so let them speak German!"

Anwaldt, tripping, made towards the toilet. There were numerous obstacles in his path: uneven floorboards, tables blocking his way, waiters bustling through thick smoke. Finally, he reached the cubicle. He dropped his trousers, supported his hands on the wall and swayed from side to side. Among the uniform murmur, he heard the dull thumping of his heart. He listened intently to the sound for quite a while then suddenly heard a cry and saw Lea Friedländer's alluring body twitching below the ceiling. He stumbled back into the room. He needed a drink to scrub the image from his eyes.

"Oh, how pleased I am to see you, Criminal Director! Only you can help me!" he shouted with joy to Mock, who was sitting at his table and smoking a fat cigar.

"Calm down, Anwaldt. It's not true, any of it! Lea Friedländer's alive," the strong hand, covered with black hair, patted him on the shoulder. "Don't worry. We'll solve this case."

Anwaldt looked at the place where, a moment ago, Mock had been. Now a waiter sat there, looking at him with an amused expression.

"Well, it's a good thing you've woken up, sir. It would have been awkward for me to throw a client out who gives such tips. Shall I order you a droschka or a taxi, sir?"

BRESLAU, SATURDAY, JULY 14TH, 1934
EIGHT O'CLOCK IN THE MORNING

The morning sun outlined Baron von der Malten's Roman profile and the wave of Eberhard Mock's black hair. They were sitting in the Baron's garden, drinking aromatic coffee.

"How was the journey?"

"Fine, thank you. Only I was a bit worried with your chauffeur driving so fast and being so tired."

"Oh, Hermann's a man of iron. Have you read Anwaldt's report?"

"Yes. Very detailed. It's a good thing you sent it to me straight away."

"It took him the whole of yesterday to write it. He says he writes well after a drinking binge."

"He got drunk? Really?"

"Unfortunately. At Orlich's, near the Operetta. What do you intend to do, Eberhard? What are your plans?"

"I intend to take care of Maass and von Köpperlingk," Mock exhaled a thick cloud of smoke. "They'll lead me to that Turk."

"And what has Maass got to do with him?"

"Olivier, Baron von Köpperlingk bribed Maass with pretty rented schoolgirls from Madame le Goef's. Anwaldt's right: Maass is too intelligent not to know that he's dealing with the daughters of Corinth, but on the other hand too egocentric to accept the fact. He's of a kind with

139

Professor Andreae, I think. Why did the Baron bribe him? That, we'll find out. Then I'll put some pressure on the Baron. I'm sure he'll serve the Turk to me on a plate. Anwaldt's not going to achieve more than he has. He doesn't know Breslau well enough and, besides, they really scared him. Now I'm stepping into action."

"How are you going to make them talk?"

"Olivier, please . . . Leave my methods to me. Ah, here is Anwaldt. Good morning! You don't look all that good. Did you fall into some hydrochloric acid?"

"I had some minor problems," said the convalescent, bowing to both men. Mock, embracing him cordially, said:

"Please don't worry. The Gestapo aren't going to harass you again. I've just sorted that out." (*"Yes, he sorted that out very efficiently,"* thought *the Baron holding out a limp hand to Anwaldt. "I wouldn't like to be in that Forstner's shoes."*)

"Thank you," Anwaldt croaked. Generally, on the third day after being drunk, the physical pains would subside and a deep depression would appear. That is how it would have been now, too, if it were not for that one human being — Eberhard Mock. The sight of that angular man in his immaculately cut pale suit had a soothing effect on Anwaldt. He glanced contritely at Mock and, for the first time in his life, had the feeling that somebody cared.

"I'm sorry. I got drunk. I've no excuse."

"Too true, you've no excuse. If you ever get drunk again, you'll stop working with me and you'll go back to Berlin. And Criminal Counsellor von Grappersdorff won't be welcoming you with open arms." Mock looked sternly at the humbly stooping Anwaldt. Suddenly, he put his arm around him. "You won't get drunk any more. You simply won't have any reason to. I'm back from Zoppot and I'm going to watch over you. We're leading this investigation together. Allow us, Baron . . ." He turned to von der Malten, who was observing this whole episode with a degree of distaste, "to take our leave. We've an appointment to see the Director of the University Library, Doctor Hartner."

BRESLAU, THAT SAME JULY 14TH, 1934
NINE O'CLOCK IN THE MORNING

Despite the early hour, the sun scorched the windows and roof of the Adler. Anwaldt was driving, Mock navigating and explaining the streets and places they passed. They drove down Krietener Weg, along which ran workmen's blocks interspersed with small, flowery houses. They passed the border post of Breslau and found themselves in Klettendorf. The sweetish stench of Liebich's sugar factory penetrated the thick air. The recently built Evangelical church, separated by a low fence from the presbytery concealed among trees, flashed past their right window. Mock grew pensive and stopped commenting on the neighbourhood. They were driving through a beautiful suburb full of gardens and villas.

"Ah, so we're in Oparów, are we? Except we've approached it from another direction, is that right?"

"Yes. It's Opperau, not Oparów."

Anwaldt did not ask the way again. He parked the car outside Madame le Goef's salon. The muffled cries of bathers – already using the sports pool some 200 metres away, despite the early hour – could be heard in the silence. Mock did not get out. He found his cigarette case and offered it to Anwaldt. The striped, blue cigarette paper grew damp to the touch.

"You've experienced great humiliation, Herbert." Clouds of cigarette smoke emerged from Mock's nose and lips with every word. "I once experienced something like that, too. That's how I know how to stifle the bitterness inside. You have to attack, throw yourself at someone's throat,

141

tear and bite. Fight! Act! Who shall we attack today, Herbert? The corruptible erotomaniac Maass. Who shall we use against him?" He did not answer, but indicated, with his head, the manor standing in its burning garden. They extinguished their cigarettes and made a move. Nobody stopped them either at the gate or on the drive. The guards bowed politely to Mock. After several sharp rings, the door opened a little. With a kick, Mock flung it wide open and roared to the terrified butler:

"Where is Madame?!"

Madame ran down the stairs, wrapping a dressing gown around her. She was no less alarmed than the doorman.

"Oh, what's happened, your Excellency? Why is your Excellency so angry?"

Mock placed one leg on a stair, put his hands on his hips and yelled so loudly that the crystals on the hall lamp swung.

"What's the meaning of this, dammit? My associate is viciously attacked here, in this place! What am I to understand by that?"

"I'm sorry. It was a misunderstanding. The young man did not have any identification. But please, please . . . Do go up to my office . . . Kurt will bring some beer, a siphon, ice, sugar and lemons."

Mock spread himself brusquely behind Madame's desk, Anwaldt on the small, leather sofa. Madame sat on the edge of her chair and glanced anxiously at one, then the other in turn. Mock lengthened the silence. The servant entered.

"Four lemonades," ordered Mock. "Two for this man."

Four tall glasses sweated on the small table. The door closed behind the servant. Anwaldt swallowed the first lemonade almost in one gulp. The second, he savoured for longer.

"Please call the pseudo-schoolgirl and some other pretty eighteen-year-old. She's to be a 'virgin'. You know what I mean? Then please leave us alone with them."

142

Madame smiled knowingly and retreated from the royal presence. A freshly made-up eye winked meaningfully. She was pleased that His Excellency was no longer angry.

The "schoolgirl" was accompanied by a red-haired angel with pale, hazel eyes and white, transparent skin. They did not let the girls sit, so they stood in the middle of the room, worried and helpless.

Anwaldt got up and, with his hands behind his back, paced the room. Suddenly, he stopped in front of "Erna".

"Listen carefully to me. Today the bearded chauffeur is going to take you to see Maass. You'll tell Maass that your friend from school wants to meet and please him. That she's waiting for him in the hotel . . . Which hotel?" he asked Mock.

"The Golden Goose on Junkerstrasse 27/297."

"You," Anwaldt turned to the red-head, "really will be waiting for him there, in room 104. The porter will give you the key. You're to play the innocent and surrender to Maass after a long time resisting. Madame will tell you what to do to make the client think he's dealing with a virgin. Then you," he pointed to "Erna", "will join them. To put it briefly – you're to keep Maass in that room for two hours. I wouldn't like to be in your shoes if you don't. That's all. Any questions?"

"Yes," the schoolgirl's alto reverberated. "Will the chauffeur agree to take us there?"

"It's all the same to him where you give yourself as long as it's with Maass."

"I've got a question, too," the red-haired angel croaked. *(Why do they all have such deep voices? Never mind. As it is, they're more honest than Erna Stange with her melodious, quiet squeak.)* "Where do I get a school uniform from?"

"Wear an ordinary dress. It's summer and not all schools make their pupils wear uniforms. Apart from that, tell him that you were ashamed of coming to a tryst in a hotel wearing school uniform."

Mock got up unhurriedly from behind the desk. "Any other questions?"

BRESLAU, THAT SAME JULY 14TH, 1934
TEN O'CLOCK IN THE MORNING

They parked the Adler in front of the Police Praesidium. After entering the gloomy building where the walls soothed with their cellar-like coolness, they parted ways. Mock went to see Forstner, Anwaldt to the Evidence Archives. A quarter of an hour later, they met at the porter's counter. Each held a package under his arm. They left the thick walls of the Praesidium regretfully and choked as they breathed in the heat of the street. The police photographer, Helmut Ehlers, whose enormous bald head seemed to reflect the sun's rays, waited beside the car. All three got in; Anwaldt drove. First, they went to Deutschmann's tobacco shop on Schweidnitzer Strasse, where Mock bought his favourite cigars, and then turned back. They passed St Dorothy's Church, the Hotel Monopol, the Municipal Theatre, Wertheim's Department Store and turned right into Tauentzienstrasse. After about twenty yards, they stopped. Kurt Smolorz emerged from the shadowy gate and approached the car. He got in next to Ehlers and said:

"She's been with him for five minutes already. Köpperlingk's chauffeur is waiting for her over there," he waved at the chauffeur who was leaning against the Mercedes, smoking a cigarette. Fanning himself with his somewhat too small, stiff cap, he was clearly suffocating in his dark livery with its golden buttons carrying the Baron's monogram. After a while, on a pavement as hot as an oven, Maass appeared – plainly excited – with the schoolgirl attached to his side. An elderly lady, walking past, spat with disgust. They got into the Mercedes. The chauffeur did not look

144

in the least surprised. The engine growled. A moment later, the elegant rear of the limousine disappeared from sight.

"Gentlemen," Mock said quietly. "We've got two hours. And let Maass enjoy himself a bit at the end. Soon he'll be with us . . ."

They got out and, with relief, hid in the shade of the gate. The short caretaker blocked their way and asked, a little frightened:

"Who have you come to see?"

Mock, Ehlers and Smolorz paid him no heed. Anwaldt pushed him against the wall and, with one hand, forcefully squashed his unshaven cheeks. The caretaker's lips rolled into a frightened snout.

"We're from the police, but you haven't seen us. Understand, or do you want trouble?"

The caretaker nodded to show he understood and scurried into the depths of the yard. Anwaldt barely managed to climb to the first floor then pressed the brass doorknob. It gave way. Although his conversation with the caretaker and his ascent had taken no more than two minutes, both policemen and the photographer had not only silently entered the apartment, but they had also begun a methodical, detailed search. Anwaldt joined them. Wearing gloves, they picked up and examined every object, replacing it exactly where they had found it. After an hour, they met in Maass' study which had been searched by Mock.

"Sit down," Mock indicated the chairs spread out around a small circular table. "You've searched the kitchen, bathroom and living-room, have you? Good work. Find anything interesting? That's what I thought. There is, however, one interesting thing here . . . This notebook. Ehlers, to work!"

The photographer unpacked his equipment, stood a vertical, portable tripod on the desk and fixed a Zeiss camera to it. On the top of the desk, he spread the rough-book found by Mock then held it in place with a pane of glass. He pressed the cable release. The flashlight shot once. The title

145

page: "*Die Chronik von Ibn Sahim*. Übersetzt von Dr Georg Maass"[†] was fixed on photographic film. The flash clicked and went off another fifteen times until all the pages covered in the even, small handwriting had been photographed. Mock glanced at his watch and said:

"My dear gentlemen, we've managed on time. Ehlers, when can you have the photographs ready?"

"At five."

"Anwaldt will collect them from you then. Only him, understood?"

"Yes, sir."

"Thank you, gentlemen."

Smolorz locked the door as easily as he had opened it. Anwaldt glanced through the stained-glass window and, in its coloured glow, made out the caretaker sweeping the yard and anxiously looking around at the windows. It was probable that he did not know which apartment they had broken into. After a few seconds, they were in the car, Mock driving. They made their way along Agnesstrasse to the Police Praesidium where Ehlers and Smolorz got out. Mock and Anwaldt turned into Schweidnitzer Strasse, and then into Zwinger Platz and, passing the coffee-roasting house and merchants' club, drove into busy Schuhbrücke. They passed the Petersdorff and the Barasch Brothers' Department Stores – the latter crowned with a glass globe – then left behind them the Museum of Palaeontology and the former Police Praesidium. They reached the Oder. Next to St Maciej's Secondary School, they turned right and soon found themselves at Dominsel. Passing the medieval cathedral and the red Georgianum Seminary building, they made their way on to Adalbertstrasse. A moment later, the bellboy of the Lessing Restaurant was bowing from the waist before them.

A pleasant coolness dominated the room, which, at first, allowed them to breathe freely again, then produced a calm sleepiness. Anwaldt closed

† *The Chronicles of Ibn Sahim*. Trans. Dr Georg Maass.

his eyes. He thought he was being rocked by gentle waves. The clatter of cutlery. Mock attacked the succulent, pink salmon swimming in horseradish sauce, with two forks. He cast an amused eye on the dozing Anwaldt.

"Wake up, Anwaldt," he touched the sleeping man's shoulder. "Your lunch will get cold."

Smoking a cigar, he watched as Anwaldt greedily consumed a beefsteak with sauerkraut and potatoes.

"Please don't be offended, Herbert," Mock placed a hand on his bloated stomach. "I've eaten too much, but you, I see, have an excellent appetite. Perhaps you'd like this piece of salmon? I haven't touched it."

"With pleasure. Thank you," smiled Anwaldt. Nobody had ever shared their food with him. He ate the fish with relish and took a fair draught of strong, black tea.

Mock built Anwaldt's character profile in his thoughts. It was not complete without the details of his torture in the Gestapo cell, but no tactical question, no trick which could provoke Anwaldt into confessing, came to mind. Several times, he opened his mouth and immediately closed it again because it seemed that what he was about to say sounded silly and flat. After a while, he came to terms with the thought that he would not be reading Anwaldt's psychological profile to Madame le Goef's girls next week.

"It's half-past one now. Before half-past four, please look through von Köpperlingk's files and consider how we can pin him down. Please look through the files of all the Turks, too. Maybe you'll find something. At half-past four, you're to give all those files to Forstner; at five, collect the photographs from Ehlers and come to see me in my apartment. I'm leaving the car with you. Everything clear?"

"Yes, sir."

"So why are you looking at me so strangely? Do you need anything?"

"Nothing, nothing . . . It's just that nobody's ever shared their food with me."

Mock laughed out loud and patted Anwaldt on the shoulder with his small hand.

"Don't take it as a sign of my particularly liking you," he lied. "It's a habit from childhood. I always had to hand in an empty plate . . . I'm taking a droschka home now. I need a nap. Goodbye."

The Criminal Director was falling asleep already in the cab. On the threshold of sleep and wakefulness, he remembered a Sunday lunch a year ago. He was sitting with his wife in the dining-room, happily nibbling spare ribs in tomato sauce. His wife was also eating with great relish, going through all the meat first. At one point, she glanced pleadingly at the plate in front of Mock, who always left the best pieces to the end.

"Please, do give me a little of your meat."

Mock did not react and stuffed all the meat still remaining on his plate into his mouth.

"I'm certain you would not even give it to your children – if you could have any, of course." She got up, angry. (*She was wrong again. I did give some to one. And to one not my own.*)

BRESLAU, THAT SAME JULY 14TH, 1934
TWO O'CLOCK IN THE AFTERNOON

Anwaldt left the restaurant and climbed into the car. He glanced at the files stamped by the Gestapo, and at the package which he had collected that morning from the archives. Unwrapping it, he shuddered: strange, curved writing. Blackened blood on blue wallpaper. He rewrapped the bloody writing and got out of the car. Under his arm, he carried the Gestapo files and the blanket used by Mock to cover the back seat. He did not feel like driving through the scorching city. He made off in the direction of the slender steeples of St Michael's Church to Waschteich Park, whose strange name Mock had explained to him during their drive: in the Middle Ages, women used to wash their linen in the pond there. Now children were shouting and running by the pond while most of the benches were occupied by nursemaids and servants. These women demonstrated an excellent capacity to divide their attention as they pursued vociferous discussions while, from time to time, shouting at the children wading in the shallow waters by the bank. The remaining benches were occupied by soldiers and local scamps proudly smoking cigarettes.

Anwaldt removed his jacket, lay on the blanket and began to examine von Köpperlingk's files. Unfortunately, there was nothing in them that he could use to pin down the Baron. What was more: everything the Baron did in his apartment and on his property took place with the Gestapo's full blessing. (Mock told me that even Kraus, although he was furious when he heard about his homosexual agent, soon realized the advantage to be gained from him.) The last piece of information filled Anwaldt with hope: it concerned the Baron's servant, Hans Tetges.

He turned on his back and, with the help of a few brutal and suggestive images, thought of a way for the Baron. Pleased with his idea, he now started looking through the files written by the Gestapo and the C.I.D. concerning Turks. There were eight Turks in all: five had left Breslau before July 9th, when the Baron's ball had taken place, the other three had to be excluded because of their age – Anwaldt's assailant, after all, could not have been twenty (like the Turkish students at the Engineering College) or sixty (like a certain merchant, included in the Gestapo files because of his uncontrollable tendency to gamble). Of course, data from the Registration Office and the Turkish Consulate, which Smolorz was to supply, might bring additional information about Turks who did not have the dubious pleasure of finding themselves included in police documents.

When the Turkish trail failed him, Anwaldt applied all his intellectual powers to conjuring up details of a "vice for the Baron". The protests of a child who, not far from Anwaldt, was insisting that he was right, were not conducive to concentration. He raised himself on his elbow and listened to the kind-hearted reassurance of the old nursemaid and the little boy's hysterical voice.

"But, Klaus, I keep telling you: the gentleman who arrived yesterday is your daddy."

"No! I don't know him! Mummy told me I don't have a daddy!" The enraged little child stamped his foot on the parched earth.

"Mummy told you that because everybody thought your daddy had been killed by Indian savages in Brazil."

"Mummy never lies to me!" The shrill voice broke down.

"Well, she didn't lie to you. She said you didn't have a daddy because she thought he was dead. Now Daddy's come . . . Well, we know he's alive . . . Now you've got a daddy," the nanny explained with incredible patience.

The little one did not give in. He thumped the ground with his wooden rifle and yelled:

"You're lying! Mummy doesn't lie! Why didn't she tell me that it's Daddy?"

"She didn't have time. They left for Trebnitz in the morning. They'll be back tomorrow evening, and they'll tell you everything . . ."

"Mummy! Mummy!" The boy screamed and threw himself on the ground, thrashing his arms and legs. As he did so, he kicked up clouds of dust which settled on his freshly ironed sailor's suit. The nanny tried to pick him up with the result that Klaus broke away and dug his teeth into her plump arm.

Anwaldt got to his feet, folded the files, rolled up the blanket and limped towards the car. He did not look behind, afraid that he might turn back, grab Klaus by his sailor's collar and drown him in the pond. The murderous thoughts had not been provoked by the child's yelling which, like a lancet, had cut through his wounded head and the blue traces of the hornet's stings; no, it was not the shouting which had infuriated him but the thoughtless, blind stubbornness with which the spoilt brat rejected unexpected happiness: the return of a parent, who had appeared after so many years. He did not even realize he was talking to himself:

"How can you explain to a pig-headed brat like that that his resistance is idiotic? He needs a thrashing, then he'll see his foolishness. After all, he won't understand anything if I go up to him, put him on my knee and say: 'Klaus, have you ever stood in the window with your face pressed up against the pane, watched men pass by and said about each and every one of them without exception: that's my Daddy, he's very busy — that's why he's put me in an orphanage, but he'll come and get me soon?'"

VIII

BRESLAU, THAT SAME SATURDAY, JULY 14TH, 1934
HALF-PAST TWO IN THE AFTERNOON

Kurt Smolorz sat on the square in Rehdigerplatz, watching for Mock and becoming more and more worried about the state of his report. He was to have included the results of his surveillance of Konrad Schmidt, the iron fist of the Gestapo known as "fat Konrad" by screws and prisoners alike. These results were to help him find an effective means of coercion, that is, a "vice for Konrad", as Mock metaphorically described it. From the information gathered by Smolorz, it could be concluded that Schmidt was a sadist in whom the number of fat cells was in reverse proportion to the grey matter of his brain. Before finding employment in the prison service, he had worked as a plumber, circus athlete and guard at the Kana alcohol distillery. From there, he had ended up in prison for stealing spirits. He was released after a year and here the chronology of his files broke off. Further files dealt only with Konrad the Screw. In this capacity, he had worked for the Gestapo for a year. Smolorz looked at his first annotation: "drinking vodka" below the heading "Weak Points", and grimaced in anger. He knew that this remark would not satisfy his boss. Vodka, after all, could only be a "vice" for an alcoholic and fat Konrad certainly wasn't one. The second entry ran: "Easily provoked into a brawl." Smolorz could

152

not imagine that this fact could be used against Schmidt, but it was not up to him, after all, to do the thinking. The third and last annotation: "Is probably a sexual pervert, sadist", brought some hope that his week-long, strenuous labour would not go to waste.

He was also cross at Mock for forbidding him to use the usual official channels of communication which meant that he, Smolorz — instead of drinking cold beer somewhere now after having left the report on his boss' desk — had to keep watch near Mock's house for Lord knows how long.

It was not, as it turned out, long. A quarter of an hour later, Smolorz was sitting in Mock's apartment with his much-desired, perspiring tankard and waiting with some impatience for his boss' opinion. The opinion was more of a stylistic nature.

"What's this, Smolorz, can't you formulate your thoughts appropriately and officially?" The Criminal Director laughed out loud. "In official documents we write 'tendency to intoxicating drink' and not 'drinking vodka'. Alright, alright, I'm pleased with you. And now, go home. I have to take a nap before I make an important visit."

BRESLAU, THAT SAME SATURDAY, JULY 14TH, 1934
HALF-PAST FIVE IN THE AFTERNOON

The newly nominated Director of the University Library, Doctor Leo Hartner, stretched his bony torso and for the hundredth time cursed the architect who had designed the Baroque Augustinian monastery, now the magnificent building of the University Library on Neue Sandstrasse. The architect's mistake, according to Harnter, lay in locating the elegant quarters, serving as the Director's study at present, on the north side, thanks to which the room was cool — pleasant to everyone but its occupant. His aversion to temperatures below 20°C was founded. This

excellent specialist of Oriental languages had returned from the Sahara a few weeks ago after having spent close to three years studying the languages and customs of desert tribes. Now Breslau, in its summer heat, provided him with much-loved warmth but this, unfortunately, ended at the threshold of his study. The thick walls, the stone, heat-resistant barriers irritated him more than the freezing Sahara nights when deep sleep had isolated him from the prevailing cold. But here – within the closed expanse of his study – he had to act, make decisions and sign masses of documents with numb hands.

The coolness which prevailed in the room acted entirely differently on the two men comfortably ensconced on the leather armchairs. Both were breathing deeply and, instead of the swelter and dust of the street, they inhaled the bacteria and spores of mould born on the yellowing pages of volumes.

Hartner strolled nervously across the room. He held the piece of wall-paper with the "death verses".

"Strange . . . The writing is similar to some I saw in Cairo in eleventh- or twelfth-century Arabian manuscripts." His intelligent, slender face froze in thought. The short, grey hair bristled on the top of his head. "But it's not the Arabic I know. To be honest, this doesn't look Semitic to me at all. Well, please leave it with me for a few days; maybe I'll break the code when I put some other language under the Arabic text . . . I see you've got something else for me. What photographs are these, Herr, Herr . . . ?"

"Anwaldt. They're copies of Doctor Georg Maass' notes, which he himself described as being a translation of the Arabic chronicle of Ibn Sahim. We'd like to ask you, sir, for some more information about this chronicle, its author, and also the translation."

Hartner skimmed Maass' text. After a few minutes, his lips twisted into a pitiful smile.

"I see a number of characteristics of Maass' academic writing in these

few sentences. But, for the time being, I'll reserve any comments as to the translation until I see the original text. You have to know, my dear sirs, that Maass is well known for his fantasizing, his stubborn dullness and a peculiar *idée fixe* which makes him perceive more or less hidden archetypes of the apocalyptic visions of the Old Testament in every ancient text. His academic publications are swarming with pathological images of annihilation, death and disintegration which he finds everywhere, even in works of love and festivity. I can also see it in this translation, but only when I've read the original can I say whether these catastrophic elements come from the translator or from the author of the chronicle, whom, by the by, I'm not acquainted with."

Hartner was a typical armchair scholar who made his discoveries alone, entrusted the results of his research to specialist periodicals and expressed his pioneer's euphoria to the desert sands. For the first time in several years, he had before him an audience which – although small – was listening attentively to his arguments. He, too, listened intently and with pleasure to his own deep baritone.

"I know Maass well, as also Andreae and other scholars analysing fictitious works, creating new theoretical constructions, moulding their heroes from the clay of their own imaginations. Which is why, in order to eliminate any fraud on Maass' part, we have to check what he's working on at the moment: whether he really is translating some ancient text or whether he's creating it himself in the depths of his own imagination." He opened the door and said to his assistant:

"Stählin, ask the librarian on duty to come and see me. Tell him to bring the register of loans with him. We'll check," he addressed his guests, "what our exterminating angel is presently reading."

He approached the window and lost himself in the cries of boys who had turned out in swarms on the grassy tuft opposite the cathedral and were bathing in the Oder. He shook his head, remembering his guests.

155

"But, dear sirs, please help yourselves to some coffee. Strong, sweet coffee is excellent in the heat — something the Bedouins know very well. A cigar perhaps? Imagine, that was the only thing I missed in the Sahara. I emphasize: thing, not person. Indeed, I took a whole trunkful of cigars, but it turned out that the Tibbu people were even more fond of them than I. I assure you that the very sight of those people is so terrifying that I would willingly hand anything over to them in order not to have to look at them. On the other hand, I bribed them with cigars so as to listen to their ancestral and tribal stories. They proved useful for my post-doctoral thesis, which I recently submitted for publication." Hartner bellowed forth a large cloud of smoke and was on the point of presenting the arguments of this thesis when Anwaldt fired a question:

"Are there a lot of insects there, Doctor?"

"Yes, a lot. Just imagine: a cold night, ragged crags, the sharp chimneys of bare rock, sand eating its way into everything, people in the rifts with faces like the Devil himself, wrapped in black cloaks, and, in the moonlight, snakes slithering and scorpions . . ."

"That's the face of death . . ."

"What did you say, Inspector?"

"Sorry, nothing. You're describing it so vividly, Doctor, that I felt the waft of death . . ."

"I too felt it many times in the Sahara. Fortunately, it did not sweep me away and I have been allowed to see them again." Here, he pointed to a slim blonde and a seven-year-old boy who had unexpectedly entered the office.

"I'm very sorry, but I knocked twice . . ." said the woman with a clear Polish accent. Mock and Anwaldt stood up. Hartner looked at his loved ones tenderly. He stroked the boy on the head, who — evidently shy — was hiding behind his mother.

"It doesn't matter, my dear. Allow me to introduce His Excellency,

Director Eberhard Mock, the Chief of the Criminal Department of the Police Praesidium and his assistant Herr Herbert, Herbert . . ."

"Anwaldt."

"Yes, Criminal Assistant Anwaldt. Allow me, sirs – this is my wife, Teresa Jankewitsch-Hartner, and my son, Manfred."

Greetings were ceremoniously exchanged. The men bowed over the beautiful, slender hand of Frau Harnter. The boy bowed politely and gazed at his father who, apologizing to his guests, was speaking to his wife in a half-whisper. Frau Jankewitsch-Hartner, with her original beauty, stirred an intense yet somewhat differing interest in the two men: Mock was driven by the instinct of Casanova; Anwaldt, the contemplation of a Titian. This was not the first Polish woman to make such an impression on him. He sometimes caught himself thinking, absurdly, that the female representatives of that nation had something magical about them. "Medea was a Slav," he thought at such moments. Looking at her delicate features, her turned-up nose and her hair tied back in a knot, listening to her amusingly soft "*bitte*", he tried to liberate the noble contours of her body, the rounded curvature of her legs, the proud lift of her breasts, from her summer dress. Unfortunately, the object of their various, but perhaps basically similar, yearnings bade them farewell and left the office, tugging the shy boy with her. In the door, she passed the old, stooping librarian whose eyes lingered on her, something which did not escape the husband's notice.

"Show me that register you're lugging under your arm, Smetana," Hartner said, not too kindly. The librarian, having done what was asked of him, returned to his duties while Harnter began to study Smetana's sloping, Gothic calligraphy.

"Yes, dear sirs . . . For over a week now, Maass has been exclusively reading a fourteenth-century manuscript entitled *Corpus rerum Persicarum*. I'll take this work for analysis tomorrow and compare the

157

translation you photographed with the original. Today I'm going to work on the writing in the saloon carriage and that unfortunate Friedländer's prophecies. I'll also find something out about this Ibn Sahim. I might possibly have the first pieces of information the day after tomorrow. I'll contact you, Criminal Director." Hartner put on his spectacles and lost interest in his interlocutors. The search for pure truth entirely extinguished his oratorical-didactic passion. He turned his complete attention to the bloody writing and, muttering something to himself, put forward his first intuitive hypotheses. Mock and Anwaldt rose and said goodbye to the obliging scholar. The latter did not reply, occupied exclusively with his thoughts.

"He's very polite, this Doctor Hartner. He must have a lot of responsibilities, yet he is ready to help us. How is that possible?" Anwaldt said, seeing that his first words provoked a strange smile on Mock's face.

"My dear Herbert, he has a debt of gratitude to repay me. And one so great that he will not — I assure you — be able to repay it even with the most laborious scholarly expertise."

IX

Baron von Köpperlingk was taking a walk in the large park on his estate. The setting sun always awoke disturbing premonitions and unclear longings in him. The sharp, brassy cries of the peacocks strutting around the manor and the splashing of water in the pool where his friends were frolicking irritated him. The dogs' barking annoyed him as did the untamed curiosity of peasant children whose eyes followed everything that happened behind the manor walls from trees and fences – even in the evenings and at night – like the eyes of animals. He loathed these impudent, unwashed brats who never averted their eyes and who, at the very sight of him, choked with mocking laughter. He glanced at the wall which surrounded the manor and thought he saw and heard them. Despite the rage which flared within him, he made his way to the manor with a distinguished gait. With the wave of a hand, he caught the attention of Josef, the butler.

"Where's Hans?" he said coldly.

"I don't know, your Lordship. Someone phoned him and he ran from the manor, very agitated."

"Why didn't you tell me about this?"

159

"I didn't consider it fit to worry your Lordship during his walk."

The Baron looked calmly at the old servant and counted to ten in his head. With great difficulty, he controlled himself and hissed:

"Josef, please pass on to me any information concerning Hans, be it — in your eyes — of the least importance. If you don't in future do this, even once, you'll be begging in front of the Church of the Sacred Heart."

The Baron ran out to the drive and, facing the setting sun, shouted the name of his favourite butler several times. Hostile eyes answered him from the fence. He set off as fast as his legs could carry him towards the iron gates. The jeering looks pursued him; the evening air thickened. "Hans, where are you?" yelled the Baron. He tripped on even ground: "Hans, where are you? I can't get up." The evening air thickened; lead thickened in the Baron's body. From behind the manor wall flashed the barrels of machineguns. Bullets whistled into the gravel alley, kicked up clouds of dust, wounded the Baron's delicate body, did not allow him either to get up or to fall to the ground. "Where are you, Hans?"

Hans was sitting next to Max Forstner in the back of the parked Mercedes, its engine still running. He was weeping. His sobs reached a crescendo when two men with smoking machineguns ran up to the car. They took the front seats. The car moved off with a screech.

"Don't cry, Hans," Forstner said with concern. "You simply saved your life. Besides, I saved mine, too."

BRESLAU, THAT SAME JULY 15TH, 1934
EIGHT O'CLOCK IN THE EVENING

Kurt Wirth and Hans Zupitza knew that they could not refuse Mock. These two bandits, before whom the entire criminal world of Breslau shook, had a double debt of gratitude owing to "good Uncle Eberhard". Firstly, he had saved them from the noose; secondly, he had allowed them to carry on with dealings both profitable and completely at odds with German law. In exchange, he sometimes asked them to do that which they did best.

Wirth had met Zupitza twenty years earlier, in 1914, on the freight ship *Prinz Heinrich*, which sailed between Danzig and Amsterdam. They became friends without the use of unnecessary words – Zupitza was a mute. The clever, short and slim Wirth, ten years his elder, took the twenty-year-old mute giant under his wing and did not regret his decision a month later when Zupitza saved his life for the first time. It happened in a tavern in Copenhagen. Three drunk, Italian sailors wanted to teach the small, thin German some good manners – meaning how to drink wine. This cultural education entailed pouring gallons of sour Danish plonk down Wirth's throat. When he was already on the floor, drunk, the Italians decided that they would not be able to civilize that Kraut anyway so it would be better if such a cad disappeared from the face of the earth altogether. They had begun enforcing this decision with the help of broken bottles when into the inn came Zupitza who, a moment earlier, had almost brought down the wooden privy where he had got his hands on one of the numerous girls who comforted sailors in Copenhagen. He had not, however, lost all of his energy in her arms. A few seconds later, the Italians had stopped moving. The following day, the gloomy waiter – whose countenance over time would frighten many – shook like jelly when, questioned by the police, he tried to put across in his unskilled tongue the sound of skin cracked open, the shattering of glass, the moans and the wheezing. When Wirth came to, he weighed out the pros and cons and in Amsterdam abandoned the sailor's profession for ever. The inseparable Zupitza likewise disembarked permanently on to *terra firma*. Yet they did not break all contact with the sea. Wirth devised a means of survival not known in Europe at the time: extortion from port smugglers. The pair formed an efficient mechanism whereby Wirth was the brain,

Zupitza the muscle. Wirth would lead the negotiations with the smugglers; if these proved not to be submissive, Zupitza would kidnap and murder them, using methods invented by Wirth. Soon all the police in post-war Europe were looking for them: in the docks of Hamburg and Stockholm, where they left their victims' mutilated remains; in the brothels of Vienna and Berlin, where they spent mountains of increasingly worthless marks. They felt the chase on their backs. Chance associates began to betray them more and more frequently in exchange for worthless promises. Wirth had a choice: either to leave for America, where the Mafia awaited them, bloodthirsty and ruthless competition in the field of extortion, or to find a quiet and peaceful place in Europe. The first choice was very dangerous, the second virtually impossible, since European policemen everywhere, dreaming of fame, carried photographs of both bandits in their pockets.

Nobody achieved that fame, but there was one man who consciously rejected it. This was a policeman from Breslau – Criminal Director Eberhard Mock – who, in the mid-'20s was in charge of so-called Vice Affairs in the Kleinburg district. It was shortly after his extraordinary promotion. All the newspapers wrote about the brilliant career of the forty-one-year-old policeman who, from one day to the next, had become one of the most important people in the city – Deputy to the Chief of the Breslau Police Criminal Department, Mühlhaus. On May 18th, 1925, during a routine check on a brothel on Kastanien-Allee, Mock, shaking with nerves, enlisted a constable from the street and, together, they burst into the room where the duo, Wirth and Zupitza, were mingling with a female trio. Mock, afraid that the arrested men might not obey him, shot them just in case, even before they had managed to clamber out from under the girls. Then, with his constable's help, he tied them up and, in a hired cart, took them to Karlowitz. There, on the flood banks, Mock presented the two bound and bleeding bandits with his conditions: he would not stand them up in front of a tribunal if they settled in Breslau and obeyed him unconditionally. They accepted the proposition without reservation. Nor were there any reservations as to the whole situation on the part of the constable, Kurt Smolorz. He was quick to pick up Mock's reasoning, not least since it most intimately concerned his own career. Both bandits found themselves in a certain friendly brothel where, hand-cuffed to their beds, they were subjected to loving first aid. After a week of convalescence, Mock made his conditions explicit: he demanded the large sum of a thousand dollars for himself and five hundred for Smolorz. He did not trust German money, which was being wasted away at the time by the fatal disease, inflation. In exchange, he proposed to Wirth that he would close his eyes on the extortion racket against smugglers who, shunting their dirty goods to Stettin, paused in Breslau's river port. It was an argument of a sentimental nature which inclined Wirth to accept these propositions unconditionally. Mock had decided to separate the insepara-ble companions and assured Wirth that — if the money was not handed over on time — Zupitza would be turned over to the hands of justice. A second important argument was the prospect of a peaceful, settled life instead of the wandering life they had led up until then. Two weeks later, Mock and Smolorz were wealthy men, while Wirth and Zupitza — sprung from the executioner's axe — entered *terra incognita*, fallow ground which they swiftly cultivated in their own way.

That evening, they were happily drinking warm vodka in Gustav Thiel's tavern on Bahnhofstrasse. The tiny man with a foxy face, slashed with scars, and the square, silent Golem accompanying him, made an unusual couple. Some of the customers laughed at them surreptitiously; one of the regulars was completely unabashed and openly expressed his amusement. The fat man with pink, wrinkled skin kept exploding into laughter and pointing his chubby finger in their direction. Since they were not reacting to his taunts, he recognized them as cowards. And there was nothing he liked more than to torment fearful people. He rose and, pushing his feet hard into the damp floorboards, made towards his victims. He stood near their table and laughed hoarsely:

"Well then, my little man . . . Are you going to have a drink with good old uncle Konrad?"

Wirth did not so much as glance up at him. He calmly drew strange shapes with his finger on the wet oilcloth. Zupitza gazed pensively at the pickled gherkins swimming in a murky solution. At last, Wirth turned his eyes to Konrad. Not of his own free will, certainly: the fat man had squeezed his cheeks and was ramming a bottle of vodka into his mouth.

"Piss off, you fat pig!" Wirth with difficulty suppressed the memories of Copenhagen.

The fat man blinked in disbelief and grabbed Wirth by the lapels of his jacket. Not noticing the giant rise from his seat, he butted his head, but before it reached the would-be victim's face Zupitza's open hand materialized and the assailant's forehead collided with it. That same hand grasped the fat man by the nose and shoved him on to the counter. Wirth, in the meantime, was not idle. He leapt on to the bar, grabbed Konrad by the collar and slammed his head into the countertop wet with beer. Zupitza took advantage of the moment. He spread his arms and suddenly clapped them together. The fat man's head found itself between two fists; blows from either side crushed his temples, soot poured over his eyes. Zupitza took the inert body under the arms while Wirth made way for him. Those present in the tavern were numb with fear. Nobody would laugh at the singular couple again. They all knew that Konrad Schmidt did not give in to just anyone.

Unusual equipment had been arranged in cell no. 2 of the investigative prison in the Police Praesidium: a dentist's chair, its arms and leg-rests fitted with leather straps and a brass buckle. At that moment, the straps tightly hugged the mighty, stout limbs of the man sitting in it, a man so terrified that he was almost swallowing his gag.

"Did you know, sirs, that what every sadist fears most is another sadist?" Mock calmly finished his cigarette. "Consider, Schmidt, these men," – he indicated Wirth and Zupitza – "they are the cruellest sadists in all Europe. And do you know what they like most? You won't find out if you answer my questions nicely."

Mock signalled to Smolorz to remove the gag from Konrad's mouth. The prisoner breathed heavily. Anwaldt asked the first question:

"What did you do to Friedländer during the interrogation that made him admit to killing Marietta von der Malten?"

"Nothing, he was simply afraid of us, that's all. He said he killed her."

Anwaldt gave the signal to the duo. Wirth yanked Konrad's jaw down, Zupitza thrust an iron rod into his mouth. He squeezed the upper first tooth with a small pair of pliers and broke it in half. Konrad screamed for almost half a minute. Then Zupitza removed the rod. Anwaldt asked the question again.

"We tied the Jew's daughter to the couch. Walter said we'd rape her if he didn't admit to slashing up that one in the train."

"Which Walter?"

"Piontek."

"And then he confessed?"

"Yes. Why in the hell is he asking that?" Konrad turned to Mock. "For you, it's . . ."

He did not manage to finish. Mock broke in:

"But you screwed that Jewish girl anyway, eh, Schmidt?"

"It goes without saying," Konrad's eyes hid in folds of skin.

"And now, tell us, who is this Turk with whom you tortured Anwaldt?"

"That I don't know. The boss simply told me that with this one here we . . . both . . . well . . ." here he indicated the Assistant with his eyes.

Mock gave Zupitza the signal. The rod found itself in Konrad's jaws again and Zupitza yanked the pliers down. What remained of the broken tooth crunched in its gum. At the next signal, Zupitza broke off a bit of the second upper first. Konrad choked on blood, wheezed and sobbed. After a minute, they removed the rod from his teeth. Unfortunately, Schmidt could not say anything because his jaw was dislocated. It took Smolorz a long time to put it back in place.

"I am asking you again. Who is that Turk? What is his name and what is he doing at the Gestapo?"

"I don't know. I swear."

This time Schmidt pressed his jaws together so tightly as to make it impossible for them to reintroduce the rod. Then Wirth took a hammer and positioned a huge nail on the hand of the bound man. He slammed at the hammer. Konrad screamed. Not for the first time that day, Zupitza demonstrated his reflexes. When the Gestapo-man's jaws flew open, the rod quickly found itself between them.

"Are you going to talk or do you want to lose some more teeth?" asked Anwaldt. "Are you going to talk?"

The prisoner nodded. The rod was removed.

"Kemal Erkin. He came to the Gestapo in order to train. The boss holds him in high esteem. I don't know any more."

"Where does he live?"

"I don't know."

Mock was certain that Konrad had told them everything. Unfortunately — even too much. Because in the broken, stifled phrase

"For you, it's . . ." he had touched on the murky secret of Mock's agreement with Piontek. Luckily, he had only brushed up against it. Mock did not know whether any of the men present could guess the rest of the sentence. He looked at the tired but clearly moved Anwaldt and at Smolorz, calm as usual. *(No, they probably haven't guessed.)* Wirth and Zupitza looked at Mock in expectation.

"We won't get any more out of him, gentlemen." He got up close to Konrad and gagged him again. "Wirth, there's to be no trace left of this man, understood? Apart from that, I advise you leave Germany. You were seen in that tavern butchering Schmidt. If you'd acted like professionals and waited for him to go outside, you could safely carry on with your business. But you got carried away. Did you have to deal with him in the tavern? I had no idea you got so violent when someone offers you vodka. Too bad. Tomorrow, when Konrad doesn't turn up for work . . . the day after tomorrow at the latest, the entire Gestapo in Breslau will be looking for your distinctive mugs. In three days, they're going to be looking for you all over Germany. I advise you to leave the country. Go somewhere far away . . . I consider your debt repaid."

X

BRESLAU, MONDAY, JULY 16TH, 1934
NINE O'CLOCK IN THE MORNING

Konrad Schmidt's body had been lying at the bottom of the Oder beyond Hollandwiesen for ten hours already when Mock and Anwaldt lit up their choice Bairam cigars from Przedecki's and were having their first sip of strong, Arabic coffee. Leo Hartner did not conceal his pleasure. He was sure he was going to surprise and interest his listeners. Pacing his office, he constructed in his mind a plan of how to present his report, appropriately distributing the turning-points, composing apt recapitulations. Seeing that his guests were growing impatient with the prevailing silence, he began his lecture with apparent retardation.

"My dear friends, in his *Geschichte der persischen Litteratur* Wilhelm Grünhagen mentioned a lost historical work from the fourteenth century describing the Crusades. This work, entitled *The War of Allah's Army against the Infidels*, was supposed to have been written by a certain educated Persian, an Ibn Sahim. Gentlemen – 'So what?' – you may say. After all, many works have disappeared . . . here's . . . yet another old manuscript . . . Such disdain would, however, be unfounded. If Ibn Sahim's work had survived to this day, we would be in possession of yet one more source of the fascinating history of the Crusades, a source all the more interesting in that it was written by a man from the other side of the barricades – a Musulman."

Mock and Anwaldt lived up to the lecturer's hopes. The epic delay of the narration did not disconcert either of the would-be Classicists. Hartner was excited. He placed his slim hand on the pile of papers:

"My dear gentlemen, the dream of many an historian and Oriental specialist has been fulfilled. In front of me lies the lost work of Ibn Sahim. Who discovered it? Yes, yes – it was Georg Maass. True enough, I don't know how he discovered that the manuscript was to be found in the University of Breslau's library, whether he was the one who found a clue or whether someone gave it to him. And it is not easy to find a manuscript which – as this one is – has been bound with two other, lesser manuscripts. To put it briefly, this discovery will bring Maass world fame . . . The more so since, working on the piece, he is simultaneously translating it into German. And – this I do have to concede – he is translating faithfully and most beautifully. The photographic prints which you gave me are a literal translation of a very interesting fragment of that chronicle. It speaks of a macabre murder committed in the year 1205 by two men – a Turk and a Crusader on the children of Al Shausi, the leader of the Yesidi sect. Those who know the history of the Crusades will be surprised, for in 1205, during the fourth Crusade, the Crusaders did not go beyond Constantinople! But one cannot exclude single sallies of at least a few detachments even into the distant territories of Anatolia or, perhaps, Mesopotamia. These seekers of adventure and riches plundered what they could, sometimes in excellent mutual understanding with the Muslims. The Yesidis frequently became the target of their attacks . . ."

Anwaldt sat listening, all ears. Mock glanced at his watch and opened his mouth politely to ask Hartner to get to the point. The latter, fortunately, understood his intention:

"Yes, yes, your Excellency, I'm just going to explain who these Yesidis were. This rather secret sect, which came into being in the twelfth century and exists to this day, is commonly considered as being satanic. This is a great simplification. Indeed, the Yesidis do worship Satan, but a Satan that is already being punished for his sins. Despite the punishment, however, he is still omnipotent. They call this god of evil Malek Tau, represent him in the guise of a peacock, and believe that he rules the world with the help of six or seven angels, also represented as iron or bronze peacocks. To put it briefly, the Yesidi religion is a mixture of Islam, Christianity, Judaism and Mazdaism, that is, all the faiths whose repre-sentatives crossed the mountains in the centre of Mesopotamia, west of Mosul, leaving behind crumbs of their beliefs. On a day-to-day basis, the Yesidis are a peaceful, honest and clean people – and this the nineteenth-century traveller and archaeologist, Austen Henry Layard, clearly empha-sized – who have been persecuted over entire centuries by everyone: the Crusaders, Arabs, Turks and Kurds. So do not be surprised that alliances against the Yesidis were forged even between those who fought each other, such as the Crusaders and the Saracens. For all these persecutors, the cult of the god of evil was a stumbling block which justified the cruellest of slaughters. The decimated Yesidis avenged themselves on their enemies in the same way, passing down the dictates of ancestral revenge from gener-ation to generation. To this day, they live on the borders of Turkey and Persia, retaining their unaltered customs and strange faith . . ."

"Doctor Hartner," the impatient Mock could no longer bear it. "What you're saying is very interesting, but please tell us, does this interesting story from centuries ago – apart from the fact that Maass brought it into the light of day – have any bearing on our case?"

"Yes. A great deal," Hartner adored surprises. "But let us be precise, gentlemen: it is not Maass who brought this chronicle out into the light of day, but the person who murdered Marietta von der Malten," he relished the astonished expression of his listeners. "I declare with full responsibility that the writing on the wall of the saloon carriage where that unfortunate girl was found comes from precisely that Persian chronicle. In translation, it reads: 'And scorpions did in their innards dance'. Keep calm, I will try to answer all of your questions presently . . . Now I'll give you one more piece of important information. An anonymous source from the end of the thirteenth century, recorded in the writings of a Frankish chronicler, states that the teenage children of the Yesidi leader, Al-Shausi, were murdered by a 'German knight'. Only two of our compatriots took part in the fourth Crusade. One of them died in Constantinople. The other was Godfryd von der Malten. Yes, gentlemen, our Baron's ancestor."

Mock choked on his coffee, black drops sprayed his pale suit. Anwaldt gave a start and experienced the action of that hormone which, in human beings, is responsible for making bodily hair stand on end. Both then smoked in silence. Observing the impression he had made on his listeners, Hartner could scarcely contain himself for joy, which contrasted rather strangely with the gloomy history of the Yesidis and Crusaders. Mock broke the silence:

"I'm lost for words to thank you, sir, for such an insightful, expert appraisal. My assistant and myself, we are deeply moved, bearing in mind that this whole story throws new light on our puzzle. Will you allow me, sir, to ask you a few questions? This will inevitably mean betraying a few secrets concerning the investigation, which you will be so kind as to keep to yourself."

"Naturally. I'm listening."

"From your expert report, one could conclude that Marietta von der Malten's murder was revenge taken after centuries. The bloody writing in the saloon carriage, taken from a work unknown to anyone and generally considered to be lost, testifies to this. My first question is: could Professor Andreae who is, after all, well acquainted with Eastern writings and languages, for some reason be unable to decipher the quotation?

Because if you exclude that, it will be clear that he deliberately misled us."

"My dear sir, Andreae did not understand the writing. It's obvious. This scholar is, above all, a specialist in Turkish studies and, as far as I know, knows no Eastern language apart from Turkish, Arabic, Hebrew, Syrian and Coptic. Whereas Ibn Sahim's chronicle is written in Persian. The Yesidis spoke Persian; today they use Kurdish. Try giving an expert – however excellent – in the Hebrew language a text in Yiddish but written in the Hebraic alphabet, and I assure you that without knowing Yiddish, he'll be helpless. Andreae knew Arabic writing because, until recently, Turkish texts used to be written only in Arabic. But he does not know Persian, I know that perfectly well because I used to be one of his students. So, he saw a text written in the Arabic alphabet, which he knows, but he hardly understood any of the text. Since he is trying, at any price, to salvage his academic prestige, he concocted a translation from, as it were, ancient Syrian. And he has, by the by, concocted more than once. He once invented some Coptic inscriptions basing his post-doctoral thesis on them . . ."

"If Maass discovered the chronicle . . ." – this time it was Anwaldt who spoke – "a fragment of which was found on the wall of the saloon carriage . . . that means he's the murderer. Unless someone else, who had dealings with the text before him, slipped it to Maass for some reason. Did anyone before Maass use any of the three manuscripts bound together?"

"I checked most meticulously the reading-room loan register of the last twenty years, and the answer is: no. Since 1913 – because that's the date the records start – no-one before Maass made use of the manuscripts which are bound together."

"Dear Herbert," Mock's voice resounded, "Maass has a cast-iron alibi. On May 12th, 1933, he gave two lectures in Königsberg, and this has been confirmed by six of his listeners. On the other hand he does undoubtedly have something to do with the murderers. Why otherwise

172

would he deceive us and translate the text from the carriage quite differently? And apart from that, how did he know that the manuscript could be found here? Maybe he stumbled on the traces of this Persian chronicle when he was researching Marietta's obituary? But, I should apologize, these questions are for Maass. Sir," he addressed Hartner again, "is it possible that someone could have read this manuscript without leaving any trace in the records?"

"No librarian will lend out a manuscript without writing it down in the notebook. Besides, only scholars with appropriate references from the university can handle the manuscripts."

"Unless the librarian colluded with the reader and did not make the rightful entry."

"Such a collusion, I cannot exclude."

"Do you employ anyone who has completed their Oriental Studies?"

"Not at the moment. Two years ago, a librarian who was a specialist in Arabic worked for me; he moved to Marburg where he was appointed to a chair at the university."

"Name?"

"Otto Specht."

"There's one question gnawing at me," Anwaldt said quietly, while putting the name in his notebook. "Why was Marietta von der Malten's murder so contrived? Is it perhaps because the children of the arch-Yesidi, so to speak, were killed in an equally cruel manner? Is it that the means used in vengeance have to correspond exactly to the crime committed centuries ago? What really happened? What does the chronicler write about it?"

Hartner shuddered with the cold and poured himself another cup of steaming coffee.

"A very good question. Let us give the voice to the Persian chronicle."

XI

MESOPOTAMIA, DJABAL SINDJAR MOUNTAINS,
THREE DAYS ON HORSEBACK WEST OF MOSUL.
SECOND SAFAR OF THE SIX HUNDRED
FIRST YEAR OF HIDJRA

*Here speaks Ibn Sahim, son of Hussain, may Allah have mercy on him.
This chapter contains information about the just vengeance taken by
Allah's soldier on the children of the Satanic pir, may his name be cursed
for ever and ever . . .*

The evening sun was slipping ever lower across the blue firmament.
The outlines of the mountains were becoming sharper and the air
clearer. Above the steep crag, the suite of riders moved slowly. At its
head rode two leaders: a Crusader and a Turkish warrior. When
they had reached the edge of the mountainous ravine beyond which
stretched a gentle slope, they brought their horses to a halt and
with obvious satisfaction stretched out beneath the stone meander-
ings of rocks which brought to mind cathedral spires. About forty
of the accompanying riders, half of them Christian, half Muslim,
did the same. With relief, the Crusader removed his helmet, called
a *salada*, the elongated back end of which had impressed a red,

swollen band on his wet neck. Rivulets of sweat escaped from beneath the basinet and ran down the tunic adorned with Maltese crosses. His mount, harnessed in a nose-band of finely wrought work, was breathing freely; white sheets of froth slipped down its sides.

Tiredness did not seem to trouble so much the Turkish knight, who was examining the Crusader's crossbow with curiosity. He wore, as did his soldiers, a basinet, a helmet bound in a piece of white material, a coat of mail, white trousers reaching just below his knees, and high, black boots. The weapons of the Turk and his men consisted of horn bows and quivers with three-feathered arrows, and Arabian swords called *saif*. On top of that, the leader wielded an iron pick-axe embossed with silver in shapes of Arabic ornaments.

After a moment had passed, the Christian knight stopped wiping away the sweat, the Saracen lost interest in the crossbow. Both attentively observed the valley which stretched beyond the rocky slope. A low yet wide temple stood among green palm trees. Small alcoves had been hewn into its walls where olive lamps burned, blackening all around with smoke. Every now and then, someone approached the fire, passed their right hand over the flame and, with blackened hand, touched their right brow. The horsemen were paying less attention to this strange behaviour; they were more interested in the number of people in the valley. With a great effort and independently of each other, they counted and arrived at a similar result: in the vicinity of the temple and houses adjoined to it, milled around about two hundred people of both sexes and all ages. The men dressed in tight hair shirts and black turbans drew their attention in particular — they were making sure that not a single oil lamp went out. When a lamp began to burn down, they dipped fresh wicks into olive oil and the flame, hissing, fired up again.

Night fell on the land. In the light of the oil lamps began rituals – wild, violent dances. Singing, full of passion, soared over the valley. Guttural cries tore the air. The Crusader was sure he was witnessing an orgy to Semiramida, the Turk felt a painful arousal. They looked each other over and gave orders to their soldiers. Slowly, cautiously, they rode down the gentle slope of the hill. The names of seven angels vibrated in the air: *"Djibrail"*, *"Muchail"*, *"Rufail"*, *"Azrail"*, *"Dedrail"*, *"Azrafil"*, *"Shamkil"*. The thunder of drums, flutes and tambourines split the valley. The women were falling into a trance. The men, as if hypnotized, spun around their own axis. The priests were now offering sheep and their extremities in sacrifice, and feeding the meat to the poor. Those waiting for their turn were nibbling on strings of dried figs.

The stampede of horses' hooves thundered; the faithful – terrified – turned their faces from the sacred fire. It had begun. The armoured horses, covered in crosses, trampled and jumped over living barriers. The Crusader, cleaving human torsos with his sword, was intoxicated by the sweet sensation of justice: here, under his loyal instrument of God's glory, were falling the worshippers of Satan and the seven fallen angels, whose names had reverberated so proudly in the air a moment ago. The Turk showered arrows into the smoke of the bonfires and oil lamps. Blood poured over brightly dyed jackets and colourful turbans. A few of those attacked drew fantastically curved weapons from their belts and tried to stand up to the enraged assailants. The hiss and whistle of crossbow strings created strange music. Arrows pierced soft flesh, crunched against bone, tore apart tense muscle fibres. A moment later, the assailants' passion was turned against the women, the only survivors. In the embraces of steel arms, the brown faces paled, the beautiful, regular features froze; under stress from abrupt and violent movement, the intricately plaited braids fell apart, the flowers decorating the hair withered, the silver and gold coins tinkled on their temples, the polished stones covering foreheads clanked, glass beads cracked. Some of the women hid in the alcoves and rocky ravines. The Crusaders and Saracens dragged them out and took them in frenzied convulsions. Those who had not yet come upon such a reward were finishing off the few men still alive. The captive women humbly accepted their fate. They knew they would be put up at the slave market. Over the valley silence gradually fell, only rarely interrupted by moans of pain or ecstasy.

Both leaders stood in the temple courtyard in front of the entrance to the home of the man for whom they had been searching so long: the holy *pir* Al-Shausi. Five symbols were hewn in the walls of the house: a serpent, an axe, a comb, a scorpion and a small human figure. Next to them appeared a delicately engraved Arabic sign: GOD. THERE IS NO GOD BUT HE, THE LOVING, THE ETERNAL. ALL THAT DWELLS IN THE HEAVENS AND ON EARTH BELONGS TO HIM.

The Turk looked at the Crusader and said in Arabic:

"It's a verse from *The Throne of the Second Sura of the Koran.*"

The Crusader was acquainted with this famous fragment. He had heard it on the lips of dying Saracens, listened to it in the evenings coming from the lips of praying Arabian captive women. But he was not put out by the lofty sacred inscription intended to protect and bless Al-Shausi's house just as a year ago he had not been troubled by the Byzantine God when, in search of loot, he had desecrated and defiled the temple in Constantinople.

They entered. Two Turkish soldiers blocked the door so that nobody could slip out; the rest went in search of the holy elder. Instead of him, they brought in two rolled carpets which were moving violently. These they unfurled and, at the leader's feet, there appeared a desperate, perhaps thirteen-year-old girl and her slightly older brother — children of the man they were looking for and who had escaped into the desert. The leader of the Crusaders threw himself at the girl without a word, pushed her to the uneven, stone floor and, very shortly afterwards, won his successive spoil of war. The girl's brother said something about their father and vengeance. In the light of the oil lamps, the rapist saw several scorpions which had crawled out of a broken clay vat. He wasn't afraid of them; on the contrary — the presence of these sinister creatures flamed his passion all the more. All around, men were yelling — aroused, olive oil stank, shadows danced on walls. The satiated Crusader had decided: the children of the satanic cult's highest priest would be punished by way of example. He ordered the boy's and the girl's bellies to be stripped bare. He raised his sword, the faithful companion in the fight *ad maiorem Dei gloriam* and dealt a sure but not very hard blow. The blade traced a semi-circle and with its tip tore the girl's velvet belly and the boy's, covered with its first growth. The skin separated, revealing their innards. The Crusader removed his helmet and very efficiently, with the help of his dagger, threw several scorpions into it. Then he tipped it like a sacrificial vessel over the victims' entrails. The enraged, arching scorpions found themselves among warm intestines. They stung blindly with the sharp thorn of their abdomens and slid around in the blood. The victims lived a long while yet and did not take their flaming eyes off their executioner.

XII

BRESLAU, THAT SAME MONDAY, JULY 16TH, 1934
FOUR O'CLOCK IN THE AFTERNOON

The heat had increased after lunch but, strangely, neither Mock nor
Anwaldt seemed to feel it. The latter, however, was troubled by a pain in
his gum where, an hour ago, the dentist had extracted a root. Both men
were sitting in their offices in the Police Praesidium. But it was not just
the place that brought them together – their minds, too, were preoccupied
by the same case. They had found the murderer. It was Kemal Erkin. Both
had confirmed their first, still intuitive suspicions, reached by a simple
association: the tattoo of a scorpion on the Turk's hand . . . scorpions in
the Baron's daughter's belly . . . the Turk is the murderer. This conclusion,
after Hartner's expert appraisal, had acquired something without which
any investigation would be groping around in the dark: a motive. In
killing Marietta von der Malten, the Turk had taken vengeance on a seven-
century-old crime which the Baron's ancestor, the Crusader Godfryd von
der Malten had committed, in 1205, on the children of Al-Shausi, leader
of the Yesidi sect. As Hartner had said, the imperative of vengeance was
passed down from generation to generation. However, some doubt did
arise: why was it committed only now, after seven hundred years? In order
to disperse the doubt and turn suspicion into unwavering certainty, it was

179

necessary to answer the question: was Erkin a Yesidi? Unfortunately it would remain unanswered as long as nothing more was known about Erkin than his name, nationality and fat Konrad's babbling "He came to the Gestapo in order to train". This could mean that the Turk was undergoing something like a practice period with the Gestapo, an apprenticeship. One thing was certain: the suspect had to be captured using all possible means. And interrogated. Likewise using all possible means.

At this point, the parallel thinking of the two policemen came up against a serious obstacle: the Gestapo guarded its secrets. In all certainty, Forstner, freed of his "vice" by the death of Baron von Köpperlingk, wouldn't want to co-operate with a man he loathed, Mock. Getting hold of basic information about Erkin, therefore, was extremely difficult, not to speak of finding any proof of his belonging to any secret organisation or sect. Mock did not even have to stretch his memory to know that he had never in the Police Praesidium met anyone resembling Erkin. The former Political Department of the Police Praesidium, which occupied the west wing of the building on Schweidnitzer Stadtgraben 2/6, after Piontek's downfall and Forstner's domination, constituted territory where Mock's feelers did not extend. Long infiltrated by Hitler's men and officially under their control after Göring's decree in February, it constituted an independent and secretive organism whose numerous sections were located in rented villas in beautiful Kleinburg, utterly inaccessible to anyone from the outside. Erkin might be working in just one of these villas and only be in the "Brown House" on Neudorfstrasse from time to time. In the old days, Mock would have simply turned to the chief of a particular department in the Police Praesidium for information. Now, there was no question of it. The Chief of Gestapo, Erich Kraus – the right hand of the notorious chief of Breslau's S.S., Udo von Woyrsch – hostile as he was to Mock, would sooner own up to being of Jewish descent than to pass even the tritest of rumours beyond the purlieus of his department.

How to obtain facts about Erkin and then arrest him was where Mock's and Anwaldt's plans – identical to this point – diverged. The Director's thoughts tended to the chief of Breslau's Abwehr, Rainer von Hardenburg; Anwaldt's hopes focussed on Doctor Georg Maass.

Remembering the warning he had received that morning – that one of the telephonists was the lover of Kraus' Deputy, Dietmar Föb – Mock left the police building and, crossing Schweidnitzer Stadtgraben, made his way to the square near Wertheim's Department Store. Suffocating from heat in the glass telephone kiosk, he dialled von Hardenburg's number.

In the meantime, Anwaldt, wandering through the Praesidium building, tried in vain to find his chief. Impatient, he resolved to take the decision into his own hands. He opened the door to the Criminal Assistants' room. Kurt Smolorz was quick on the uptake and followed him into the corridor.

"Take one man, Smolorz, and we'll go and get Maass. Maybe we'll sit him in the dentist's chair."

Mock and Anwaldt simultaneously felt the heat turn tropical.

BRESLAU, THAT SAME JULY 16TH, 1934
FIVE O'CLOCK IN THE AFTERNOON

An indescribable mess reigned in Maass' apartment. Anwaldt and Smolorz, tired after their hurried search, sat in the games room and panted heavily. Smolorz kept going to the window and peeping out at the drunk who, glued to the wall, swept his strangely sober eyes all around. Maass was not coming yet.

Anwaldt stared at the typing paper, covered in handwriting, which lay in front of him. It was something like an unfinished draft of a report, two chaotic sentences. On the top of the paper was written: "Hanne

Schlossarczyk, Rawicz. Mother?" Underneath: "Investigation in Rawicz. Paid to Adolf Jenderko Detective Agency: 100 marks". Anwaldt no longer paid attention to either the heat, or the sound of a piano upstairs, or the too-tight shirt which clung to him or even the throbbing pain caused by the extraction of the tooth nerve. He sunk his eyes into the sheet of paper and desperately tried to remember where, in the not too distant past, he had come across the name "Schlossarczyk". He glanced at Smolorz, who was nervously shuffling the papers which lay on the cake platter, and emitted Archimedes' cry. He knew: the name had appeared in the dossier of von der Malten's servants, which he had gone through the previous night. He sighed with relief: Hanne Schlossarczyk would not be an unknown factor, as was Erkin. He muttered to himself:

"I'll find everything out from the Adolf Jenderko Agency."

"Pardon?" Smolorz turned from the window.

"Oh, nothing. I was simply thinking aloud."

Smolorz peered over Anwaldt's shoulder. He read Maass' note and burst out laughing.

"What are you laughing at?"

"It's a funny name, Schlossarczyk."

"Where is the town of Rawicz?"

"In Poland, some fifty kilometres from Breslau, just across the border."

Anwaldt fastened his loosened tie, put on his hat and glanced with distaste at his dusty shoes.

"You, Smolorz, and your pseudo-drunk are to take turns and sit in Maass' apartment until he returns. When our scholar appears, please keep him here and inform Mock or myself."

Anwaldt carefully closed the door behind him. After a while, he returned and looked at Smolorz with interest:

"Tell me then, why did the name Schlossarczyk make you laugh?"

182

Smolorz smiled, embarrassed.

"It reminded me of the word Schlosser — 'locksmith'. Just think: a woman has the name 'locksmith'. Ha, ha . . . what kind of a locksmith is that, without a key . . . ha . . . ha . . ."

BRESLAU, THAT SAME JULY 16TH, 1934
SIX O'CLOCK IN THE EVENING

Teichäcker Park, behind Main Station, was seething with life at this time of day. Its coolness was sought by travellers changing trains in Breslau, and white-collar workers from the Railroad Administration, working overtime before their longed-for holiday in Zoppot or Stralsund; children made a noise by the ice-cream kiosks, servants made room for themselves on the benches using their huge bottoms as wedges, the less sick from Bethesda Hospital reclined, fathers of families, refreshed by a shower in the shower baths and time spent with newspapers in the reading room on Teichäckerstrasse, smoked cigars and leered at the prostitutes lazily passing. A one-legged veteran played his clarinet outside Our Saviour's Church. Seeing two elegantly dressed, middle-aged gentlemen taking a walk, he played a couplet from an operetta, expecting more generous alms from them. They left him behind with indifference. He heard only a fragment of one statement expressed in a fairly high, sure voice: "Alright, Criminal Director, we'll check up on this Erkin." The veteran adjusted his sign-board "Verdun — we will avenge" and stopped playing. The men sat on a bench vacated by two teenage boys, watching for a while as the boys in brown shirts and armed with shovels walked away. They were talking. The musician-beggar strained his ears. The falsetto of the very distinguished tall gentleman interwove with the bass murmurs of the shorter, stocky man in a suit of pale cord. The veteran's excellent hearing easily picked out the high-toned lines which penetrated the street noise; the bass tones, on the other hand, were lost in the clatter of cabs, the roar of cars and the screech of trams rattling on the corner of Sadowa and Bohrauer Strasse:

"I'll find out, if you wish, whether the man we're looking for speaks . . . What? Ah, fine . . . Kurdish."

". . ."

"My dear Criminal Director, our lamented Emperor Wilhelm already called Turkey his 'Eastern friend'."

". . ."

"Yes, yes. Military relations were always very much alive. Just imagine, my father was a member of the military mission led by General von der Goltz, who helped — probably in the '80s — the modern Turkish army. Following him, Deutsche Bank marched triumphantly into Turkey and built the new section of the Baghdad Railway."

". . ."

"And today, we Germans remember that in 1914 the highest spiritual leader of Islam declared a 'holy war' against our enemies. So it is not surprising that higher Turkish officers get their schooling from us. I knew some myself when I was in Berlin."

". . ."

"Rest assured. I don't know when, but I will certainly hand you that Erkin on a plate."

". . ."

"Think nothing of it, Criminal Director. I rest in the hope that you will kindly repay me."

". . ."

"Until we meet again in that pleasant place we both know so well."

The veteran lost interest in the two men who were at that moment shaking hands for he had seen a group of tipsy teenage lads with rubber truncheons approaching. As they passed by, he played "*Horst-Wessel-*

Lied". For nothing. Not a single fenig dropped into his hat, perforated by French bullets.

* * *

In the meantime, at Freiburgstrasse 3, Franz Huber, joint owner of the Adolf Jenderko Detective Agency, had suddenly stopped being mistrustful or refusing stubbornly to co-operate. In a flash, he had ceased wanting to see Anwaldt's police identification, no longer wanted to call the Police Praesidium to confirm his identity, had stopped examining the detective from a Criminal Department staff which spread over eighteen police precincts under Breslau's Criminal Police Station. Franz Huber had suddenly become very helpful and extremely polite. Staring into the black hole of a muzzle, he replied exhaustively to all the questions:

"What did Maass want exactly? What instructions did he give you?"

"He found out from the Baron's old caretaker about the illegitimate child whom Olivier von der Malten had fathered with a chambermaid. The only woman who had served the Baron now lives in Poland, in Rawicz. She's called Hanne Schlossarczyk. My instructions were to find out whether she really did have a child by the Baron and what has happened to the child now."

"Did you go to Rawicz yourself?"

"No, I sent one of my men."

"And?"

"He found Hanne Schlossarczyk."

"How did he persuade her to talk? After all, people aren't usually very willing to admit to such a sin."

"My man, Schubert, presented himself as a lawyer looking for any heirs to the supposedly deceased Baron. That's what I thought up."

"Clever. And what did your man find out?"

"The rich, old lady, on learning of a great inheritance awaiting her, readily admitted to the misdeed of her youth, then started crying so much that Schubert could hardly calm her."

"So she was sorry for her sin."

"Not quite. She was furious at herself for not knowing anything about her son, who would have been the Baron's heir. That's why she was crying."

"So she had qualms of conscience?"

"So it would appear."

"And so the Baron has an illegitimate son by her. That's a fact. What is his name, how old is he and where does he live?"

"Schlossarczyk worked for the Baron from 1901–1902. That's presumably when she got pregnant. Thereafter, Baron Ruppert von der Malten, Olivier's father, never again employed a woman, not even as cook. So her son must be thirty-one or thirty-two. His name? We don't know. Certainly not the same as the Baron. His mother got a handsome sum to keep quiet, enough for her to live comfortably to this day. Where does the bastard live now? That we don't know either. And what do we know? That until he became of age, he lived in an orphanage in Berlin, where he landed up as a baby from his loving mother's arms."

"What orphanage?"

"She doesn't know herself. Some merchant took him there. An acquaintance of hers."

"The merchant's name?"

"She didn't want to give it to us. She said he had nothing to do with it."

"And your man believed that?"

"Why should she lie? I told you she cried because she didn't know her son's name. If she did, she'd have been pleased. She'd got an inheritance, after all."

Anwaldt automatically asked another question:

"Why did she hand him over to an orphanage? She could have lived comfortably with her son on the money the Baron gave her."

"That my man didn't ask."

The detective put his pistol in his pocket. He could barely breathe through his parched throat. His gum was aching and swelling. The hornet stings, too, were playing up again. He opened his mouth and did not recognize his own voice:

"Was Maass happy with you?"

"Yes and no. Because, after all, we only partially carried out his instructions. My man established that Hanne Schlossarczyk had a child by the Baron. But he did not establish either his name or his whereabouts. So we only got a half from Maass."

"How much?"

"A hundred."

Anwaldt lit a Turkish cigar which he had bought in the covered market by Gartenstrasse. The pungent smoke took his breath away for a moment. He mastered the spasm in his lungs and exhaled a huge ball of smoke towards the ceiling. He unbuttoned his shirt collar and loosened his tie. He felt embarrassed: a moment ago he had held the man in his sights and now he was smoking in his company as with an old friend. (*I got carried away needlessly and terrorized this man. My gun opened nothing but his lips. That's all it did. It didn't guarantee the truth. Huber could have simply made it all up.*) He glanced up at the certificates and photographs hanging on the wall. On one of them, Franz Huber was shaking hands with a high-ranking officer in a spiked helmet. Under the newspaper photograph the legend read: "The policeman, Franz Huber, who saved the child, receives the congratulations of General Freiherr von Campenhausen. Beuthen 1913." Anwaldt smiled in conciliation. He was resigned.

"Herr Huber, I apologize for pulling out that pop gun. You used to be a policeman (how do you people in Breslau call it? *Schkulle?*), and I treated you like the suspect's associate. It is no surprise that you were suspicious of me, especially as I do not have my identification with me. All it resulted in was my leaving now without knowing whether you lied to me or not. In spite of that uncertainty, I'll ask you one more question. Without the gun. If you answer, it might just be the truth. May I speak?"

"Go ahead."

"Doesn't it seem strange to you that Maass dispensed with your services so easily? It's obvious, after all, that he's looking for the Baron's illegitimate son. Why did he stop halfway, pay half your fee and not try to look for him any more with the help of your agency?"

Huber took off his jacket and poured himself some soda water. He remained silent for a moment and gazed at the framed photographs and certificates.

"Maass laughed at me and my methods. He thought I had bungled it, that I could have put pressure on the old woman. He decided to find it all out for himself. I knew he liked to brag, so I asked him how he was going to find the man he was looking for. He said that he would restore the old bag's memory with his friend's help and that she would tell him where her little son was." Huber opened his mouth and sighed loudly. "Listen to me, son. Your pop gun didn't frighten me. I've got that old Jew Maass and you up my arse," he panted angrily. "I didn't lie to you because I didn't want to. And do you know why? Ask Mock. I'll have a word with him about you. And you'd better get yourself out of here if it turns out he doesn't know you."

XIII

Anwaldt was, indeed, leaving Breslau, but not because of Huber's threats. He sat in a first-class carriage, smoking cigarette after cigarette and watching with indifference the monotonous, Lower Silesian landscape in the orange light of sunset. (*I've got to find that descendant of von der Malten's. If some curse really is hanging over the Baron's descendants, then they're in mortal danger from Erkin. But why am I really looking for him? After all, Mock and I have found the murderer. No, no we haven't, we've only identified him. Erkin works through Maass; he's watchful, knows we're looking for him. There's no doubt that Erkin is the "friend" who's going to squeeze the information out of Schlossarczyk. So, looking for Schlossarczyk's son, I'm looking for Erkin. Dammit, he might be in Rawicz already. I wonder what orphanage the boy was at in Berlin. Maybe I knew him?*) Lost in thought, he burnt his fingers on his cigarette. He swore — not only in his thoughts — and swept his eyes over the compartment. All the travellers on the night train had heard his crude expletive. A boy of around eight, podgy, very Nordic and dressed in a navy-blue suit was standing in front of him and holding a book in his hand. He said something in Polish and put the book on Anwaldt's lap.

189

Suddenly, he turned round, ran to his mother – a young, stout woman – and sat on her knees. Anwaldt glanced at the title of the book and saw that it was a school edition of *Oedipus the King* by Sophocles. It was not the little boy's book; some secondary school pupil going on holiday must have left it in the compartment. The boy and the mother watched him expectantly. Anwaldt gesticulated that it was not his book. He asked his fellow passengers about it. Apart from the lady with the child, there were a student and a young man with pronounced Semitic features. Nobody owned up to the book and the student, seeing the Greek text, reacted with a "God forbid". Anwaldt smiled and thanked the boy by tipping his hat to him. He opened the book at random and caught sight of the familiar Greek letters which he had once so loved. He was curious whether, after so many years, he would be able to understand anything. He read under his breath and translated verse 685: *"There was the voice of dark suspicions which gnaw at the heart". (I still remember Greek well; I did not know two words; it's a good thing there's a little dictionary at the back of the book.)* He turned over a few pages and read verse 1068 – Jocasta's lines. He did not have the least problem with the translation. *"Unfortunate one, may you not know who you are."* The aphoristic character of these sentences reminded him of a certain game he used to play with Erna: Biblical fortune-telling, so called. They would open the Bible at random and point to the first verse that came to hand. The sentence thus found was to constitute a prophecy. Laughing quietly, he closed Sophocles then opened him again. The game was interrupted by the Polish guard asking for his passport. He examined Anwaldt's documents, touched the peak of his cap with his finger and left the compartment. The policeman returned to his divination, but he could not concentrate on the translation because of the fixed and stubborn gaze of the boy who had presented him with *Oedipus the King*. The lad was sitting and staring at him without blinking. The train moved off. The boy continued staring.

190

Anwaldt lowered his eyes to the book then glared at the boy. It did not help. He wanted to attract the mother's attention, but she was fast asleep, so he went out into the corridor and opened the window. Pulling out the cardboard box of cigarettes, he touched – with relief – the new police identification card which he had picked up from the Police Praesidium Personnel Department after leaving Huber's office. *(If a little brat can manage to make me so anxious, there is something wrong with my nerves.)* One inhalation and nearly a quarter of the cigarette was burned down. The train drew into a station. A large sign announced RAWICZ.

Anwaldt bid his fellow passengers goodbye, slipped Sophocles into his pocket and jumped down to the platform. He left the station and stood beside a few well-tended flower beds. He opened his notebook and read: *Ulica Rynkowa, 3*. At that moment, a droschka drew up. Anwaldt, pleased, showed the cabman the paper with the name of the street on it.

Rawicz was a pretty, neat little town, full of flowers and dominated by red-brick prison watch towers. The falling dusk was inviting people out into the street so there were groups of noisy, teenage boys hanging around and proudly accosting strolling girls, women on little stools sitting in the entrances of white washed houses, whiskered men in tight waistcoats, treating themselves to frothy tankards and discussing Polish foreign politics as they stood outside restaurants.

The cab stopped near one such gathering. Anwaldt threw the cabby a handful of fenigs and glanced up at the number of the house. *Rynkowa 3*.

He entered the doorway and looked around, searching for a caretaker. Instead there appeared two men in hats. Both had very determined expressions. They asked Anwaldt something. He spread his arms and – in German – presented his reason for being there. He mentioned the name of Hanne Schlossarczyk, of course. The men's reaction was simply peculiar. Without a word, they cut off his way out and shepherded him upstairs. Anwaldt climbed the solid, wooden stairs tentatively and found himself on the first floor where there were two small apartments. One was open, lit and crowded with a number of men whose expressions betrayed self-assurance. Anwaldt's instinct did not fail him: that is what the police look like all over the world.

One of the guardians urged Anwaldt delicately towards the lit apartment. Once inside, he indicated the long kitchen with his hand. Anwaldt sat on a wooden stool and lit a cigarette. He had not even managed to look around when an elegant man entered the kitchen in the company of another with a walrus-like moustache, who wielded a broom in his hand. The moustached man looked at Anwaldt, then at the dandy, shook his head and left. The dandy approached the stool and spoke in correct German:

"Documents. Name, surname. Purpose of visit."

Anwaldt handed the man his passport and replied:

"Criminal Assistant Herbert Anwaldt from the Police Praesidium in Breslau . . ."

"Do you have relatives in Poznań?"

"No."

"Purpose of visit?"

"I'm pursuing two murder suspects. I know they intended to visit Hanne Schlossarczyk. Now I would like to know who is questioning me."

"Police Officer Ferdynand Banaszak from the Poznań police. Your official identification, please."

"Here," Anwaldt tried to give his voice a hard edge. "And besides, what kind of interrogation is this? Am I accused of something? I would like to see Hanne Schlossarczyk on a private matter."

Banaszak laughed out loud.

"Say what you wanted to see her about or we'll invite you to a building which has made our town famous throughout Poland." And in so saying, he did not stop smiling.

Anwaldt realized that if a policeman from west Poland's main city had appeared in this small town, then the affair in which Schlossarczyk was mixed up must be serious. Without unnecessary introduction, he told Banaszak everything, keeping secret only the reason why Erkin and Maass were searching for Schlossarczyk's illegitimate son. The police officer looked at Anwaldt and sighed with relief.

"You asked whether you could speak to Hanna Ślusarczyk.† My answer is: no, you can't speak to Hanna Ślusarczyk. She was chopped up with an axe this morning by a man whom the caretaker described as being a German-speaking Georgian."

POZNAŃ, TUESDAY, JULY 17TH, 1934
THREE O'CLOCK IN THE MORNING

Anwaldt stretched his numb limbs. He breathed with relief in the cool interrogation room at the Poznań Police Praesidium on ulica 3 Maja. Banaszak had almost finished a German translation of the report of Hanna Ślusarczyk's case and was getting ready to leave. After returning to Poznań from Rawicz, it had taken them half the night to prepare official reports by which the investigation into the woman's murder was to be shared between the Police Praesidium in Breslau, represented by Criminal Assistant Herbert Anwaldt, and the State Police Praesidium in Poznań in whose name acted Ferdynand Banaszak. The reasoning was long and intricate, and based on Anwaldt's statements.

This record, together with Banaszak's German translation – signed by both men – was to wait until morning to be signed by the President of the Poznań Police. Banaszak reassured Anwaldt that this was a mere formality and offered him a small, beefy hand. He was clearly pleased with the turn of events.

† 'Schlossarczyk' is the German form of the Polish surname 'Slusarczyk'.

"I'm not even going to pretend that I would be only too glad to throw this whole stinking case on to your shoulders, Anwaldt. But I don't have to. It's your case anyway, a German-Turkish case. And, you're the one who is mainly going to lead the investigation. Goodbye. Do you really intend to sit up all night over this? I've still got half a page left to translate. I'll translate it for you tomorrow. I'm very sleepy now. You've all the time in the world to relish the case!"

His laughter boomed in the corridor for a long time. Anwaldt drank his strong coffee, which was now cold, and started to read the case files. He grimaced as he did so, feeling the sour taste in his mouth. Too much coffee and too many cigarettes were taking their toll. Police Officer Banaszak spoke fluent German, but his writing of it was atrocious. He had mastered only professional police terminology and phrasing – he had served in the Prussian Criminal Police in Poznań from 1905 to the outbreak of the war, as he had told Anwaldt – the rest of his vocabulary was very poor, and this together with the numerous grammatical errors, created a comical combination. Anwaldt read the short, clumsy sentences with genuine amusement. He closed his eyes to the stylistics. The most important thing was that the files were comprehensible to him. It appeared that Walenty Mikołajczak, the caretaker of the building where the deceased had lived, had, at about nine o'clock in the morning, July 16th, 1934, been asked in German by a "well-dressed, Georgian-looking" stranger – which, according to the caretaker, meant black hair and an olive complexion – for Hanna Ślusarczyk's apartment. The caretaker imparted the information and returned to his work. (He was repairing the cages where tenants kept their rabbits.) But the visit of such an unusual guest caused him unease. Ślusarczyk was a loner. Every now and again, he went up to her door and eavesdropped. But he neither heard nor saw anything suspicious. At about ten o'clock, he got thirsty and went into the nearby Ratuszowy bar for a beer. He returned at about eleven-thirty and knocked on Ślusarczyk's door. Surprised by the sight of her open window – the old spinster, the crank, never opened her windows, fanatically afraid as she was of draughts and murderers; the latter because of the fame she enjoyed as "a rich woman". According to Mikołajczak, "everybody knew that Miss Ślusarczyk had more den de mayor hisself". Since no-one answered, the caretaker opened the door with a spare key. He found her quartered remains in the wooden washtub. He closed the door and informed the police. Three hours later, Police Officer Ferdynand Banaszak arrived in Rawicz with five detectives. They pronounced that death had been caused by loss of blood. Nothing was discovered that could point to burglary as being the motive. Nothing, apart from a photographic album, had disappeared from the apartment, which was confirmed by Mrs Amelia Sikorowa, a friend of the deceased. He testified, furthermore, that the deceased had no relatives or, apart from Sikorowa, any friends. She had corresponded with no-one except a merchant in Poznań, but she kept his name a secret. (The neighbour suspected that he was Ślusarczyk's former loved one.)

Anwaldt felt immensely tired. In order to banish the tiredness, he shook the last cigarette from his packet. He inhaled and looked anew at Banaszak's neat annotations. He did not understand anything because this was the page half-covered in Polish writing which Banaszak had not yet translated into German. Anwaldt examined the Polish text with fascination. He had always wondered about the mysterious diacritical marks: the flourishes beneath the "a" and "e", the little wave over the "l", the oblique accents over the "s", "z" and "o". Among these letters, he found his name written twice. This did not surprise him in the least, for in the arguments as to why the German police were to take over the investigation, Banaszak had often referred to its assignation. But the error in his name did surprise him. The name was written without a "t". He leaned over the page so as to add a "t", but withdrew his hand. A drop of ink flowed from the nib and splattered on the green felt which covered the table. Anwaldt could not pull his eyes away from his surname swimming among Polish squiggles, oblique lines and gentle waves. Only the surname was his. Not the first name: that sounded unfamiliar, foreign, proud: the Polish name "Mieczysław".

He got up, opened the door and entered the main part of the station where, behind a wooden barrier, nodded a sleepy duty constable. His assistant, an old policeman just short of retirement, was arguing with some queen of the night in a flowery dress. Anwaldt walked up to him and discovered that the old man spoke German. Mentioning Police Officer Banaszak, he asked him if he would translate the Polish text. They went back to the interrogation room. The old policeman started stammering:

"According to Walenty Mikołajczak's testimony . . . he carried Ślusarczyk's letters to the post office . . . He read and contemplated the name of the addressant . . . no . . . how do you say it?"

"Addressee. What does 'contemplated' mean?"

"Yes . . . addressee. 'Contemplated' means that he has it in his brain, he knows."

"Addressee: Mieczysław Anwald, Poznań ul. Mickiewicza 2. Walenty Mikołajczak was surprised that she was sending letters addressed to a shop. The name of the establishment announces . . ."

"Reads, surely."

"Yes. Reads. The name of the establishment reads 'Mercer's Goods. Mieczysław Anwald and Company'. Then is goes . . . well . . . I know . . . something about a photographic album . . . But what's it to you? He's asleep . . . sleeping . . ."

The old policeman abandoned his duties as translator with relief, went out of the room and left Anwaldt alone. Closing the door, he cast a concerned eye back at the tired German policeman who had rested his forehead on the coarse, green felt.

He was wrong. Anwaldt was not asleep at all. It was easier for him to transport himself in time and space with eyes closed. He was now sitting in Franz Huber's agency with the old detective in his sights. In the agency, its walls covered in wood, floated specks of dust which settled as a powdered carpet on the thick files and glass panes behind which old photographs were turning yellow. Franz Huber was tapping the top of his desk with his engraved cigarette holder and slowly drawling out his words:

"Schlossarczyk worked for the Baron from 1901–1902. That's presumably when she got pregnant. Thereafter, Baron Ruppert von der Malten, Olivier's father, never again employed a woman, not even as cook. So her son must be thirty-one or thirty-two. His name? We don't know. Certainly not the same as the Baron. His mother got a handsome sum to keep quiet, enough for her to live comfortably to this day. Where does the bastard live now? That we don't know either. And what do we know? That until he became of age, he lived in an orphanage in Berlin, where he landed up as a baby from his loving mother's arms."

"What orphanage?"

"She doesn't know herself. Some merchant took her there. An acquaintance of hers."

"The merchant's name?"

"She didn't want to give it to us. She said he had nothing to do with it." (*I'm better than Schubert, the detective from Huber's agency. I know what that merchant was called. The same as me except without a "t". An orphanage in Berlin and a mercer from Poznań, Mieczysław Anwald. Two cities, two people, one surname, one death sentence.*)

The establishment of Mieczysław Anwald's blue textiles on Ulica Północna near the Goods Station was already rumbling with life at this hour. Workers were carrying bales of material, carts and delivery vans were driving up to the ramp, a Jew was pushing a trolley constructed out of planks nailed together, the trade representative of the Bielschowsky establishment was waving his business card in front of the manager's nose, abacuses were clattering in the counting-room, Police Officer Banaszak was puffing away at a small ivory pipe and Anwaldt was repeating in his mind: "it's a pure coincidence that Schlossarczyk's and Baron von der Malten's son was brought up in a Berlin orphanage as I was, it's pure coincidence that he was taken there by a man with the same surname as mine, I'm not the Baron's son, it's pure coincidence that Schlossarczyk's and the Baron's son was brought up . . ."

"Can I help you?" the well-built fifty-year-old squeezed a fat cigar between his fingers. "What do our dear police want from me?"

Banaszak got up and, with reluctance, glanced at the unshaven Anwaldt who was muttering something to himself. He pulled out his identification and, stifling a yawn, said:

"Police Officer Banaszak, and this is Criminal Assistant Klaus Überweg from the Breslau Police. Did you know Hanna Ślusarczyk of Rawicz?"

"No . . . no, I don't . . . where . . ." the merchant glanced at the cashier women who were suddenly counting more slowly. "Let's go to my apartment. It's too noisy here."

The apartment was large and comfortable. From the agency, the way in was through the kitchen door. Two servants threw a flirtatious eye at the young man for whom the night had been too short; under their

198

employer's glaring eyes, they immediately reverted to their plucking of a fat duck. The men's footsteps rang on the sandstone floor. The merchant invited the policemen into the library where the spines of untouched books glittered and the green armchairs standing under a palm spread their soft insides. Through the open window wafted the nauseating, sweetish smell of a slaughterhouse. Mieczysław Anwald did not wait for Banaszak to repeat his question.

"Yes, I know Hanna Ślusarczyk."

"Do you speak German?" the police officer's pipe was blocked.

"Yes."

"Perhaps we could switch to that language. It will save us time since Assistant Überweg doesn't speak Polish."

"Certainly."

Banaszak finally blew his pipe through and the library filled with scented smoke.

"Let's be exact, Herr Anwald. You knew her. Yesterday morning your friend was killed."

Mieczysław Anwald's face contorted in pain. There was no verbal reaction. Anwaldt ceased to repeat his mantra and started to ask questions:

"Herr Anwald, is it you who took Hanne Schlossarczyk's illegitimate child to the Berlin orphanage?"

The merchant did not reply. Banaszak moved uneasily and said in Polish:

"My dear fellow, if you want your family to find out about your romance with a woman of ill repute, if you want to walk out of your establishment led to the police station by two uniformed policemen, then persist in your silence."

The host looked at the unshaven man with flaming eyes, and answered in German with a Silesian accent:

"Yes. It was me who took the child to the orphanage in Berlin."

"Why did you do so?"

"Hanna asked me to. She could not part with the child herself."

"So why did she part with it at all?"

"My dear Assistant," Banaszak bit his tongue at the last instant so as to not say "my dear Anwaldt". He was angry at himself for having agreed to Anwaldt's strange request to introduce him under a fictitious name. "Please forgive me, but this question has nothing to do with the case. Firstly, it should have been addressed to the deceased; secondly, the answer won't give you what you're looking for: the son's address."

"I'm not, sir, going to come to Poznań again in order to ask something you've not allowed me to ask."

Anwaldt examined the books through the yellow glass and admired the large collection of Greek literature in translation. A verse from *Oedipus the King* roared in his ears: *"Terrible though it is, Sir, while the witness/ Does not the truth confess, hold fast still to your hope."*

"She was young. She still wanted to get married."

"Which orphanage did you take the child to?"

"I don't know. Definitely a Catholic one."

"How's that, were you in Berlin or not? You went there at random with the child, not knowing where you were going to leave it? How did you know they would take him in anywhere?"

"Two nuns were waiting for the child at the station. It had been decided by the family of the child's father."

"What family? Name!"

"I don't know. Hanna kept it absolutely secret and never told anyone. I expect she was generously rewarded for her silence."

"Had anything else been decided?"

"Yes. The family paid in advance for the boy to be educated at a secondary school."

200

Anwaldt suddenly experienced a painful spasm in his chest. He got up, strolled across the room and decided to put an end to the pain by means of its cause. So he lit another cigarette. But the effect was such that he was gripped by a dry cough. When it had passed, he quoted Sophocles: "Terrible though it is, Sir, while the witness/ Does not the truth confess, hold fast still to your hope."

"I beg your pardon?" Anwald and Banaszak asked simultaneously, looking at the Breslau policeman as if he were mad. The latter walked up to Mieczysław Anwald's armchair and whispered:

"What name did they give the child?"

"We christened the boy in Ostrów. The kind-hearted priest took our word that we were married. He only asked to see my passport. The godparents were some chance people who got paid for it."

"Tell me, dammit, what was the child's name?!"

"The same as mine: Anwald. We gave him the name Herbert."

POZNAŃ, THAT SAME JULY 17TH, 1934
TWO O'CLOCK IN THE AFTERNOON

Herbert Anwaldt sat comfortably spread out on the plush couch in the saloon carriage. He was reading *Oedipus the King* and not paying the slightest attention to the crowded Poznań platform. Suddenly, the conductor appeared and politely asked what the gentleman would like to eat during his journey. Anwaldt, not taking his eyes off the Greek text, ordered pork knuckle and a bottle of Polish Baczyński vodka. The conductor bowed and left. The Breslau train moved off.

Anwaldt got up and looked at himself in the mirror.

"I'm doing well with my money. But what the heck. Did you know," he said to his reflection "that my daddy has a lot of money? He's very good. He paid for me to go to the best Berlin secondary school specializing in the Classics."

He stretched out on the couch and covered his face with the open book. He drew in with pleasure the faint odour of printer's ink. He closed his eyes so as to bring to mind more readily the blurred future, an image persistently knocking at the threshold of consciousness, stubbornly jumping like a photograph in a peep-show which does not want to slip into the correct frame. It was one of those moments when the humming in his ears and dizziness announced an epiphany, a prophetic dream, a flash of clairvoyance, a shaman's transformation. He opened his eyes and looked around the delicatessen with interest. He felt a stinging pain. The wounds left by the bee-stings were pulsating. The portly shopkeeper in a dirty apron laughed as he handed him some onion peelings. The smile did not leave his face. You pig, shouted Anwaldt, my daddy's going to kill you. The shopkeeper threw himself across the counter at the boy hiding behind his tutor, who had just entered the shop. *(Sir, please look at the tower I've built with the bricks. Yes, you've built a lovely tower, Herbert, the tutor patted him on the shoulder. Again. And again.)* "Here you are, sir, your vodka and pork knuckle." Anwaldt threw the book aside, sat up and uncorked the bottle. He shuddered: a child was shouting. Little Klaus in Waschteich Park, like an upside down, poisoned cockroach, was thrashing his legs against the ground. "He's not my daddy!" The wheels rumbled rhythmically. They deafened Klaus' cries. Anwaldt tipped the bottle. The burning liquid had an almost immediate effect on his empty stomach, clarified his mind, calmed his nerves. The policeman dug his teeth into the trembling pink meat with relish. A few moments later, only a thick bone lay on his plate. He stretched out comfortably on the couch. The alcohol conjured up an image in his mind of a dark green forest and the crooked figures of Soutine's exiled children. Not all are exiled, he explained to himself. That little Pole from the train to Rawicz, for example, will never be expelled anywhere by anyone. You're a Pole, too. Your mother was Polish. He sat up and drank two glasses of vodka in a row. The bottle was empty. (*Scorching desert sand is settling on the stone floor. Into the ruined tomb peers a hairy goat. Hoof marks in the sand. Wind blows sand into zigzag gaps in the wall. From the ceiling fall small, restless scorpions. They surround him and raise their poisonous abdomens. Eberhard Mock tramples them methodically. I'll die just like my sister died. Sophocles: "Unfortunate one, may you not know who you are."*)

XIV

BRESLAU, THAT SAME TUESDAY, JULY 17TH, 1934
SEVEN O'CLOCK IN THE EVENING

Eberhard Mock sat shirtless in his apartment on Rehdigerplatz, resting after a heavy and nerve-racking day. He spread out the chessboard, positioned out the pieces and tried to immerse himself in Überbrand's *Chess Traps*. He was analysing a particular master hand. As usual, he put himself in the defence's position and, to his satisfaction, found a solution which led to stalemate. He looked at the chessboard again and instead of the white king, which was not being pinned down in check but which nevertheless could not move, he saw himself, Criminal Director Eberhard Mock. He stood retreating, under fire from the black knight, who bore the face of Olivier von der Malten, and the black queen, who resembled the Chief of Gestapo, Erich Kraus. The white bishop, looking like Smolorz, stood useless in one corner of the board, and the white queen, Anwaldt, was curled up somewhere on his desk far from the chessboard. Mock did not answer the telephone which rang persistently for the fourth time already that evening. He expected he would hear the Baron's cold voice summoning him to give a report. What was he to tell von der Malten? That Anwaldt had disappeared who knew where? That the owner of the tenement and his new tenant had entered Maass' apartment and found

204

Smolorz there? Yes, he could of course say that he had identified the murderer. But where was that murderer? In Breslau? In Germany? Or maybe the mountains of Kurdistan? The telephone rang persistently. Mock counted the rings. Twelve. He got up and crossed the room. The telephone stopped ringing. At that moment, he threw himself at the receiver. He remembered von Hardenburg's principle regarding telephones: wait until the twelfth ringing tone. He went to the kitchen and took a piece of dried sausage. Today was the servant's day off. He tore a fair piece of sausage with his teeth, then ate a spoonful of hot horseradish. As he chewed, his eyes watered abundantly – the horseradish was hot – and he thought about the young Berliner who, humiliated and maltreated in the Gestapo cells, had surrendered under his torturers' threats and left this over-heated and evil city. The telephone rang again. (Where can Anwaldt be?) A second ringing of the telephone. (I'll sort that cursed Forstner out yet!) Third. (A nerve-racking day, but nothing really happened.) Fourth. (That's exactly why). Fifth. (It's a pity about Anwaldt; it would be good to have someone like him among my men.) Sixth. (Too bad, he too had found himself in a "vice".) Seventh. (I've got to get a whore for myself. That'll calm me.) Eighth. (I can't pick it up with my mouth full.) Ninth. (Yes, I'll call Madame.) Tenth. (Maybe it's von Hardenburg?) The telephone rang for the eleventh time. Mock dashed into the hall and picked the receiver up after the twelfth bell. His ear heard a drunk babbling. He brusquely interrupted the stream of incomprehensible justifications.

"Where are you, Anwaldt?"

"At the station."

"Wait for me on platform one. I'll come and collect you right away. Repeat – which platform?"

"Plaaaatform . . . One."

* * *

Mock did not find Anwaldt on platform one or on any other platform. Guided by his intuition, he went to Bahnschutz Police Station. Anwaldt was lying in a cell, asleep and snoring loudly. Mock showed the astounded duty constable his identification and politely asked for help. The constable eagerly barked some instructions to his men. They grasped the drunkard under the arms and carried him out to the Adler. Mock thanked the obliging constable and his colleagues, started the engine and a quarter of an hour later was back at Rehdigerplatz. All the benches on the square were occupied. People, resting after the day's heat, watched with amazement as a stocky man with a sizeable belly, panting loudly, dragged an inert creature from the back seat of his car.

"He's sozzled," laughed a passing teenager.

Mock removed the drunken man's jacket, soiled with vomit, rolled it up and threw it into the front of the car. Next, he threw the man's left arm over his own sweaty neck, with his right he took him by the waist and, under the eyes of the mocking rabble, hauled him through the doorway. The caretaker, as if out of spite, was nowhere to be seen. "Anyone could walk through the door and that idiot's probably drinking beer at Kohl's," he muttered furiously. He advanced step by step. His cheek rubbed against Anwaldt's dirty, sweaty shirt. He shuddered every now and then as a sour cloud of breath swept over him, stopped on the half-landings and swore like a trooper, careless of the neighbours. One of them, the lawyer Doctor Fritz Patschkowsky, taking his dog for a walk, stood stock still, amazed, and the large Pomeranian practically tore itself from its leash. Mock glanced at the man with some hostility and did not respond to the haughty "good evening". At last he reached his door and stood Anwaldt next to it. With one hand, he held him up; with the other, he struggled with the lock. A minute later, he was in the apartment. Anwaldt lay on the floor in the hall. Mock, sitting at the mahogany dressing-table, was breathing heavily. He closed the door and calmly smoked a cigarette.

Next, he grasped Anwaldt by his shirt collar and tugged him to the games room. He took him under the arms, put him on to the gently sloping chaise longue, and searched his pockets. Nothing. *(Some pick-pocket has already robbed him.)* He loosened the tie, unbuttoned the shirt and removed the shoes. Anwaldt's clothes were in a dismal condition, stained by grease and ash. On the thin cheeks, a two-day stubble fell like a shadow. Mock observed his subordinate for a while, then went out to the kitchen and ran his eyes thoughtfully over the green jars standing on the top shelf in the larder. Each of them had a parchment cap held in place by a pale rubber band. Finally, he found a jar containing dried mint. He poured two handfuls of the herb into a jug and then, with some difficulty, lit a fire under the stove. He fiddled with the stove lids for a long time until he found the right one and stood a shining, polished kettle on it. From the bathroom, he brought a tin basin and stood it next to Anwaldt's bedding just in case, then returned to the kitchen. He lifted the steaming kettle and filled the jug containing the leaves with boiling water. Not knowing how to extinguish the fire, he drowned it with tap water. Then he took a cool bath and changed into a dressing gown. He sat at his desk, lit a fat Turkish cigar – one of the ones he kept for special occasions – and looked at the chessboard. Stalemate continued to paralyse the king-Eberhard Mock. He was still threatened by the knight-von der Malten and the queen-Kraus. But here, at the chessboard, appeared the white queen-Anwaldt – recovered from somewhere – and came to the king's aid.

BRESLAU, WEDNESDAY, JULY 18TH, 1934
EIGHT O'CLOCK IN THE MORNING

Anwaldt opened his swollen eyes and immediately saw the jug and glass standing on the little table. With shaking hands, he filled it with strained mint tea and raised it to his lips.

"Shall I give you a knife to separate those lips?" Mock was tying his tie, spreading a spicy scent of quality eau de cologne and smiling kind-heartedly. "Do you know, I'm not even furious with you. Because how can you be furious with someone who's just miraculously been found? Click, Anwaldt was here and Anwaldt's gone. Click, and Anwaldt's here again." Mock stopped smiling. "Nod if you had a good reason to disappear from my sight."

Anwaldt nodded. Fireworks lit up inside his skull. He poured himself some more mint. Mock stood astride, observing his hung-over assistant. He clasped his hands and twiddled his thumbs.

"Good. I see you feel like drinking. That means you won't be sick. I've run a bath for you. There's one of my shirts in the bathroom and your cleaned and pressed suit. You certainly took care of it yesterday. I paid the caretaker's wife an arm and a leg for her efforts. It took her half the night. She also cleaned your shoes. You'll pay me back when you've got some money. Someone robbed you yesterday. Take a shave because you look like an alcoholic tramp. Use my razor," Mock was harsh and decisive. "And now listen to me. In three-quarters of an hour you're to sit here and tell me your adventures. Briefly and concretely. Then we'll go to John the Baptist's Cathedral. There, at nine-fifteen, Doctor Leo Hartner's going to be waiting for us."

* * *

They sat in the cool darkness. The violence of the sun stopped short of the coloured filter of stained-glass windows; walls of ashlar muffled the noise and bustle of the sweating city; Silesian princes slept in silent niches; and Latin signs on the walls invoked the contemplation of eternity. Mock's watch showed nine-twenty. As agreed, they sat in the front row and watched out for Hartner. Instead of him, a short priest with a crew-cut and silver-framed spectacles walked up to them. Without a word, he

208

handed Mock an envelope, turned and left. Anwaldt wanted to follow him, but Mock held him back. He took the typed letter from the envelope and passed it to his assistant.

"You read. I can't see properly in this light and we're not going out into that cursed heat." On saying this, Mock realized that he was speaking in familiar terms to Baron von der Malten's son. (If I was on familiar terms with Marietta, I can be the same with him.)

Anwaldt looked at the sheet of paper embossed with the University Library's golden crest beneath which appeared the elegant letters of the Director's typewriter.

Dear Excellency,

I apologize for not being able to attend our appointment personally, but family reasons prompted me to leave suddenly yesterday evening. I called Your Excellency several times, but you were not in. So let me speak through this letter for I have several important things to impart. All that I am now going to say is based on the admirable book *Les Yesîdîs* by Jean Boyé, published ten years ago in Paris. The author, a well-known French ethnographer and traveller, stayed with the Yesidis for four years. They liked him and respected him to such a degree that he was admitted to some sacred rituals. Among the many interesting descriptions of the religious cult of this secret sect, one is particularly significant. And so, our author stayed somewhere in the desert (he doesn't say exactly where) with several of the Yesidi elders. There, they visited an old hermit who lived in a grotto. This elderly eremite would frequently dance and fall into a trance like the Turkish dervishes. While he did so, he pronounced prophecies in an incomprehensible tongue. Boyé had for a long time to implore the Yesidis to clarify these prophetic cries. They eventually agreed and explained them. The hermit proclaimed that the time of vengeance for the murdered children of Al-Shausi had come. Boyé, knowing the history of the Yesidis very well, knew that these children had died at the turn of the twelfth and thirteenth centuries. He was surprised, therefore, that these born avengers had waited so long to fulfil their sacred duty. The Yesidis explained to him that, according to their law, vengeance is only valid if it corresponds exactly to the crime which it is to avenge. So that if someone's eye had been gouged out with a stiletto, then his avenger had to visit the same barbarity on the criminal or his descendant, and not just with any ordinary knife but with a stiletto and — best of all — the very same one.

Vengeance for Al-Shausi's murdered children would only be in keeping with their law if the children of the murderer's descendant were killed in the very same way. But this could not come about for centuries, up until the moment that the deity Malak-Taus manifested himself to the hermit and announced that the awaited time had come. These hermits are profoundly venerated by the Yesidis and are considered to be the guardians of tradition. And the duty to avenge belongs to the sacred tradition. So that when the eremite announced that the time was right, the gathering chose an avenger whose right hand was tattooed with the symbol of vengeance. If this avenger did not fulfil his task, they hung him before everybody's eyes. So much for Boyé.

Dear Excellency, I too, unfortunately, am unable to answer the question which so troubled Jean Boyé. I looked through the entire genealogy of the von der Malten family and think I know why the Yesidi's vengeance could not be fulfilled for so many centuries. In the fourteenth century, the von der Maltens branched into three: the Silesian, the Bavarian and the Netherlandish. In the eighteenth century, the last two dried out. The Silesian branch did not propagate abundantly – mostly singleton boys were born to this well-known junker's family, and the vengeance – let me remind you – could only be considered valid if it was carried out on siblings. In that family's entire history, siblings were born only five times. In two cases, one of the children died when still an infant, in two others, the boys died in unknown circumstances. In the last one, Olivier von der Malten's aunt, his father Ruppert's sister, spent all her days in a strictly closed, sequestered convent, so that vengeance on her was effectively hindered.

Dear Excellency, I wrote that I know why revenge has not been taken. Unfortunately, I do not know why this elder had insight and announced ceremoniously that the moment of vengeance had come. The only living male descendant of Godfryd von der Malten, Olivier, did not, at the time of the hermit's insight, have any other children apart from the hapless Marietta. So that her terrible murder is a tragic mistake of a demented old shaman, caused by the hashish which is so popular in his country.

I finish my overly long letter and apologize for not verifiying Maass' translation of Friedländer's last two prophecies. A lack of time rendered it impossible; much time was spent in my examining the Yesidi's curse and on complicated family matters which un-expectedly hastened my departure. I remain sincerely yours, Doctor Leo Hartner.

Mock and Anwaldt looked at each other. They knew that the prophecies of the holy elder from the desert were not the drug-induced babble of a demented shaman. They left the cathedral and, without a word, got into the Adler, which was parked in the shade of an enormous chestnut tree, of which many grew in the Cathedral Square.

"Don't worry, son," Mock looked at Anwaldt with compassion. This was no slip of the tongue. He had uttered the word "son" consciously. He remembered the Baron, clinging to the train window and shouting: "He is my son". "I'll take you home now. Your apartment may not be safe. I'll send Smolorz to get your things. You stay at my place, get some sleep, do not answer any telephone calls and do not open the door to anyone. In the evening, I'll take you somewhere where you'll forget about your daddy and all insects."

XV

BRESLAU, THAT SAME WEDNESDAY, JULY 18TH, 1934
EIGHT O'CLOCK IN THE EVENING

Wednesday frolics at Madame le Goef's salon were kept in the style of
Antiquity. In the evening, a naked slave, painted the colour of mahogany,
struck an enormous gong, the curtain rose and the set was revealed in
front of the audience: the façade of a Roman temple with naked men and
women dancing against this background amidst rose petals floating from
the ceiling. These Bacchanalia – where dancers only mimicked sexual
congress – lasted about twenty minutes, after which there followed an
interval of a similar duration. During this time, some guests retreated
to discreet rooms while others fortified themselves and drank. After the
break, the slave struck the gong once again and on stage there appeared
several "Roman men and women" dressed in thin tunics, which they
promptly discarded. More rose petals fell, the room became airless; this
time, the bacchanalia were real. After half an hour of such games, the
actors and actresses left the stage – exhausted, the hall emptied while
the withdrawing rooms burst at the seams.

That evening, Rainer von Hardenburg, Eberhard Mock and Herbert
Anwaldt sat in a small gallery, observing the introductory mimicry of a
Bacchanalian orgy from above. At the very outset of the performance,

already, Anwaldt was clearly stirred. Seeing this, Mock got up and went to Madame's office. He greeted her effusively and presented her with his request. Madame agreed without hesitation and picked up the telephone. Mock returned to his seat. Anwaldt leaned over to him and whispered:

"Where does one get the keys to one of the rooms?"

"Wait a minute. What's the hurry?" Mock laughed coarsely.

"Look: all the prettiest ones are being taken."

"They're all pretty here. See: those coming in our direction, for example."

Two girls in school uniforms were approaching their table. Both policemen knew them well; the girls, on the other hand, pretended to be seeing the men for the first time. Both gazed at Anwaldt with rapture. Suddenly, the one resembling Erna touched his hand and smiled. He got up, put his arms around the girls' slender backs, turned to Mock and said "thank you". The three withdrew to a room in the middle of which stood a round table with a beautifully embossed chessboard. Von Hardenburg glanced at Mock with a smile. He relaxed in Madame le Goef's salon and was not so exacting with titles.

"You knew how to make that boy happy. Who is he?"

"A close relative from Berlin. Also a policeman."

"So we'll hear a Berliner's opinion of the best club in Breslau. Or rather just outside of Breslau."

"What do Berliners know? They'll always laugh at us. But not my relative. He's too well behaved. You know, they have to treat their complexes somehow. Especially those who come from Breslau. You know the saying 'a true Berliner has to come from Breslau'?"

"Yes. Take Kraus, for example," von Hardenburg adjusted his monocle. "He spent two years in Berlin then, after Heines', Brückner's and Piontek's downfalls, von Woyrsch transferred him to Breslau as Chief of Gestapo. Kraus took his promotion as a kick upstairs. So, to hide his disappointment, our spiteful and wooden-headed eager beaver started to turn his nose up. And here is the two-year-old Berliner criticizing Silesian provincialism at every step. I checked – do you know where he's from? From Lower Silesian Frankenstein."

The men laughed out loud and clinked their wine glasses. The actresses on stage bowed, generously bestowing the audience with their charms. Mock pulled out some Turkish cigarettes and offered them to von Hardenburg. He knew that the Chief of the Abwehr did not like to be hurried and would reveal all the information he had managed to acquire on Erkin of his own free will and at the moment that suited him. Mock expected to hear more than he had deduced from Hartner's expertise and letter. He wanted to learn Kemal Erkin's whereabouts.

"People like Kraus cannot stand our tradition of nobility, family and culture," von Hardenburg continued on the subject of Silesia. "All those von Schaffgotsches, von Carmers and von Donnersmarcks. That's why they boost their self-esteem by deriding the fossilization of junkers and coal Barons. Let them laugh . . ."

Silence fell. Von Hardenburg watched the "performances"; Mock wondered whether today's light-hearted evening was a good opportunity to touch on important, practical matters. After much thought, he decided:

"*A propos* Kraus . . . I've a favour to ask of you . . ."

"Eberhard," von Hardenburg was becoming increasingly familiar. "I still haven't granted you the first favour, the Turkish-Kurdish one, and you already have another . . . No, no, that was a joke. Proceed."

"Count," Mock, in contrast to his interlocutor, had become formal. "I would like to work for the Abwehr."

"Oh, and why is that?" von Hardenburg's monocle reflected the glint of candles and discreetly dimmed table lamps.

"Because my department is being infiltrated by Kraus' rabble," Mock replied. "He's already looking down on me, soon he's going to be giving me orders. I'll become a nominal Chief, a dummy, a puppet dependent on uncouth thugs, barbarians from the Gestapo. Count, I come from a poor, craftsman's family from Waldenburg. But in spite of that, or maybe because of it, I want to be *integer vitae scelerisque purus*."[†]

"Oh, Eberhard – despite your descent, you are in spirit a true aristocrat. But surely you realize that working for us, it is not easy to behave according to Horace's maxim."

"My dear Count, I lost my virginity a long time ago and have been working for the police since 1899 with a break during the war when I fought in Russia. I saw many things, but you will surely agree with me that there's a difference between a man who's defending the state using what might not always be conventional methods and an executioner's helper."

"You do know," the monocle glinted with amusement, "that I wouldn't be able to offer you a position of any authority."

"I'll answer by changing the gist of Napoleon's famous saying: 'It's better to be second or even fifth or tenth in Paris, than first in Lyons.'"

"I can't promise you anything at the moment," von Hardenburg examined the menu assiduously. "It's not only up to me. There, I'll order spare ribs in mushroom sauce. And now the other matter. I've got something about Kemal Erkin for you. Firstly, he's a Kurd. He comes from a rich merchant family. In 1913, he graduated from the élite school for cadets in Istanbul. He was good at his studies and applied himself most ardently to German. Our language was then, as it is today, compulsory in every business and military school in Turkey. During the war, he fought in the Balkans and Armenia. There, too, he was surrounded by the grim fame of executioner and sadist during the slaughter of Armenians. My Turkish informer was not inclined to give more detailed information on the subject of this shady page in Erkin's life and Turkey's history. In 1921, as a young

[†] *"Man pure, by crime untouched." (Horace, Hymns 1, 22, 1)*

216

officer in the Turkish Intelligence Service, Erkin was sent on two years' supplementary studies to Berlin. There he made numerous friends. On his return, he climbed ever higher in the Turkish political police. Suddenly, in 1924, the day before he was to be promoted as Chief of this force in Smyrna, he requested a transfer to the German Consulate in Berlin where the position of Deputy Military Advisor had just been vacated. Erkin, like you, preferred to be second in Paris rather than first in Lyons. His request was considered favourably and since 1924 the ambitious Turk has been in Germany. He has been living all the time in Berlin, leading a quiet, mono-tonous administrative-diplomatic existence, varied only by excursions to Breslau. Yes, yes, Mock, he's been greatly interested in our city. He visited it twenty times in six years. We kept an eye on him initially. His file is thick, but you would be disappointed in its contents. So Erkin dedicated himself, in our city, to what you could call artistic pleasures. He diligently went to concerts, regularly visited museums and libraries. Nor did he disdain the brothels where he was famous for his tremendous vigour. We have a statement from a prostitute who claimed that within half an hour Erkin had had intercourse with her twice without, so to speak, leaving her body. He even made friends with a certain librarian at the University Library, but I've forgotten his name. In December of 1932, he asked if he could undergo training at the Staatspolizeileistelle in Oppeln. Just imagine: having a cosy position in Berlin, he suddenly decides to move to the forlorn countryside and have Silesian provincials teach him! It looks as if he prefers to be tenth in Oppeln rather than second in Berlin!"

Von Hardenburg wiped his monocle and ordered spare ribs from a passing waitress. He tapped his cigarette against the lid of his gold cigarette case with its engraved crest, and looked intently at Mock.

"But maybe you can explain this strange love Kemal Erkin has for the beautiful Silesian land, our Switzerland of the North?"

Mock lit his cigarette, without a word. Rituals in honour of Bacchus had begun on the stage. Von Hardenburg put his monocle in place and followed the spectacle with intent: "Look at that red-head on the right. A true artist!"

Mock did not look. All of his attention was concentrated on the sparks flashing in the dark red wine. Deep thought was expressed by the horizontal lines on his forehead. Von Hardenburg turned his eyes away from the stage and raised his glass.

"Who knows, maybe your explanation would help both me and my superiors in Berlin to make a decision favourable to you? Apart from that, I hear you've got quite a large file of character profiles of various people . . ."

A powerfully built girl walked up to their table and smiled at von Hardenburg. Mock smiled at him too and raised his glass. They clinked glasses, almost noiselessly.

"So, maybe we can meet tomorrow in my office? And now, please forgive me. I have an appointment with this Maenad. Bacchus beckons me to his mysteries."

* * *

That evening Mock did not play chess with his girls for the simple reason that chess was a marginal activity to them, and they were now performing their primary role in quiet boudoirs with other clients. Mock, therefore, did not play the royal game which does not mean that he did not satisfy his other, non-chess-related needs. At midnight, he said goodbye to a stout brunette and went to the boudoir which he usually occupied on Friday evenings. He knocked several times, but nobody answered. So he opened the door a little and swept his eyes across the room. Anwaldt, entirely naked, was lying on the divan among Moorish cushions. The schoolgirls were slowly getting dressed. With one gesture, Mock hastened their movements. The embarrassed Anwaldt also pulled on his shirt and trousers. When the giggling girls had disappeared, Mock stood a bottle of

Rhein wine and some glasses on the table. Still feeling the effects of his hangover, Anwaldt swiftly knocked back two glasses.

"How are you feeling? Has the oldest and best therapy for depression worked?"

"This painkiller works on a very short term."

"Did you know that the vaccine against any disease is nothing other than the virus causing it?" Mock obviously liked this medical metaphor. "And so I'll infect you for good: von Hardenburg confirmed that our suspicious Erkin is a Yesidi who has come to Breslau on a sinister mission. He's completed half of it *par excellence*."

Anwaldt leapt up from the chair, catching his knees on the chess table. The glasses danced on their thin legs.

"Mock, sir, you're playing at rhetorical games here, but what hangs over me is no game. Somewhere not far from me, maybe even in this brothel, a fanatic who wants to stuff me with scorpions is lying in wait. Just look at that wallpaper, how well Persian verses would look written on it in my blood. You prescribe brothel therapy for me . . . But what therapy can help a man for whom having a father — his deepest longing — has at one and the same time become his greatest curse?"

The words broke up, the grammar was confused — Anwaldt started weeping like a child. His abused and stung face was contorted by wrenching sobs. Mock opened the door to the corridor and looked around. A drunken client was kicking up a row between the tables downstairs. Mock closed the door and approached the window to open it wider. The garden was bursting with the warm scent of lime trees. Some Bacchante was groaning in the next room.

"Don't exaggerate, Anwaldt." He bit his tongue. (He had wanted to say: "Don't whine; you're a man".) His irritation was expressed by a loud puff. "Don't exaggerate; it's enough for you to take great care until we catch Erkin. And then the curse will not be fulfilled."

219

The young man now sat with dry eyes. He avoided Mock's gaze, nervously snapped his knuckles, rubbed the small cut on his chin, whipped his eyes from side to side.

"Don't worry, Herbert," Mock understood the state he was in all too well. "Who knows, maybe our neuroses are caused by us holding back our tears. After all, Homer's heroes cried, too. And bitter tears at that!"

"And you . . . do you sometimes cry?" Anwaldt looked at Mock hopefully.

"No," he lied.

Anwaldt was gripped by anger. He got up and shouted: "Well, right . . . because why should you want to cry? You weren't brought up in an orphanage . . . Nobody made you eat your own excrement when you couldn't swallow the spinach! You didn't have a whore for a mother and a cursed Prussian aristocrat for a father who did nothing more for his child than put him in a Catholic orphanage and secondary school specializing in the Classics! You don't wake up happy to have survived one more day because somehow no-one's torn your belly apart and poured vermin into your guts! Listen to me, man, they waited seven centuries for a boy and a girl . . . Why should they let an opportunity like this go by now? Their possessed shaman is even now undergoing a revelation . . . The deity is approaching . . ."

Mock was no longer listening; he was feverishly searching through scrolls of memory, like someone who, at a stiff, official reception cannot bear silence at the table and is trying to find some joke, anecdote, pun in his head . . . Anwaldt yelled; someone knocked at the door. Anwaldt screamed; the knocking intensified. A fake groan resounded in the other room and spilled out into the garden through the open window. Anwaldt was hysterical; someone thumped on the door.

Mock got up and took a swing. His small palm bounced off his yelling assistant's cheek. Silence. Nobody was knocking at the door; the Maenad next door gathered her clothes which lay scattered on the floor; Anwaldt froze; Mock found his lost thought in the darkness. He heard his own voice resound in his head: "Don't exaggerate; it's enough for you to take great care until we catch Erkin. And then the curse won't be fulfilled . . . curse won't be fulfilled . . . curse won't be fulfilled . . ."

He was standing very close to Anwaldt and looking him in the eyes: "Listen, Herbert, Doctor Hartner wrote that their vengeance is invalid if it is not executed in exactly the same circumstances as the crime to be avenged. The Yesidis waited centuries for a son and a daughter to be born to the von der Malten family . . . But there have already been siblings of mixed sex in the family. Olivier von der Malten's aunt and his father, Ruppert. Why didn't the Yesidis kill *them*, rape her and sew scorpions into their innards? Hartner suspects that revenge could not be taken in a closed convent." Mock shut his eyes and experienced self-loathing. "I don't think so. Do you know why? Because their father was no longer alive. Those twins were born after the death of their father who was killed at Sadowa. I know that perfectly well. My university colleague, Olivier von der Malten, told me about his grandfather-hero. So the curse was not fulfilled . . . But if von der Malten were to die . . ."

Anwaldt walked up to the table, grabbed the bottle of wine and knocked it back. Mock watched as the wine ran down his chin and dyed his shirt. Anwaldt drank to the last drop. He hid his face in his open hands and hissed out:

"Alright, I'll do it. I'll kill the Baron."

Mock choked on his own self-loathing.

"You can't. He's your father."

Anwaldt's eyes flashed between his fingers.

"No. You are my father."

The black Adler stopped in front of von der Malten's manor. A man got out and staggered towards the gate. The sound of the doorbell tore through the silence. The Adler drove off with a screech of tyres. The man at the wheel looked into the rear window and contemplated his own reflection for a while.

"You're the lowest son-of-a-bitch," he said to the tired eyes. "You pushed that boy into committing a crime. He has become a tool in your hands. A tool to remove the last witness of your masonic past."

* * *

Baron Olivier von der Malten stood on the threshold of his enormous hall. It looked as if he had not been to bed at all. He wrapped the crimson dressing gown around himself and watched the swaying Anwaldt severely.

"What are you thinking of, young man? That this is a police station, a hostel for drunks?"

Anwaldt smiled and – in order to hide his stammering speech – said as quietly as he could:

"I've got some new, important information for you . . ."

The host entered the hall and indicated for Anwaldt to do the same, after which he dismissed the sleepy servant. The spacious, panel-covered room was hung with portraits of the von der Maltens. Anwaldt did not see sternness and gravity in them but rather cunning and vanity. He looked around – in vain – for a chair. The Baron made as if not to notice.

"What do you want to tell me about this case that's new? I had lunch with Counsellor Mock today so I am more or less up to date. What could have happened this evening?"

Anwaldt lit a cigarette and, for lack of an ashtray, shook the ash on to the polished floor.

222

"And so Counsellor Mock told you about the Yesidi's vengeance. Did he mention that the vengeance had not been wholly fulfilled?"

"Yes. 'The mistake of an old demented shaman,'" he quoted Hartner. "Did you come to see me, drunk as you are, at four o'clock in the morning to ask me about my conversation with Mock?"

Anwaldt scrutinized the Baron and noticed quite a few shortcomings in his dress: the button on his vest, the strings of his long johns slipping out from under the dressing gown. He burst out laughing and stayed in this strange, doubled-up position for a while. He imagined the elderly gentleman sitting on the toilet and panting heavily, when here comes his drunken little son and destroys the sacred peace of the elegant residence. Laughter was still contorting his lips when he let loose words, swollen with anger:

"Dear Papi, we both know that the dervish's revelations are startingly consistent with family realities. The unofficial ones, of course. The god of the Yesidis has finally grown impatient and taken bastards into account. On the other hand, how is it that in this knightly family no warrior inseminated any captive, no landowner got hold of a comely peasant girl in a haystack? All were temperate and faithful to their marriage vows. Even my dear Papi. After all, he begat me before getting married."

"I would not joke in your position, Herbert," the Baron's tone was inalterably haughty — but his face had shrunk. In one moment he had changed from a proud junker to a fearful old man. His neatly combed hair had slipped to the sides, his lips sunk to reveal the absence of dentures.

"I don't wish you to call me by my first name," Anwaldt had stopped smiling. "Why didn't you tell me everything at the beginning?"

The father and son stood face to face. Delicate streaks of dawn began to creep into the hall. The Baron remembered the June nights of 1902 when he would creep into the servants' quarters, and the sheets — drenched with sweat — when he left; he remembered the disciplinary whipping which

223

Ruppert von der Malten had personally bestowed on his twenty-year-old son; he remembered Hanne Schlossarczyk's terrified looks as she left the lordly residence, literally booted out by the servants. He broke the ringing silence with a matter-of-fact answer.

"I found out about the Yesidi's curse today. And I wanted to tell you about our close relationship were the investigation to come to a dead stop. That would have encouraged you to go on."

"Close relationship . . . *(Do you have a relative, asked the tutor, even a distant one? Pity, you could have spent Christmas away from the orphanage at least once.)* Even now you're a hypocrite. You can't call it by its name. It's not enough for you to have dropped me off in some refuge, paying nine years of fees at a secondary school: an offering for your peace of mind. How much did you pay that merchant from Poznań, Anwald, for his name? How much did you pay my mother to forget? How many marks does corrupting a conscience cost? But it called out in the end. It shouted: summon Anwaldt to Breslau. He'll be useful. He happens to be a policeman so let him lead the investigation into his sister's murder. But I'll tell him about the family ties to mobilize him, right? Conscience is conscience, but practicalism is practicalism. Was it always like that with the von der Maltens?"

"What you call practicalism," the Baron proudly raised his eyes to the portraits of his ancestors, "I would term family pride. I summoned you to catch your sister's murderer and avenge her terrible death. As a brother you had the absolute right to do so . . ."

Anwaldt pulled out his gun, released the safety catch and aimed at the head of the first ancestor in the gallery. He pulled the trigger. The dry crack of the firing-pin resounded. He started to rummage through his pockets feverishly. The Baron caught him lightly by the shoulder, but quickly removed his hand. The policeman looked at him with hazy eyes.

"I can't stand . . . German Yesidi . . ."

The Baron drew himself up as taut as a string. They continued to stand face to face in the misty, orange glow.

"Please behave correctly and hear me out to the end. I told you about our family pride. It results from centuries of tradition, from the history of our ancestors. All that would cease to exist. My death would mean the end of the family, the last, Silesian branch of the von der Maltens would dry up." He grabbed Anwaldt by the shoulders and spun him round so that the elegant, syphilitic faces gyrated. "But in this way our family will continue to exist in the person of Herbert von der Malten."

Suddenly, he ran up to the wall and took down a somewhat jagged sword with a golden hilt embossed with mother of pearl. Holding it on outstretched arms, he approached Anwaldt. He looked at him for a moment, holding back his emotions. As a man should. As a knight should.

"Forgive me, son," he bowed his head. "Gaze at all this around you. You are heir to it. Receive our coat of arms and our sacred family symbol, the sword of our great-grandfather Bolck von der Malten, a knight of the Thirty Year War. Bury it in the murderer's heart. Avenge your sister."

Anwaldt received the sword ceremoniously. He stood astride and bowed his head as if he were going to be anointed. From his lips emerged a thin, derisive giggle.

"Dear Father, your pathos makes me laugh. Did the von der Maltens always talk like that? I speak far more simply: I'm called Herbert Anwaldt, I've got nothing to do with you and I don't give a damn about this pantheon of yours, which you're going to end. I'm going to start my own. I'm going to give it a beginning, I, the bastard of a Polish chambermaid and an unknown father. So what? Nobody will know about it in seven centuries, and corrupt chroniclers will write up a polished life history. But I have to live, start my own family. And my life means the extinction of the von der Malten family. My life will blossom on your ruin. Do you like the metaphor?"

225

He raised the sword and struck. The skin on the Baron's head split, revealing the bare bone of the skull. Blood stuck to the neatly combed hair. Von der Malten threw himself on the stairs with the cry: "Police!"

"I am the police," Anwaldt climbed the stairs in his father's tracks. The old man tripped and fell. He thought he was lying on a wet sheet in the servants' stuffy quarters. The beige carpet covering the stairs sucked in the brownish-red gore. The pitiful strings of his long johns wound around the leather slippers.

"I beg you, don't kill me . . . You'll go to prison . . . but here you've got a fortune . . ."

"'I am relentless and cannot be bought' replies death." Anwaldt rested the sword's blade under the Baron's rib. "You know that treatise? It was created when your ancestor Godfryd cut into the bellies of Arabian virgins with his Durendal." He felt the blade hit upon an obstacle. He realized it had got stuck in the carpet. Behind the Baron's back.

He left the trembling sword and curled-up body on the stairs and turned to face the old servant who had been watching the spectacle with dumb horror.

"Look, old man, here the knight Heribert the Invincible von Anwaldt has punished the lecherous one, the follower of Satan, the Yesidi . . . Give me the scorpions and we'll fulfil the eternal prophecy . . . Aren't they here? . . . Wait . . ."

As Anwaldt, on all fours, was searching for scorpions on the floor, the Baron's chauffeur, Hermann Wuttke, appeared in the hall and, without second thoughts, grabbed a heavy, silver candlestick. The sun was rising. The people of Breslau looked up at the sky and cursed yet another stifling day.

226

XVI

The Breslau–Oppeln train was two minutes late, which to Mock, who was used to the punctuality of German trains, seemed unpardonable. *(It's no surprise that in a state governed by Austrian sergeants, everything breaks down.)* The train slowly drew in to the platform. Mock saw a man in a carriage window laughing and gesticulating wildly to he did not know whom. He glanced at Smolorz. He, too, had noticed the jester; he dashed towards the waiting room with the high, ornamental vault. The train came to a halt. Mock spied Erkin in the same window and right behind him the grinning man helping a lady take down a heavy suitcase. Erkin jumped briskly out of the carriage and made towards the waiting room. The jester threw the travelling valise of the unpleasantly surprised lady roughly on to the platform and swiftly followed him.

There were only a few travellers in the waiting room. The Turk walked towards the underground tunnel leading to the city. The way down was divided lengthwise by an iron barrier. He walked down on the right. After years of living in Germany, he had managed to get to know Prussian *"Ordnung"* so that, on seeing a man climbing in the opposite direction yet on the right hand side of the barrier and against the current, his hand

227

instinctively flew to his inside pocket where he kept a gun. After a moment, he withdrew it. The man was nearing Erkin, manoeuvring his body in such a way as not to deviate from a straight line. Parallel to the drunkard, but on the correct side of the barrier, walked four S.S.-men and a hunched pen-pusher in a hat. The drunkard got close to Erkin and blocked his way. Swaying to all sides, he was attempting to put a crooked cigarette in his mouth. The Turk, laughing to himself at his suspicions, said he did not have a light and tried to pass him, but he felt such a powerful blow to his stomach that he had to double over. Out of the corner of his eye, he caught sight of the S.S.-men leaping over the barrier. He did not have time to lean against the wall before they came up to him from the back. The abusive lady approached, tugging her heavy suitcase. The stocky man in a tight coat and a hat shoved her roughly aside. In his hand, he held a revolver. Erkin slipped his hand into his pocket, but it was the last move he managed to make. Pushed forcefully, he fell on to the barrier and hung there a moment. Two of the S.S.-men pressed him down and the pen-pusher aimed a terrible blow with a rubber truncheon. Erkin did not lose consciousness, but grew numb. He saw the stocky man in the overly tight coat walk up slowly, reassuring the Railway Protection Officer by holding up his identification. He was grinning broadly. The office worker with the rubber truncheon, clearly enraged by the mediocre results of his first blow, pursed his lips and took another, mighty swing.

OPPELN, WEDNESDAY, NOVEMBER 14TH, 1934
ONE O'CLOCK IN THE MORNING

The wind blew through the gaps in the garage door. The cold restored Erkin's consciousness. He was in an unnatural half-sitting position, both hands handcuffed to iron grips protruding from the wall. He shuddered with the cold. He was naked. Blood had coagulated over his eyes.

Through a red fog, he saw the stocky man. Mock walked up to him and said quietly:

"The day has finally come, Erkin. Who will avenge poor Marietta von der Malten? I will. You can understand that very well, can't you? Vengeance, after all, is your sacred duty. I really do like your customs as far as vengeance is concerned." Mock searched his pockets and pulled a disappointed face.

"I have no hornets or scorpions with me. Somehow I forgot them. But, you know, your death is going to be like Marietta's in one respect. You won't be a virgin any more . . ." he glanced to the side. A man emerged from the darkness. In a face covered with pustules, burned tiny eyes. A shudder ran through the Turk. It ran through him again when he heard the clatter of a belt buckle and the sound of trousers being lowered.

Schlesische Tageszeitung, July 22nd, 1934, p.1

THE MISERABLE DEATH OF A MASON

On Thursday, in the early hours of the morning, Baron Olivier von der Malten, one of the founders and members of the Freemasons' Lodge, "Horus", was killed in his residence on Eichen-Allee 13, Breslau. The killer is his illegitimate son Herbert Anwaldt from Berlin. According to witness Mattias Döring, the Baron's butler, Anwaldt arrived at von der Malten's residence in the night so as to impart some important news to the Baron. According to our informant, he had that very day learned that he was the Baron's unlawful son and it was on that subject that he had wanted to talk to him at this unusual hour. The despair of a rejected child, the strong feelings of a scorned foundling, took the upper hand over reason, and Anwaldt, after a sharp altercation, pierced his father-not-father with a stiletto and was then incapacitated by H. Wuttke, the Baron's chauffeur, who practically battered the killer to death with a candlestick. The accused, in a very serious condition, was taken to the University Clinic where he will remain under police surveillance.

One conclusion can be drawn from this sad story; Freemasons are morally dirty. They should be eliminated from society.

Tygodnik Ilustrowany, December 7th, 1934, p.3
(frag. from article *Abyss of Foolishness*)

. . . Our western neighbours are using all they can in their campaign against the Jews and Freemasons, even the most repulsive of crimes. Here is an example. Last month, a mentally ill policeman murdered, in Breslau, a generally respected aristocrat, a member of the Freemasons' Lodge, "Horus", whom he considered to be his own father. Newspapers which are loudspeakers of German propaganda, such as the *Völkischer Beobachter*, are bursting with anti-Masonic hysteria. The alleged father (there is no mention of the mother) is presented as being scum who threw his own child into a cesspool; the latter, on the other hand, is considered by all and sundry as the just one who had avenged his own father's wrongs. The effect is such that the demented knifeman, after a tribunal farce, has been sentenced to two years' imprisonment.

Breslauer Neueste Nachrichten, November 29th, 1934, p.1

PATRICIDE CONVICTED TO TWO YEARS' IMPRISONMENT
After a trial lasting almost four months, former Criminal Assistant

Herbert Anwaldt — whom the people call the bastard-avenger — has been convicted to two years' imprisonment and, on his release, to compulsory psychiatric care for the murder of his father, Baron Olivier von der Malten. The court, when presenting its grounds for such a conviction, pointed to the burning harm caused to his child — raised in an orphanage — by the well-known aristocrat and liberal philanthropist. This discordance between the Baron's words and his actions, his glaringly heinous injustice, appeared — to the court — to partially justify the crime committed under severe provocation by Anwaldt, who suffers a nervous disorder . . .

Breslauer Zeitung, December 17th, 1934

FAREWELL TO HEAD OF CRIMINAL DEPARTMENT OF BRESLAU POLICE, EBERHARD MOCK. MERITORIOUS POLICEMAN TAKES ANOTHER STATE POSITION

Today, to the sound of marches played by the garrison orchestra, Breslau's Police Praesidium bid a ceremonious farewell to Director Eberhard Mock, who is to take over a different government post. Mock, plainly moved, said goodbye to the institution with which he had been associated since youth. We have unofficially learned that he is not leaving the city which owes him so much . . .

Schlesische Tageszeitung, September 18th, 1936, p.1

AVENGER RELEASED FROM PRISON TODAY

Today a large crowd of Breslau's citizens waited outside the prison on Kletschkau Strasse for Herbert Anwaldt, perpetrator of the memorable vengeance bestowed on Freemason Olivier von der Malten, his unlawful father. Some of those present at this greeting held banners with anti-Masonic slogans. It is praiseworthy that the people of our city react so actively to the blatant injustice dealt by some crypto-Masonic judge in convicting this righteous man to two full years of imprisonment.

Anwaldt was released at twelve o'clock and was immediately driven away in an awaiting car to – as we learned – a certain clinic where, in accordance with the court's verdict, compulsory hospitalization awaits him. This verdict must be changed! The liquidator of Freemasons deserves a medal, not a stint in a psychiatric hospital. His action was proof of a great presence of mind. Jews and Freemasons! Don't make a madman of this honest German!

XVII

BRESLAU, FRIDAY, OCTOBER 12TH, 1934
TEN O'CLOCK IN THE MORNING

The monstrous, modernistic office block on the corner of Ring and Blücherplatz, where the administration of many municipal offices and a bank were housed, was equipped with an unusual lift. It was made up of numerous small single cubicles, one above the other, strung as if on a rope. This pulley was constantly on the move so that people entered and left the small, open cubicles in flight. If someone was lost in thought and did not get out on time, they would pass through the attic or basement in perfect safety. Complete darkness would suddenly fall, and the cubicle, shuddering and grating, would move – with the help of massive chains – horizontally, after which it found itself appropriately vertical again. As soon as the reinforced concrete monster had been built, this lift was the cause of much excitement, especially among the children who overpopulated the surrounding dirty streets and dilapidated yards. Caretakers had their work cut out for them and little rascals had their heads full of ideas as to how to outwit them.

That day, caretaker Hans Barwick was particularly vigilant because, since morning, several scamps had been trying to make the exciting journey through the floors, attic and basement. He observed each

233

entering client carefully and a moment earlier a man, his hat pulled over his brow and wearing a leather coat, had arrived. Barwick had wanted to check his identification but rapidly had changed his mind: dealing with such an individual foretold inevitable problems. A few minutes later, he was passed by a policeman whom he knew, Max Forstner. Barwick had first met him the previous year when giving a statement concerning a case which involved an unsuccessful bank robbery and since then had greeted Forstner with great deference. He did this every Friday, since on that day this official regularly visited the bank for reasons unknown to Barwick.

Forstner entered the lift, losing the obsequious porter from view. The lift moved at a leisurely pace. It passed the first floor and found itself between flights. Forstner disliked these moments. He was pleased when the level of the lift floor was at one with the level of a landing; he would then jump out sprightly, smiling like a man of the world. When the lift neared the second floor, Forstner was initially surprised, then furious. On the threshold to the floor stood a man in a leather coat who obviously had no intention of moving aside in order to allow the policeman to leave.

"Get out of my way," Forstner shouted and threw himself at the obstacle. His momentum, however, was incomparably lesser and weaker than the strength with which the pushy nuisance barged into the lift. He crowded Forstner into the depth of the cubicle and pressed him hard against the wall. The lift was reaching the third floor. Forstner tried to draw his gun. At that moment, he felt a painful prick in his neck. The lift was approaching the ninth floor. Sensual impressions such as the hammering of machinery and the rocking of the cubicle no longer reached Forstner. The lift crossed the attic in utter darkness and found itself on the ninth floor again. The man in the leather coat then got out and went down by way of the stairs.

Hans Barwick suddenly heard the wailing of the mechanism and the high squeak of chains. The racket was so piercing that only one, gloomy thought came to his mind: "Dammit, someone's got their leg crushed again." He stopped the lift and conquered the stairs, flight by flight, but it was not until the very top that he realized his suspicions had been somewhat optimistic. Between the ceiling of the lift and the threshold of the ninth floor shuddered the unnaturally contorted body of Max Forstner.

DRESDEN, MONDAY, JULY 17TH, 1950
HALF-PAST SIX IN THE EVENING

The square next to the Japanese Palace, not far from Karl-Marx-Platz swarmed with people, dogs and prams of yelling children. Those who had managed to find a bench in the shade could speak of great happiness. To the happy ones belonged the Director of the Psychiatric Hospital, Ernst Bennert, and an elderly man immersed in his newspaper. They sat at opposite ends of a bench. The elderly man did not show the least surprise when Bennert started to talk to himself in a half-whisper, but when a young woman with a little boy toddling beside her approached and politely asked whether she could sit down, the men looked at each other and, in unison, refused. She left, muttering something about old men, and Bennert immediately resumed his monologue. The elderly man listened through to the end, revealed his scar-ridden face from behind the newspaper and quietly thanked the doctor.

* * *

Extract from the secret report of a U.S.A. intelligence agent
in Dresden M-234 May 7th, 1945
. . . during the bombing of Dresden, among others died . . . former Chief of the Criminal Department of Breslau Police, later Deputy Chief of the Abwehr Department of Internal Affairs, Eberhard Mock. He was under the care of agent GS-142 from whose reports it appears

235

that between 1936 and 1945 Mock came to Dresden every two months and visited his relative, Herbert Anwaldt, in various hospitals. According to information obtained by agent GS-142, from 1936 Anwaldt stayed at the psychiatric hospital on Marien-Allee. When the hospital was closed down by the S.S. in February, 1940, Anwaldt did not suffer the fate of other patients shot somewhere in the forests near the village of Rossendorf: he ended up in the hospital for war veterans on Friedrichstrasse. Official hospital records contain fictitious information about the part played by Anwaldt in the campaign against Poland. The pseudo-veteran survived the bombing of Dresden in this same hospital. As of March this year, he is once more at the psychiatric hospital on Marien-Allee. Agent GS-142 did not succeed in establishing the nature of the relationship between Anwaldt and Mock since information offered by hospital staff was of a gossipy and scandal-mongering nature: because of the frequent visits, some claimed that Anwaldt was Mock's illegitimate son, others that he was his lover.

* * *

DRESDEN, MONDAY, JULY 17TH, 1950
MIDNIGHT

Director Bennert walked in absolute silence down by the side staircase used only during apparent evacuations which thankfully had not recently been declared all that frequently. The shaft of torchlight cut through dense darkness. Ever since the city had been bombed, these narrow stairs had filled him with dread. On that memorable thirteenth day of February in 1945, as the noise of the first bomb resounded, Bennert had run down them to the cellar which had been turned into a provisional shelter. He had shouted his daughter's name, searching for her among the crush on

236

the stairs, but in vain. His cries had been lost in the din of the bomb and the horrific wailing of the sick.

He rejected the painful memories and opened the door leading out to the hospital park. Major Mahmadov was standing in the door. He patted Bennert jovially on the shoulder, passed him by and made his way upstairs. After a while, the sound of his footsteps disappeared. Bennert did not lock the door. He took his time going up. On the half-landing, he peered out of the window. Across the grass, flooded with moonlight, strode briskly an elderly man in uniform. Bennert would remember that walk for the rest of his life. Again he heard the noise of bombs, the wailing of the sick and through this same window saw an elderly man with sparks of fire in his hair and a burned face, carrying his unconscious daughter in his arms.

Nurse Jürgen Kopp sat down at a table with two colleagues, Frank and Vogel, and started to deal cards. Skat was a passion shared by all the lower ranks of the hospital staff. Kopp bid a bottle of wine and turned out a jack of clubs to draw trumps. He did not have time to win a hand, however, before they heard an inhuman cry from across the dark courtyard.

"Who's that yelling his head off?" wondered Vogel.

"Anwaldt. His light's just gone on," Kopp laughed. "Seen another cockroach, I expect."

Kopp was right in part. It *was* Anwaldt shouting. But not because of a cockroach. Along the floor of his room, comically twitching their abdomens, paraded four handsome, black, desert scorpions.

FIVE MINUTES LATER

Scorpions crawled over army trousers and hands covered in dark, thick hairs. One of the scorpions straightened its abdomen and climbed up to a double chin. It swayed on the half-open lips and stood on the gentle peak of a chubby cheek. Another, exploring an earlobe, strolled through thick, black hair. Yet another slid along the floor as if it wanted to escape from the puddle of blood pouring from Major Mahmadov's throat.

BERLIN, JULY 19TH, 1950
EIGHT O'CLOCK IN THE EVENING

Anwaldt woke in a dark room. Before his eyes, he saw a ceiling with dancing reflections of water. He got up and, with an unsteady step, approached the window. Below flowed a river. On a barrier sat a couple tenderly embracing. In the distance flashed the lights of a great city. Anwaldt knew this city from somewhere, but his memory refused to obey him. The tranquillizers had reduced the speed of his association to zero. He swept his eyes over the room. The greyness of the floor was cut by a yellow streak of light coming in through the partially open door. Anwaldt pushed the door open wide and entered an almost empty room. Its severe, ascetic décor consisted of a table, two chairs and a plush sofa. On the floor and on the sofa articles of clothing lay strewn. He started to examine them and, after a while, segregated them clearly in his mind, using gender as the decisive criterion. From his analysis, he concluded that the man who had thrown his clothes about should have remained in nothing but one sock and underpants and the woman in stockings. He caught a glimpse of the couple sitting at a table and was pleased with the precision of his analysis. He was not far wrong: the plump blonde was indeed wearing nothing but a pair of stockings and the elderly man with a red, scarred face had on only his underpants. Anwaldt stared at him for a while and cursed his feeble memory yet again. He shifted his eyes to the middle of the table and remembered a frequent motif in Greek literature: *anagnorismos* – the motif of recognition. And so someone's smell, wave of hair, some object would unravel a whole chain of associations, restore an obliterated likeness to features, generate past situations. Gazing at the chess-board laid out on the table, he stretched the string of his memory and experienced his *anagnorismos*.

Anwaldt woke up on the plush sofa. The girl had disappeared, along with her exquisite clothes. By the sofa sat the old man, clumsily holding a cup of steaming broth. Anwaldt leaned over and drank half a cup.

"Could you give me a cigarette, sir?" he asked in a strangely strong, resonant voice.

"Don't call me 'sir', son," the man extended a silver cigarette case towards Anwaldt. "We've been through too much together to play at such formalities."

Anwaldt collapsed on to the pillow and inhaled deeply. Without looking at Mock, he said quietly:

"Why did you lie to me? You set me on the Baron but that didn't stop the Yesidi's revenge in any way! Why did you incite me against my own father?"

"It didn't hold the Yesidis back, you say. And you're right. But how was I to know that at the time?" Mock lit up yet another cigarette even though the previous one was still smoking in the ashtray. "Do you remember that muggy July night in Madame le Goef's brothel? It's a shame I didn't stand you up in front of a mirror then. Do you know whom you'd have seen? Oedipus with his eyes gouged out. I didn't believe you'd escape the Yesidis. There were two ways I could have saved you from them: either give you hope and isolate you – at least for a while – or kill you myself and in this way protect you from the Turkish scorpions. Which would you have preferred? You're in such a state of mind at

239

the moment that you'll say: I'd have preferred to die . . . Am I right?"

Anwaldt closed his eyes and, squeezing them tight, tried to prevent the tears from falling.

"Interesting, my life . . . One hands me over to an orphanage, the other – to a madhouse. And claims it's for my own good . . ."

"Herbert, sooner or later you'd have ended up with the lunatics. That's what Doctor Bennert said. But to the point . . . I set you up to kill the Baron so as to isolate you," Mock lied again. "I didn't think you'd escape the Yesidis. But I knew that thanks to that you'd be relatively safe. I also knew what to do to make sure you didn't get a long sentence. I thought: Anwaldt will be protected by the prison walls and I'll have time to catch Erkin. After all, getting rid of Erkin was your only hope . . ."

"And what? Did you get rid of him?"

"Yes. Very effectively. He simply disappeared, and his holy dervish continued to believe that he was tracking you down. He believed it until recently when he sent another avenger who is now lying in your room in Bennert's Dresden clinic. And you've won a bit of time again . . ."

"Very good, Mock. So you've protected me for the time being," Anwaldt raised himself from the sofa and drank the rest of his broth. "But another Yesidi will come . . . And will get to Forstner or Maass . . ."

"He won't get to Forstner. Our dear Max met with a terrible accident in Breslau – he was crushed by a lift . . ." Mock's face turned even redder and the furrows paled. "What do you think? I'm protecting you as best I can, and you keep on thinking about the curse. If you don't want to live, you've got a gun, kill yourself. But not here, because you'll betray an apartment belonging to the Stasi . . . Why do you think I'm protecting you?"

Anwaldt did not know the answer to that question, while Mock wanted to drown it out by shouting.

"And what happened to you?" Anwaldt had never been afraid of shouting. "How did you get into the Stasi?"

"That institution gladly took on high-ranking officers from the Abwehr, where I had moved at the end of '34. But I told you about that when I visited you in Dresden."

"*Scheisse*, I was in that Dresden a long time." Anwaldt smiled bitterly.

"Because there was no possibility in all that time to get you to a safe place . . . I knew from Bennert that you weren't ill any more . . ."

Anwaldt got up suddenly, spilling the rest of his broth on the floor.

"I didn't think of Bennert . . . He knows everything about me . . ."

"Calm down." Stoic peace beamed from Mock's scarred face. "Bennert won't squeak a word to anyone. He has a debt of gratitude to repay me. I pulled his daughter out from under the ruins. This is a souvenir," he touched his face. "A blind shell exploded and flaming tar paper from the roof seared my head."

Anwaldt stretched and peered out of the window: he saw militia men dragging along a civilian drunk. He grew weak.

"Mock, now I'm going to be hunted down by the militia for the murder of that Turk who's lying dead in my room at Bennert's!"

"Not quite. Tomorrow, you and I are going to be in Amsterdam and in a week's time in the United States," Mock did not lose his self-control. He took a small piece of paper covered in masses of numbers from his pocket. "This is a coded cable from General John Fitzpatrick, a senior official in the C.I.A. The Abwehr was a way into the Stasi, and the Stasi into the C.I.A. You know what the cable says? 'I give permission for Mr Eberhard Mock and his son to enter the U.S.A.'" Mock laughed out loud. "Since your papers give your name as being Anwaldt and we haven't got time to make up new ones, let's agree that you're my illegitimate child . . ."

But the "illegitimate child" did not feel at all like laughing. He did feel joy, but it was marred by the gloomy, sad satisfaction experienced after finishing off a despised enemy.

"Now I know why you've been protecting me all your life. You wanted a son . . ."

"You know sod all," Mock feigned indignation. "Amateur psychologist! I was deeply involved in the case myself and am afraid, first and foremost, for myself. I value my belly too much to make a home for scorpions of it."

Neither of them believed it.

XVIII

NEW YORK, SATURDAY, MARCH 14TH, 1951
FOUR O'CLOCK IN THE MORNING

The Hotel Chelsea on 55th Street was, at this early hour, silent and sleepy. Most of the residents were permanent – travelling salesmen and insurance agents who went to bed early on weekdays so as to leave for work the next morning without sand in their eyes or their breath stale from alcohol.

The exception to this general rule was an inhabitant of a large, three-roomed apartment on the sixteenth floor. He was believed to be a writer. He worked at his desk by night, slept until noon, went out somewhere in the afternoons and frequently enjoyed female company in the evenings. This evening stretched to three in the morning – at which hour, a tired girl in a navy-blue dress with a large sailor's collar left the "literary man's" apartment. Closing the door, she sent a kiss into the depths of the apartment and walked to the lift. Out of the corner of her eye, she caught sight of two men advancing down the long hotel corridor. She shuddered as they passed. One of them instilled fear with his monstrous face covered in scars, the other with his flaming eyes of a fanatic. The girl sighed with relief when she found herself in the company of the dozy lift-boy.

The men walked up to the door of 16F. Mock knocked softly. The door opened just a little. The face of an elderly man appeared in the gap. Anwaldt grabbed the handle and with all his strength pulled the door towards him. The old man's head was caught between the door and the frame; the steel casing crushed his ear. He opened his mouth to cry out but was instantly gagged with a handkerchief. Anwaldt let go of the door. The old man stood in his hall and pulled the improvised gag out of his mouth. The swelling on the ear was already growing. Anwaldt dealt him a swift blow. His fist squashed the hot ear. The old man fell. Mock closed the door, dragged the assaulted man into the room and sat him in an armchair. Two silencers stared at the man unwavering.

"One move, one raised voice, and you're dead," Anwaldt tried to keep calm. Mock, in the meantime, went through the books on the desk. Then he turned and looked derisively at the defenceless man:

"Tell me, Maass, can you still get it up? You still like schoolgirls, I see . . ."

"I don't know what you're talking about." Maass rubbed his burning ear. "You've taken me for somebody else. I'm George Mason, Professor of Semitic Languages at Columbia University."

"We've changed, eh, Maass? I, Mock, was scalped by flaming tar paper falling from a roof and Herbert Anwaldt has grown fat on dumplings, his favourite meal in the lunatic asylum." He turned the pages on the table. "You, on the other hand, your jowls have sunk and the rest of your once so beautiful locks have fallen out. But the temperament remains the same, eh, Maass?"

The questioned man stayed silent, but his eyes grew larger. He opened his mouth in horror, but did not manage to cry out. Mock firmly pressed his arms into the armrests and Anwaldt, quick as lightning, pushed the handkerchief almost down his throat. After a few minutes, Maass' terrified eyes had dimmed. Anwaldt removed the gag and asked:

"Why did you betray me to the Turk, Maass? When did they buy you? Why weren't you loyal to Baron von der Malten? His gratitude and money would have freed you of the trouble of seeking private tuition for the rest of your life. But you've always liked private tuition . . . Particularly with debauched schoolgirls . . ."

Maass reached for the bottle of Jack Daniel's on the table beside him and took a long swig straight from the bottle. Tiny drops appeared on the bald head.

"What in your view, Anwaldt, is the most important thing in the world?" he had stopped hiding behind his fictitious name. Without waiting for a reply, he continued: "The most important thing is truth. But what's truth to you when you curse your burning masculinity at night, when the swaying of a passing female's hips destroys ingenious pyramids of conclusions which give rise to each other, and unaffected levels of syllogisms. You can only experience peace when the most renowned scholarly periodicals long for your articles and the exquisite nymphs for your phallus to subjugate them every night . . . Have you ever experienced that, Anwaldt? Because that's what I experienced sixteen years ago in Breslau when Kemal Erkin sent undiscovered manuscripts for me to look at and compliant houris at my feet in return for one simple expert opinion. I know the girls did not love or desire me. So what? It was enough that they fulfilled all my whims every day. They assured me peace in my work. Thanks to them I could free myself of the furious and capricious lord hiding within my loins. Not having to think about him, I got on with my work. I published a manuscript which was considered lost and the discovery brought me world fame. When endowed by Erkin with an enormous sum of money and a photocopy of the manuscript – the one supposedly lost – I fled Breslau. I knew that every department of Oriental Studies would be open to me." He took another swig of whisky and grimaced. "I chose New York, but you found me even here. Just tell me: why? Primal revenge? You're Europeans, after all, Christians . . . What about your commandment to forgive?"

"You're mistaken, Maass. But Anwaldt and I have a great deal in common with the Yesidis or − to be more precise − after what we've been through, we believe in the power of fate." Mock opened the window and gazed at the huge neon sign advertising Camel cigarettes. "And you, Maass, do you believe in destiny?"

"No . . ." Maass laughed, revealing snow-white teeth. "I believe in coincidence. It's a coincidence that my pupil introduced me to Erkin, a coincidence that I discovered your real parentage, Anwaldt . . ."

"Again you're mistaken, Maass," Mock settled himself comfortably in the armchair and spread out his elegant file. "I'll prove the existence of fate to you in a moment. Do you remember Friedländer's last two prophecies? In your translation, the first of them went: *arar* 'ruin', *chavura* 'wound', *makak* 'fester', *afar* 'rubble', *shamayim* 'heaven/sky'. That prophecy referred to me. *Makak* is nothing other than my name − Mock. The prophecy proved true. Captain Eberhard Mock of the Abwehr died and an officer of the Secret Communist Police, Stasi, Major Eberhard Mock, was born. Different face, different person, same name. Destiny . . . And now look at that second prophecy, Maass. It goes: *yeladim* 'children', *akrabbim* 'scorpions', *amotz* 'white', and *chol* 'sand' or *chul* 'to wriggle, to fall'. I thought that this prophecy referred to Anwaldt (*yeladim* sounds like Anwaldt). And it almost proved true. A major from the Stasi, a hefty Uzbek with pockets full of scorpions, arrived at the psychiatric hospital so as to accomplish the secret mission. Anwaldt was to die within white walls (*amoc* − white), in a room where windows were fitted with bars (*sevacha* − a grille), with his belly full of scorpions wriggling (*chul* − to wriggle). But I interpreted that prophecy differently and altered destiny. Anwaldt became a language specialist who − in hospital − taught himself to be a pretty good expert in Semitic languages. And the Uzbek and his brothers from the desert stayed in the Dresden hospital . . ."

Mock strolled up and down the room, proudly thrusting his hefty chest forward.

"So you see, Maass? I am destiny. Yours too . . . Do you want to know my interpretation of that last prophecy? Here it is: *amoc* is 'Maass', then – *jeladim* 'children', *akrabbim* 'scorpions', *chul* 'to fall'. 'Children', 'scorpions', and 'to fall' are omens of your death."

Mock stood in the middle of the room and raised his arms above his head. He froze in this position of a pagan priest and in a grave voice proclaimed:

"I, Eberhard Mock, relentless fate, I, Eberhard Mock, impending death, ask you, son, do you prefer to fall to the street from this floor or die from the venom of little scorpions, children still, scorpion children but with murderous poison already in their tails?"

Mock clearly emphasized the words "scorpion children" and "to fall out". Maass could not understand what scorpions he was talking about until Anwaldt opened a small medical box. Maass peered inside and paled. Little, black arachnids were rotating their pincers and flexing their abdomens as they tried to clamber out of the box. The German language long unheard by him repeated itself in his ears. The verb *ausfallen* – "to fall out" – hissed and vibrated. He made towards the open window.

In the darkness of the night, the neon smoker on the sign opposite blew a series of smoke rings.

Ⓜ MELVILLE INTERNATIONAL CRIME